"Very few authors can build chemistry like Grace Burrowes."

—*Books Like Breathing*

"Burrowes creates a character-driven novel... The slowly simmering sensuality and strong bonds of family hold readers' interest and hearts."

—*RT Book Reviews*

"Charming... Expert prose, likable characters, realistic relationships, and believable complications."

—*Publishers Weekly*

"Burrowes has a talent for filling traditional romance situations with depth and the unexpected."

—*Booklist*

"Grabs your heartstrings and doesn't let go... I will read anything Grace writes!"

—*Under the Boardwalk*

"There is just something about Burrowes's romances that makes me want to read and read and not put them down."

—*Book Girl of Mur-y-Castell*

"Burrowes excels when she mixes family sagas and tender, heartwarming romance."

—*The Royal Reviews*

"Burrowes deftly builds the romantic tension amid lovely layers of domestic tranquillity and honest conversations…[an] engrossing story."

—*Publishers Weekly*

"[Grace Burrowes] is a brilliant mastermind… A very satisfying, heartfelt read."

—*Romancing the Book*

"Once again, Grace Burrowes captivated me with a wonderful story and a tender romance featuring a thoroughly engaging central couple."

—*All About Romance*

"All Grace Burrowes novels…have a hint of mystery and a love story that will wind itself around your heart. This author has a way of luring you away for a few hours of utter bliss."

—*BookLoons*

Also by Grace Burrowes

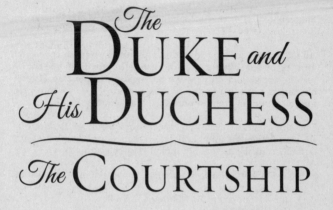

The DUKE and His DUCHESS

The COURTSHIP

Two Novellas of the Windham Family

GRACE BURROWES

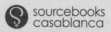

sourcebooks
casablanca

Published by Sourcebooks Casablanca, an imprint of Sourcebooks, Inc.
P.O. Box 4410, Naperville, Illinois 60567-4410
(630) 961-3900
Fax: (630) 961-2168
www.sourcebooks.com

The Courtship was originally published individually in ebook format in 2012 by Sourcebooks Casablanca.

The Duke and His Duchess was originally published individually in ebook format in 2013 by Sourcebooks Casablanca.

Printed and bound in Canada.
MBP 10 9 8 7 6 5 4 3 2 1

Contents

The Courtship

This story is for every woman who thinks she doesn't fit in and isn't worthy of notice. You may not fit in, but that's precisely because you are indeed worthy of notice.

One

"ONE HEARS HE TAKES SNUFF ONLY FROM HIS MISTRESSES' naked breasts."

Esther Himmelfarb rearranged her cards and stifled a snort at one of Charlotte Pankhurst's more ridiculous observations.

Herodia Bellamy tossed the queen of diamonds onto the table. "One hears that he bathes frequently, but seldom alone."

"A crowded undertaking," Esther murmured, "given the man's size in relation to the average bathing tub. Your turn, Lady Zephora."

"I know for a *fact*," Lady Zephora said softly, "that both Lord Anthony *and Lord Percival* have been ordered by Her Grace, their mama, to take brides this year."

So much for whist. Esther continued to study her cards while the ladies catalogued Colonel Lord Percival Windham's many positive attributes.

Their raptures matched Esther's list of the man's shortcomings almost exactly.

"He's soooo handsome," Charlotte cooed. "And it's all genuine—the golden hair, the muscles, the height."

"The dreamy blue eyes," Herodia added. "When he looks at you, it's as if he's trying to convey that he loves you simply in the way he regards you."

Not to be outdone, Zephora stated what Charlotte and Herodia had no doubt heard repeatedly from their mamas. "His wife would always have a courtesy title, and someday she might become the next *Duchess of Moreland*."

Which was the outside of too much, since it contemplated the death of the present duke—a gentleman as vigorous as he was dignified—as well as the death of the current ducal heir, Lord Pembroke, an upright soul whose greatest sin was that he'd fathered only two girl children in ten years of marriage.

"Consider," Esther said, gathering up the cards, "the present duchess would be your mama-in-law when you married Lord Percival. If she has the authority to recall commissioned officers from their billets in service to His Majesty, imagine the power she'd wield over a mere daughter-in-law."

"Lord Percy wouldn't allow her to intrude." Charlotte sniffed. "You are just jealous, Esther, because a girl without a title or a dowry can't look so high."

The jab was unexpected, since these conclusions were seldom spoken aloud. They were accepted as common knowledge, which usually allowed Esther the backhanded gift of a nonentity's privacy.

"Esther is pretty, well-spoken, well-educated in the domestic arts, *and* wellborn," Herodia pointed out. "Cease carping, Charlotte, lest the gentlemen overhear you."

This rebuke did not feel to Esther like a defense,

because it wasn't. Herodia was seizing an opportunity to appear superior to Charlotte, nothing more.

"I can *look* as high as I please," Esther said, shuffling the deck into a neat stack. "Though looking alone holds little gratification. Shall I deal again?"

As long as lords Percival and Anthony Windham were in the room chatting up the hostess by the punch bowl, Esther would have to remain as the fourth in the game. Play—or what passed for it—resumed, while Esther sent up a silent prayer that the next three weeks went by as quickly—and as painlessly—as possible.

❧

"I know that look, Percy." Tony kept his voice down, thank God, because Lady Morrisette was only several yards away, latched on to the arm of His Grace the Duke of Quimbey.

Percival Windham did not pause in his perusal of the blond young lady seated at a card table across the parlor. She had a stillness to her, a serenity that drew the eye more than all the flirtatious glances and powdered bosoms in the room.

"What look?" Percival asked.

"You're falling in love again. I've seen it a dozen times at least. Her Grace will rejoice to hear of it."

"I do not fall in love, Anthony. I fall into bed, or occasionally into linen closets, private boudoirs, secluded bowers, that sort of thing." Percival took a sip of decent punch and turned a direct stare on his younger brother. "And Her Grace will not be hearing a peep out of you, not unless you want me to apprise her of a certain tryst you had with Miss Gladys Holsopple before leaving Town."

Tony's smile was hopelessly unguarded. "Gladys Holsopple is toothsome and not too much concerned for propriety when nobody's looking. An estimable female. And you don't have to worry about my peaching on you—we've Mannering for that."

Mannering, the valet they'd be sharing for the duration of the house party. Percival turned his thoughts in a more sanguine direction and gestured slightly with his glass.

"Who's the pretty card player, Tony?"

While appearing to arrange the lace at his cuff, Tony glanced across the room. "Herodia Bellamy. Well dowered, her papa is said to have Bute's ear. Dances nicely and doesn't titter."

Tony was one of the best reconnaissance officers ever dispatched to Canada—where his talents had clearly been wasted. "Not her. She damned near tried to dance her way into my bedroom at Heckenbaum's last week. The *pretty* one." The one who made even arranging her cards an exercise in grace.

"Lady Zephora Needham. Her papa's Earl Needham, and they say it takes two hours to arrange all them bows in the chit's hair."

Tony in a teasing mood was a burden, indeed.

"Not her, and not that gossiping Pankhurst twit, either. The one with the unpowdered hair. I haven't seen her before."

"Her." Tony's smile was replaced by a frown. "Not your type at all, Perce. Esther Himmelfarb. Well-bred, well-read. The poor relation invited to make up the numbers when somebody cancels—at the very last minute. Grandpapa's an earl, but she didn't take, according to Gladys. She's the sort to play chaperone when the proper chaperones are off in the butler's pantry with the likes of you and me."

Himmelfarb, a prosaic Teutonic name, suggesting connections to the heavily Germanized royal court.

Or suggesting... Percival studied the young lady. Blond hair was severely braided into a coronet that would accentuate her height when she stood. A single spray of rosebuds had been woven into the back of her coiffure, the barest ornamentation, when fashion allowed women to adorn their hair with birds' nests and battleships.

Northern lights came to mind. Cool, beautiful, unexpected, and ethereal. Miss Esther Himmelfarb had a complexion other women sought to achieve with cosmetics and generally failed. Perfect pale skin with more rosebud pink tingeing her high cheekbones, and not a beauty patch to be seen. Her dress was a sky-blue gown de chemise, no panniers, and not much bustle, of soft velvet and expertly tailored.

All in all, a lovely woman, one upon whom primness sat more temptingly than all the wiles of a beckoning siren.

Percival watched as she shuffled the deck in tidy, economical moves. "Dallying with her would be a great deal of effort." A *challenge*.

Tony's eyes narrowed. "And yet you're considering it. Ruin that girl's reputation, and she has nothing left. I'll call you out myself, tattle to Her Grace—"

"You are feeling the effects of the punch, Anthony. I do not dally with ladies barely out of the schoolroom."

"Unless they're widowed, fast, or fairly determined."

Percy's lips quirked up. "And very, very discreet."

A moment of fraternal silence fell, during which the Duke of Quimbey, a handsome single man yet in his prime, laughed merrily at something Lady Morrisette said. The ladies at the card table all turned to regard Quimbey, the greatest prize on the marriage market for the past several Seasons.

"Thank God for Quimbey," Percival said.

He'd spoken a trifle too loudly. Esther Himmelfarb swiveled her gaze to regard him, while the other ladies continued to ogle Quimbey with longing glances.

God in heaven, Anthony, I do believe you're right this time.

Green eyes regarded the Moreland spare with a blend of humor, condescension, and...*pity?* There were depths in Esther Himmelfarb's gaze, depths of reserve and self-possession that made a red-blooded male want to take down all that golden, shot-silk hair. To provoke her to blushes and sighs and...*passion.*

"Right about what, Perce?"

Had he spoken aloud?

"We'd best find a housemaid who can provide a distraction for Mannering. Can't have any tales getting back to Her Grace when she's decreed we're both to be wed by year's end."

※

House parties entailed dancing. This was Holy Writ.

What better opportunity to look over the possible flirts and affairs, and to show oneself off to same, than the endless rotation of partners encountered on the dance floor?

Esther loathed the dance floor as her personal purgatory, until the final set concluded, and she found herself on the arm of—Everlasting Powers forefend!—Percival Windham. For her, the Almighty was now fashioning circles even of purgatory.

"Miss Himmelfarb, I believe?" His lordship winged an arm and smiled graciously. "Shall I have us introduced, or in the informality of the occasion, will you allow me to join you at supper?"

A more calculating man would have offered to escort her to whoever had the honor of dining with her, but then, Lord Percival likely did not have to be calculating.

"I will happily accept your escort to the buffet, my lord." Where Michael might rescue her or Lady Morrisette would find some dowager needing company. Esther laced her gloved hand around Lord Percival's arm, only to encounter a small surprise.

Or not so small.

Gossip had not lied. The man was muscular in the extreme, and this close, he was also of sufficient height to uphold the fiction that he'd protect Esther from any brigands or wolves wandering about Lady Morrisette's parlor.

"Does your family hail from Kent, Miss Himmelfarb? I know most of the local families and cannot recall Himmelfarbs among them."

The question was perfectly pleasant, and so too was his lordship's scent. Not the scent of exertion or the standard rose-scented rice powder—he wasn't wearing a wig—but something elusive…

"You're twitching your nose like a thoughtful bunny,

Miss Himmelfarb. Are you in anticipation of something particularly succulent among the supper offerings?"

He smiled down at her as he spoke, and for a moment, Esther could not fashion a reply. Of all the times for Charlotte Pankhurst to be right about a man's blue, blue eyes… "I'm trying to fathom the fragrance you're wearing, my lord. It's pleasant."

"If I didn't know better, I'd think from your expression that you do not approve of men wearing pleasant scents." His tone, amused, teasing, suggested that sometimes, *all* he wore was a pleasant scent—and that just-for-you smile.

They came to a halt in the buffet line, which meant…Esther was doomed to sharing a meal with the man.

Lord Percival leaned nearer, as if confiding something amid the noise and bustle of the first night of a lively, extended social gathering. "Bay rum lacks imagination, don't you think? I shall wear it when I'm a settled fellow with children in my nursery. There's cedar in the scent I wear, reminds me of Canada. You're partial to spicy scents yourself."

He was inviting a reciprocal confidence from her with that observation. The notion of trading secrets with Percival Windham made something beneath Esther's heart twang—disagreeably, of course. "Lavender, with a touch of a few other things."

While Esther stood beside Lord Percival, he leaned even closer and subtly inhaled through his patrician nose. Horses did that, gathered each other's scent upon acquaintance. And like a filly, Esther held still for his lordship's olfactory inspection and resisted the urge—the unladylike, disconcerting, thoroughly inappropriate urge—to treat him to a similar examination.

"My dear"—his lordship had straightened only a bit—"why is My Lady Hair Bows staring daggers in this direction?"

My lady…? Then…*my dear?*

He was a very presuming fellow, even for a duke's spare, and yet Esther felt the urge to smile back at him. "I'm not sure what you mean, my lord."

"You know exactly what I mean, Miss Himmelfarb." He picked up a plate, though they were still some distance from any sustenance. "Now the Needy girl is at her elbow, pouring brandy on the flames of gossip. You and I will be engaged by this time tomorrow, I don't doubt."

Did one correct a duke's spare when he made light of marriage to a woman within staring distance of professional spinsterhood?

Yes, one did.

"Her name is Needham, my lord. And I should think an engagement unlikely when you have yet to ask for my hand and I have given no indication I would accept your suit."

The light in his eyes changed, going from friendly— yes, that was the word—to something more intent. "You are an impertinent woman." This did not, unfortunately, sound as if it put him off.

"As compared to you, my lord, who are somehow a *pertinent* man? Or perhaps pertinacious might apply?"

That was rude, intended to put the perishing idiot in his place, but it only added approval to the warmth in his gaze. His eyes crinkled at the corners, his lips

curved up to reveal perfect, straight white teeth in a
dazzling, alarmingly intimate smile.

"We're going to get on famously, Miss Himmelfarb.
I adore impertinent women."

Esther knew not what to say to that. The line shuffled forward while Charlotte, Herodia, and Zephora
glared a firing squad of daggers, and Esther tried to
ignore the scent of cedar and spices.

❧

"You most assuredly do not look like you're enjoying
yourself."

Esther glanced around the ballroom, where guests
were milling before the dancing resumed, then cast a
brief, exasperated look at her cousin, the Honorable
Michael Adelman.

"Could you enjoy yourself while the tops of your
breasts were engaged in conversation by one man after
another, and half those men married to wives busily
ogling some other fellow's falls?"

Michael's lids drooped in a manner he likely did not
intend to be seductive, though it made his good looks
even more alluring. "I think the Needham girl might
accept my suit. She's said to be well dowered. The
party lasts only three weeks, Esther."

Remorse had Esther patting Michael's sleeve. "Three
weeks is nothing. We shall contrive. Compliment her
coiffure lavishly." That was the purpose of the outing,
in fact—to secure an advantageous match for Michael,
and as expeditiously as possible. Michael shuddered
beside Esther on a gilded green-velvet sofa set into an
alcove off the ballroom's dance floor.

"How does one consummate a union with a wife who must sleep with a wooden pillow, lest she disturb the architecture of her hairstyle? I lie awake at night and fret over this, you know."

He was her cousin, and Esther loved him, but he was only a man and therefore not much afflicted with insight.

"You capture her heart so completely that for you she'll give up hours of torment having her hair dressed and content herself with elaborate wigs, while leaving her crowning glory in the state intended by the Almighty. We'd best mingle. Lady Morrisette has twice smiled this way."

Michael rose and assisted Esther to her feet. "God help me," he murmured. "Our hostess is reported to hold these gatherings mostly as a means of seeing to her own entertainment." He bowed over Esther's hand. "Say nice things about me to the Needmore girl."

"Needham."

And of course Esther would, for despite his dark good looks, height, and charm, without a decent match, Michael's future held little worth looking forward to.

"Miss Himmelfarb."

With effort, Esther did not grimace, for it appeared the tops of her breasts were again to engage in conversation. "Sir Jasper." She gave him her hand, and because he was standing so close, when he bowed over it, his nose nearly touched her décolletage.

"The sets are forming, Miss Himmelfarb, and I would happily partner you."

Something in his tone implied that his partnering was available in locations other than the dance floor, and on short notice. Sir Jasper Layton was not yet thirty, had all his teeth, and was as handsome as a bad bout with smallpox could leave a man. Three beauty patches and a heavy hand with the face powder did more to call attention to his scars than hide them, though.

Esther manufactured a smile. "Thank you, sir, and tell me how your sisters go on."

He appeared surprised to recall he had sisters, though both attended the same court functions as Esther and many of the ladies present at the house party. Soon enough the steps of the dance saw him partnering other women, and Esther could breathe a sigh of relief.

"Are you concentrating on the steps, or have you taken me into dislike?" Percival Windham bowed to her jauntily, took both of her hands, and as the dance called for, moved closer. "Or is Sir Jasper overstepping?"

Esther dropped his hands, turned her back, smiled over her shoulder—*who* had chosen this particular dance?—and turned back to take Lord Percival's hands. "I'm concentrating on the steps."

They promenaded down the line, hands joined before them. "You'd rather be in the library, curled up with a book by the fire, reading French poems, or possibly German. Tell me, Miss Himmelfarb, do Germans write poetry?"

He was teasing, but also studying her as he smiled that particular, personal smile.

Esther dropped his hands and turned a full circle. "I'd be reading Shakespearean sonnets up in my room. Anybody can come upon a lady in the library."

Though her room would be stuffy and dank

because Esther lacked sufficient strength to pry open its single window.

"There's a full moon tonight, Miss Himmelfarb. Why not walk with me in the garden instead?"

He turned to his corner and whisked her down the line, leaving Esther to wonder if twenty more days—*and nights*—of this nonsense was worth the effort of seeing her cousin suitably matched.

As she slipped up to her room an hour later on aching feet, she also spared a thought to wonder whom Percival Windham would entice into the garden, and if he'd truly limit his activities there to walking.

❧

"The trouble is, we ain't got a proper dam."

Dear Tony was sliding past pleasantly foxed and barreling on to true inebriation, so Percival waved away the footman plying the card room's decanter.

"You're insulting the Duchess of Moreland, Tony, if you're saying our mother is anything less than proper. One does this at considerable peril to his well-being."

Tony continued to stare morosely at his brandy. "That's what I'm saying. She's all duchess and no mama. Not mama, not dame, not mother. We'd be back in Canada if His Grace had a notion how to foil her queer starts."

"Do you honestly expect me to believe you're missing Canada?"

"Not missing it, exactly, but there ain't any debutantes in Canada, no levees, no duchesses."

In vino, veritas. "There are bears and wolves, or have you forgotten?"

Tony offered his brother a rueful grin. "Wolves don't sing any worse than those sopranos at the opera."

"The sopranos are a good deal better smelling and friendlier."

"That they are." Tony blinked at his drink, perhaps wondering how the thing had gotten so quickly empty. "There's one little Italian gal from the chorus, and I swear that mouth of hers could devour—"

"Anthony, we're in proper company." To the extent a card room of reprobates and dowagers could be considered proper at the end of a long evening.

At the peremptory note in Percy's voice, Tony blinked. "Is it time to go home?"

Not for another twenty days. "We're certainly not going back to Canada tonight."

"Bloody cold in Canada," Tony observed, apropos of nothing.

"True." Percy set his drink aside and debated whether to leave Tony to his own devices at such a late hour. "At least in Canada the raiding parties announce themselves as such, observe certain rules of engagement, and don't use the minuet to scout out the opposition."

"That's exactly what I mean!" Tony gestured with his glass a trifle wildly, then paused as if he'd heard an arresting sound. "I'll be stepping to the gents' retiring room for a moment."

"Of course." And Percy would not allow his younger brother to stumble through the corridors, half-disguised, in charity with the world, only to be pulled into a convenient broom closet by some enterprising debutante.

They negotiated the dimly lit passages without incident—unless a giggle from a secluded alcove on the second floor could be considered an incident. As Tony unbuttoned his falls and took a lean against a handy wall in the men's retiring room, he aimed an oddly sober look at his brother.

"I've had this notion lately, Perce."

The man could piss and philosophize at the same time—a true exponent of the aristocracy. "Any particular notion?"

"It's a queer notion, as queer as considering a vocation in the church."

"Which you did for about fifteen minutes, until you recalled that bit about poverty, chastity, and obedience." For Percy, five minutes' contemplation of a life in the church had seen him buying his colors. "For God's sake, button up if you're done."

"What? Oh, indeed."

This late in the evening, Tony's fingers were clumsy, though his brain apparently continued to lumber around and his mouth danced attendance on it. "I've had the notion Her Grace might be right. Petey ain't getting any younger, and his lady ain't dropped a bull calf in ten years of marriage."

Tony was the only person in the whole of the realm who could refer to the Marquess of Pembroke, heir to the Moreland ducal title, as "Petey."

"Lady Pembroke could yet conceive a son."

"Canada is cold, Perce. It's full of wolves, and full of colonials with very big guns and little allegiance to good King George too."

When Tony had fumbled a few buttons closed in

relevant locations, Percy linked his arm through his brother's. "Are you thinking of selling out and joining the ranks of retired bachelors?"

That would solve a significant problem for Percy, true, but the idea of boarding a ship for the colonies at the end of the Season and not having Tony there to provide his inane commentary was disquieting.

"I'm thinking of taking a bride," Tony said, much of the bonhomie leaving his voice. "You like all that military whatnot, the pomp and nonsense, for King and Country. I like to be warm and well fed, to tup pretty girls, and spend my quarterly in two weeks flat."

And so had Percy, until a few years in charge of several hundred younger sons and rascals like Tony had somehow soured the allure of returning to an idle existence. Then Her Grace had taken this notion to recall her sons from the provinces and lecture them about Duty to the Succession, Familial Loyalty, and Social Responsibility.

The woman put the average gunnery sergeant to shame with her harangues.

"You are not ideal husband material, Tony." Percy spoke as gently as he could. "The ladies like some constancy for the first few years of marriage. They like to show off their trophy and drag a new husband about on calls. You've got the place in Hampshire, and you'd be expected to tend your acres for much of the year."

Tony was silent until they reached the head of the stairs. "You're saying I'd have to leave my bed before noon. Save the drinking until after supper, show up for parade inspection, the same as in Canada. Scout the terrain, deal with the locals."

Put like that, civilian life didn't sound like much of an adjustment.

"A wife would take umbrage at the opera singers. She'd expect pin money and babies."

"Babies aren't so bad."

Tony sounded wistful, though he was right: babies were dear and about as easy to love as a human being could be. A man with two adorable nieces could admit such a thing easily—to himself. On the one hand, if Tony married and produced babies—male babies in particular—then Percy could sail back to the regiment despite Her Grace's harangues and blustering.

And yet, on the other hand, to leave Tony behind in the clutches of a duchess-in-training, no older brother to seek consolation and counsel with, Her Grace looming over the marriage with a calendar in one hand and a receiving blanket in the other...

The Marquess of Pembroke was a decent fellow, but he hadn't been able to hide from his younger brothers what the duchess's interference had done to an otherwise civil and sanguine union.

"You'll not be marrying anybody just yet, Tony Windham. As a duke's son, you're a prime catch. At least look over the possibilities at some length and think of your chorus girl."

"Right-o, dear, sweet, little...the Italian—whatever her name is."

"The one with the devouring mouth."

❧

A room to oneself was a mixed blessing at a gathering like Lady Morrisette's. On the one hand, Esther had a little privacy in those rare moments when she wasn't stepping and fetching for her betters, and particularly for Lady Morrisette.

On the other hand, a lady with a room to herself had to guard doubly against the gentlemen who "accidentally" stumbled into her chambers late at night. She also had no one with whom to discuss the day's small revelations, such as how hard it had been not to watch Lord Percival Windham as he showed one lady after another how to hold her bow and let fly her arrows.

While Esther had lost the archery contest only by deliberately aiming her last shots wide of the bull's-eye, Charlotte's accuracy with a barbed comment was not to be underestimated, regardless of how desperately she'd needed Lord Percy's assistance with her bow.

Esther flipped back the covers and eased from the bed—the cot. She'd had a choice of sleeping with Lady Pott's maid in a stuffy little dressing room, or taking this glorified closet under the eaves. The closet had appealed, though on a warm night, it was nigh stifling, and on a cool night it would be frigid.

"I need a posset."

Closets did not sport bellpulls, so Esther slid her feet into slippers, belted a plain dressing gown over her nightgown, and headed down the maids' stairs to the kitchen.

A tired scullery maid frowned only slightly at Esther's request before preparing a cup of hot, spiced, spiked milk.

"There ye be, mum. Will there be anything else?"

Esther took a sip of her posset. "My thanks, it's very good. Does that door lead to the kitchen garden?"

"It do, and from thence to the scent garden and the cutting garden. The formal garden lies beyond that, and then the knot gardens and the folly." The maid shot a longing glance at the stool by the hearth, as if even giving these directions made a girl's feet ache.

Ache worse. After eighteen hours on her feet, the maid was no doubt even more tired than Esther.

"I'll take my posset to the garden."

"The guests don't generally use the kitchen garden, mum."

"All the better."

This earned Esther a small, understanding smile. The girl sought her stool, and Esther sought the cooler air of the garden by moonlight—the garden where she'd be safe from wandering guests of either gender.

Kitchen gardens bore a particular scent, a fresh, green, culinary fragrance that tickled Esther's nose as she found a bench along the far wall. Percival Windham's comment the day before about the moon being full came to mind, because the garden was limned in silvery light, the moon beaming down in all its beneficent glory.

"So you couldn't sleep either?"

Esther's first clue regarding the garden's other occupant was moonlight gleaming on his unpowdered hair.

"My lord." She started to rise, only to see Percival Windham's teeth flash in the shadows.

"Oh, must you?" He approached her bench, gaze trained on the cup in her hand. "Might I join you? I fear the farther reaches of the garden are full of predators stalking large game."

He sounded tired and not the least flirtatious. Esther

pulled her skirts aside when what she ought to be doing was returning to the stuffy, mildewed confines of her garret.

She took a sip of her posset and waited.

"How do you do it, Miss Himmelfarb?"

"My lord?"

He sighed and stretched long legs out before him, crossing his feet at the ankles and leaning back against the wall behind them. Moonlight caught the silver of his shoe buckles and the gold of the ring on his left little finger.

"How do you endure these infernal gatherings? They are exhausting of a man's fortitude if not his energy. If one more young lady presses a feminine part of her anatomy against my person, I am going to start howling like a wolf and wearing my wig backward."

His lordship sounded so put-upon, Esther found it difficult not to smile. "May I ask you a question, your lordship?"

"Lord Percy, if you must stand on ceremony—or sit upon it, as the case may be."

"Do you take snuff?"

He peered over at her in the moonlight. "I do not. It's a deucedly filthy habit. Nor do I use smoking tobacco. I'm convinced my father's frequent agues of the lungs are related to his fondness for the pipe. If you were to ask to borrow my snuffbox, you'd find it holds lemon drops."

He reached over and plucked Esther's cup from her grasp, raising it up. "May I?"

What was she to say to that? "You may."

He helped himself to a sip of her posset, and the

idea of it, of this handsome lordling drinking so casually from her cup, was peculiar indeed.

"Are you flirting with me, my lord?"

He set the cup down between them, his lips quirking. "If you have to ask, Miss Himmelfarb, then I'm making a poor job of it, aren't I?"

He hadn't said no. "May I ask you another question?"

His lordship closed his eyes and leaned his head back. "I'd rather it be a flirtatious sort of question now that you raise the subject. You're very pretty, you know, and I've lately concluded the entire purpose of this gathering is to develop one's stamina as a flirt. Like field maneuvers, I suppose." He cracked open one eye. "I apologize if I'm being rude. That's a truth potion you've slipped me."

He settled back against the wall, shifting broad shoulders as if to get more comfortable. With his eyes closed, Percival Windham by moonlight was...

Handsome. Still, yet, more...deucedly handsome, to use his word. Lord Percival was the spare, but he had "duke" stamped all over him. The height, the self-possession, the charm...

"So you're not averse to another question, my lord?"

"If we're to be drinking companions, Miss Himmelfarb, then the 'my lording' has to cease. Mind you, I am not flirting with you."

He was humoring her, though. Or something. "Do you frequently bathe in company?"

A beat of silence went by, while Esther wondered if perhaps that posset wasn't truth potion after all.

"Miss Himmelfarb, this version of not-flirting holds a man's interest. Whyever would you ask?"

He sounded amused and genuinely intrigued.

"I am appeasing my curiosity. Young ladies gossip almost as much as young men do."

"They couldn't possibly. To answer your question, it might have escaped your notice, but my dimensions are such that I rather take up the available space in most tubs. I am not in the habit of entertaining callers when I'm at my bath, despite what our hostess appears to have told half the women in the realm. You never did answer my question."

Esther cast back over their short, odd conversation. "How do I endure house parties?"

"Without committing hanging felonies on your fellow guests, all of whom seem intent on mischief. It's worse than an entire regiment of Scottish recruits on leave."

He wasn't simply tired, he was exasperated and not a little bewildered. Esther picked up the posset and handed it to him.

"Do you miss Canada?" This was what she should have asked him, not those other questions—the ones that Herodia, Charlotte, and Zephora would not believe the answers to.

He drank deeply from her cup and kept it in his hands. "I *wish* I missed Canada. The land is so beautiful it makes your soul ache, but pitiless too. In any season, Canada has ways to kill a man—snakes, locals, diseases, itching vines, and lunatic commanding officers."

Perhaps he was a little drunk, or a little homesick for somewhere neither Canada nor Kent.

"You could transfer elsewhere."

"And it would be the same, Miss Himmelfarb,

because it would still be His Majesty's military, and I would still be the Moreland spare." He fell silent, Esther's cup held in his two hands on his flat belly.

"You were treated differently because your father is a duke?"

"I was. By some I was treated worse, by others better. At my last post, I was bitterly resented by my superior officer."

This was far, far worse than flirting, or even that whispering-in-her-ear thing Percival Windham could do in a room full of people. Still, she asked the next question.

"What happened?"

He grew still, the darkness seemed to gather closer, and Esther caught a whiff of his cedary scent on the soft night air.

"I will tell you, Esther Himmelfarb, because I am a just a wee bit in my cups, or perhaps it's the moonshine loosening my tongue. In any case, we will both wish—and in the morning pretend—that I had kept my own counsel." Another pause, another sip of her posset. "My unit was between posts—there are no roads worth the name—and we came upon an encampment of natives. There are all stripes of Indians in the Canadian woods, some friendly, some murderous, and some both, depending on the day of the week. We encountered not even a gesture in the direction of hostility from this group, which upon inspection turned out to be a function of their menfolk being off on a trapping expedition."

Rape. He would not use the word in her presence, but Esther felt it lurking on the edges of the conversation.

"General Starkweather ordered the women and children rounded up, declared them prisoners, and started marching them through the woods. He did this to goad me, I'm fairly certain. We were not to provoke the locals without cause, and shivering in the woods while praying for spring did not constitute cause in the opinion of any man in that company."

He set the cup aside, apparently having finished Esther's posset.

"We got about two hours' march from the encampment, and were not likely to make our billet by dark. The general ordered the prisoners lined up in a ditch and declared himself unwilling to be slowed down by such a lot of filthy, murdering savages when the weather might turn foul at any point."

Murder now joined rape in the part of the conversation Lord Percival was not speaking aloud. Murder, rape, and offense to the honor of any officer, any honest man, present on the scene. Esther wanted to touch him, to stop him from speaking more words that would hurt him and forever haunt her.

"General Starkweather assembled a firing squad. He made sure I was directly on hand when the lads were given the command to shoulder arms. If I interfered, I was, of course, guilty of insubordination of a magnitude that would earn me a conclusion to my troubles in the same manner our captives were facing."

Rape, murder, dishonor, *execution*.

While all around him, gossip wanted to accuse Percival Windham of frivolousness and debauchery.

"You did not give the order to fire. Not on helpless women and children."

He sat up, set the cup on the ground, and peered over at her for a long moment before he resumed speaking, his words addressed to a patch of rosemary growing across the walk.

"There was an old woman, a stout little thing with a brown face as wrinkled as a prune. She'd been carrying an infant the entire distance, and the child had begun to fuss, likely from hunger. I sat there on my horse, wrapped from head to toe in thick layers of wool, while that old woman shivered, her own blanket given up to keep the child warm. I have never seen such fortitude before or since.

"The men figured out what Starkweather was up to, and the quality of their silence was as chilling as the wind in those woods. Picture this: snow all around us, two hundred of His Majesty's finest poised to witness murder, and the only sounds the wind in the pine boughs and that crying baby."

Rape, murder, dishonor, hanging, dread, and no options.

"The old woman tickled the baby's chin."

Lord Percival reached over and brushed a knuckle twice over the point of Esther's chin. "She tickled the baby's chin, jostled him and jollied him, until he was laughing as babies will. Despite the cold, despite his hungry belly, despite the firing squad several yards away, the baby laughed. Starkweather gave the command to take aim, then told me to take over."

"You did not do murder. I know you did not."

How did she know it, though? From the kindness in his eyes when he flirted? From the weariness he'd let her see by moonlight? From the fact that he'd even noticed an old woman with the courage to tickle a baby while death loomed?

"I did not give the order to fire, Esther Himmelfarb. I will admit to you I was insubordinate, and Tony was there to witness it. As I opened my mouth and gave the command to order arms, the air was filled with a shrieking such as I hope never to hear again. The trapping party had tracked us, circled around front and taken their position in the trees above the trail. I regret to report that though casualties on both sides were minimal, General Starkweather did not survive the affray."

Had he killed his superior officer? Esther did not think so, but neither did she care if he had. "Good. The man was not fit to command."

Lord Percival regarded her again for a long, long moment, until his lips curved up in a grave, sweet smile. "A court martial would not have rendered that decision, my dear."

"Then a higher court intervened in a timely fashion, my lord. Surely you cannot argue my conclusion?"

"I cannot—I will not, given your insistence, but neither will I be romanticizing the appeal of the military. If I retain my commission, I'll likely ask for and get an administrative position. I excel at recall and application of rules and regulations—I should probably have become a barrister, except the inactivity would have bored me silly."

In the past five minutes, they'd gone from an uneasy discussion on a hard bench, to a conversation between two refugees from…life. "You'll hate working at a desk, my lord."

"I'd hate even more the vapid existence of a younger son dancing about on the end of Her Grace's leash. My sister-in-law begged us to come home, and Tony and I could refuse Bella nothing."

"You are fond of Lady Pembroke?"

"I was eight years old when I met her, and yes, she is the first woman I fell in love with, if you discount Mrs. Wood."

He was perfectly, astoundingly serious. "Mrs. Wood was your governess?" This was safer ground, no awful words lurking unsaid, but in some ways the honesty he offered was equally dangerous.

"The very one. A dear old soul who made Latin and French into games and declared sums fit only for naughty boys on rainy days. Tony and I adored her. My father intervened when the tutors took over and said Mrs. Wood must stay on as our French instructor because her accent was superior."

"Can you speak any French at all?"

"*Je vous adore*, Miss Himmelfarb, will that do? I enjoy languages, but find sums a bloody lot of work, particularly in a commercial context. You know, you never did tell me how you endure these infernal house parties. Tony thinks we've been sent here to convince us to take brides out of sheer self-preservation. A bachelor's pillorying earned by our failure to become engaged this past winter."

A little dart of pain lanced through the sense of commiseration Esther had been fancying she shared with Lord Percival. A man who complained of being marital prey did not regard present company as a threat.

Which she wasn't. He was a duke's son, after all.

"I do as little as possible to burden the help, for one thing. These parties are very trying for them, and they can be unexpected allies."

"Sound advice. Mannering has to do double duty, serving both myself and Tony. But how do you...*endure?*"

His tone held genuine consternation, a sentiment Esther could share all too easily.

"Nap in the middle of the day, my lord. Don't drink to excess *ever*, and keep a chair wedged under your door latch if you're alone in your room. If your drink tastes the least bit strange, set it aside, the same with your food. Retire to your room on the pretext of seeing to correspondence, and you should be given some privacy. I also ride out on the fine days but take a groom with me, even when I'd prefer a solitary outing."

His examination of her this time was not accompanied by a smile. "I see you are a veteran of these gatherings, Miss Himmelfarb. Why aren't you married, if you find them so tedious?"

"Maybe for the same reasons you aren't married." Even that was probably saying too much. Esther retrieved her empty cup from where it sat on the ground between them. "I ought to be going in, my lord."

"Percival, or Percy to my friends. We can be friends, can we not?"

He was offering something—friendship, of some offhand, passing variety—even as he removed from consideration the curious, budding, silly notion that he might have noticed her as a man notices a young woman.

"I must be going." Esther scooted to the edge of

the bench only to find her companion on his feet, his hand under her elbow.

"I'd see you in, Esther Himmelfarb, and even up to your room, but we both know what gossip that might cause. My thanks for your company and for sharing your posset."

She turned to go, but his hand was still on her arm and his fingers closed around her wrist. A few beats of silence went by while Esther cataloged impressions.

He was wonderfully tall and substantial, a man upon whom even an Amazon like herself could lean, confident of his support.

At the end of a long day, his scent was still beguilingly pleasant. Not overwhelming, not cloying, just a teasing hint of cedar and spices that made her want to close her eyes and breathe slowly through her nose.

And he was near enough that Esther could feel the heat of his body in the moonlit shadows.

"Good night, Esther."

"Good night, my—Percival."

Would he kiss her? She hoped he would, a token kiss to her cheek, a small memory of pleasure in the midst of purgatory, a touch to make all that had been shared before a little more real.

His lips brushed her forehead before he dropped her wrist. "Sweet dreams, my lady."

She was being dismissed. Esther stepped back— did not curtsy—and left him standing in the garden, bathed in cool, silvery moonlight and solitude.

Two

"MORELAND! YOU WILL ATTEND ME! HIPPOLYTA Morrisette has sent news!"

Her Grace's trajectory into the breakfast parlor was checked by the need to turn sideways to fit her panniers through the doorway, though this did nothing to stop her prattling. "Not four days into the house party, and both boys are already much admired by several young ladies."

George, His Grace the Duke of Moreland, rose from his place at the table. "Good morning, Your Grace. I trust you slept well?" He tossed a meaningful glance at old Thomas standing at attention by the sideboard.

Her Grace's lips thinned as she allowed her husband to seat her. "I slept abominably, though I find this morning there is cause for cautious optimism."

She would not be silenced, not by the presence of a servant, not by the open door, not by anything less than the hand of Almighty God slapped over her mouth, and even then she'd give the Deity a struggle for form's sake. Her Grace was a determined woman and always had been.

His Grace flicked a glance at one of his oldest retainers. "Thomas, if you'll excuse us?"

The barest hint of commiseration showed in the old man's eyes before he bowed once to the duke, again to the duchess, and withdrew, closing the door behind him.

"His knees creak, Moreland. You should pension him before he keels over in his livery."

And lose one of few allies under the ducal roof? "Thomas serves loyally, Your Grace, and has some good years left in him. May I fix you a plate?"

Her Grace fluffed her skirts just so. "Please. I'll have eggs, toast, ham, a portion of apple tart, and half a scone with butter and strawberry jam."

Determination apparently built up an appetite, and yet the woman still had a fine figure—from what His Grace could gather. They'd had separate apartments for more than twenty years, and what happened in the early hours of the day behind the closed door of Her Grace's dressing room remained a mystery.

As well it should.

His Grace needed two plates to hold the food his wife had requested. He set the plates down before her and took his place at the opposite end of the table. "What news have you had from Lady Morrisette?"

The duchess tucked into her breakfast, gesturing with her fork for the teapot. "I don't know as I can trust Hippolyta Morrisette's veracity, but she claims both Tony and Percy are quite as sought after as Quimbey himself."

Then the boys are to be pitied. "Is that so?"

"You will not take that tone with me, Moreland. We need grandsons, and it's my duty to ensure we get

them. Criticize me for many things, but I am dutiful."
She glowered at him for a moment for emphasis—
unnecessary emphasis—before returning to her meal.

They hadn't started out sniping at each other.
They'd started out two young, lusty people who'd
hoped and prayed their parents had found them a suitable mate. And for a time…

And then little Eustace had fallen from his pony,
and it had become clear that they'd buried marital happiness along with their firstborn son. Thank a merciful
God the accoucheur had told the duchess that Tony
was the last child she could safely carry. Ten years of
Her Grace's grim focus on marital duty had about
given His Grace's interest in procreation a permanent
tendency to wilt.

Shrugging that thought aside, the duke tried for a
tone that was conciliatory without being condescend-
ing. "You have become determined on grandchildren
only since Twombly took a child bride, Your Grace.
He should be shot for mistreating your sensibilities, but
you'll soon be surrounded by other gallants. Did Lady
Morrisette mention any young ladies in particular?"

Her Grace stirred sugar into her tea with vengeance. "Twombly deserves his fate, marrying a mere
girl. She'll be the death of him, mark me on this,
Moreland. And of course I will have other gallants, but
Twombly was a fine dancer."

Twombly was an aging hanger-on, not worthy of
Agatha Venetia Drysdale Windham's notice, though it
was none of His Grace's affair where or with whom
his wife spent her time. Still, a husband was entitled to
the occasional protective gesture.

"Shall I call him out for you when he's back from his wedding journey?"

The duchess shifted on her seat. "Wouldn't that be a fine thing if he prevailed, leaving me a dowager duchess with no grandsons? No, thank you, Moreland. And yes, Hippolyta says Lady Zephora Needham is spending as much time as possible with Percy and Tony, and Charlotte Pankhurst is pitching for whichever son is not escorting the Needham girl. Needham is an earl, but Pankhurst is in line for a marquessate, and those are not to be sneezed at. Pass the cream."

His Grace obliged, and then—knowing it was folly—gave his wife the benefit of his thinking regarding the entire campaign to see the younger sons wed.

"You know, Pembroke may yet have more children. We needn't be hasty with Percival and Tony, and might regret forcing their hands."

Her Grace paused in mid-chew and raised her head, like a grazing animal scenting an intruder in its grassy paddock. "That useless twit Pembroke married will produce nothing but girls, Moreland. What use are girls, tell me?"

You were a girl once. I had rather more use for you then, and you for me.

"Girls provide the Crown an opportunity to modify the letters patent, to entertain the notion of special remainders, the viscountcy—"

"The Morefield viscountcy can be preserved through the female line, but why, why on earth, should this family revert to a lesser title when, for nearly two hundred years, a dukedom has been ours to command?"

Oh, woe to the duke who provoked Her Grace on the subject of "our" dukedom. While her eggs grew cold and His Grace's digestion became tentative, Her Grace prosed on for a good five minutes about duty, chits, twits, and sons who ought to accept the guidance of a mother devoted—*dee-voted, I tell you!*—to nothing but their lifelong happiness.

"So," she concluded with a stab of the butter knife toward her husband, "I'd prefer the Pankhurst girl, though the Needham heiress as a contingency plan will do nicely."

A concerned father had to ask, regardless of the risks involved. "And what about Tony? Is he to have the contingency plan for his bride if Percy can win the Pankhurst girl?"

"Of course not." Her Grace tore off a bite of scone and eyed it like a hawk might eye a lame mouse. "Gladys Holsopple has had two seasons, she has eight strapping brothers, and her mama assures me the girl is a very high stickler and well dowered too. She'll do for Tony, though convincing him to take on a young lady so enamored of propriety will involve effort. I expect your support in this, Moreland."

She popped the bite of scone into her maw and started chewing like a squirrel.

His Grace did not by word or deed give away certain information brought to his ears privately by loyal staff. "Somehow, my dear, I will convince Tony that a woman of unimpeachable character holds his best hope for marital happiness."

"See that you do, and pass the butter, if you please."

His Grace sent up yet one more prayer for the

happiness of his younger sons and passed his duchess the butter.

≈

A week in purgatory was a very long time, particularly when Michael was more enamored of the card room than of any of the young ladies present. Esther told herself he was biding his time, waiting for the allure of Quimbey, Lord Tony, and Lord Percival to fade.

Which ought to occur in no less than three decades at the latest, provided each man developed a tendency to flatulence.

"Lady Zephora believes her bellpull is not working correctly." Esther put as much apology into her tone as she could when she addressed the Morrisette butler. "I'm on my way to the kitchen to bring up another tea tray, for the young ladies have assembled in her drawing room this morning."

Hayes did not roll his eyes. He smiled beneficently, maybe even consolingly. "These things do happen, Miss Himmelfarb. I'll see to it and have a tea tray sent along posthaste."

The bellpull was not broken, and they both knew it.

"I wouldn't want to trouble the kitchen staff unnecessarily, Mr. Hayes. I'm on my way there, as it happens, and will cheerfully retrieve a tray for Lady Zephora."

The smile lurking in his eyes disappeared, because now they both knew the object of Zephora's complaint had been not only to criticize the house staff for a slow response to incessant demands, but also to force Esther to fetch and carry like a servant.

"If you say so, miss." He gave her a deliberate

formal bow and let her hustle along the corridor. Was it lying if the other party knew the falsehood for what it was? Esther hoped not, because another day—another hour—in purgatory would have her...

What had Lord Percival said? Howling like a wolf and wearing his wig backward.

She brushed aside the memory while she waited for the scullery maid—Patricia—to put together the tea tray. Percival Windham hadn't so much as smiled at her in the past three days. He'd smiled at everyone else—servants, horses, dogs, debutantes, they all merited his smiles—while Esther had earned only a few brooding glances.

And she hadn't set one slippered toe in the kitchen garden after dark. As the full moon waned, so had the glow of that encounter with Lord Percival.

Esther picked up the tray—the blasted thing was heavy—and headed for the maids' stairs.

"Miss." Patricia's voice had Esther pausing. "Not them stairs."

The front stairs, the ones used by family on their rare sorties to the lower regions of the house, would be longer, though Esther understood Patricia's point: the maids' stairs were for the help.

The damned tray was heavy. Esther shook her head and started for the maids' stairs, only to understand halfway up that Patricia's warning hadn't been about appearances and self-respect, or not only about those things.

"Miss Himmelfarb." Jasper Layton lounged on the first landing, elbows propped on the banister as he gazed down at her. "What on earth could cause a proper young lady to lurk on the back stairs so early in the day?"

Noon approached, but it was early by Sir Jasper's standards. Without paint and powder, his appearance improved somewhat, though late nights in the card room had left dark circles beneath his eyes. Regardless of his toilet, he was still inclined to have his conversations with the tops of Esther's breasts.

"Sir Jasper. If you'll excuse me, Lady Zephora will not want her tea cooling. I'll wish you good day."

He shifted, lazily, just enough to trap Esther two steps beneath the landing. The superior position clearly appealed to him too, so Esther let him enjoy it for a moment while she dropped her gaze to the tea tray.

He stepped aside, allowing her to pass, and then she realized why. With the tray in her hands, she faced a closed door on the far side of the landing. Her choices were to wait for Sir Jasper to open the door, to try to balance the tray on her hip and open the door herself, or to set the tray on the floor, open the door, and then pick the tray up.

While Sir Jasper ogled her backside, of course.

"A small dilemma," Sir Jasper observed from much too close behind her. "You study the dilemma, while I study the opportunities it presents."

A male hand slid around Esther's waist. She closed her eyes and discarded options: she could scream, which would result in her being compromised if anybody heard her; she could stomp on the blighted man's foot, which would anger him and not solve the problem; she could dump hot tea on his falls, which was social suicide though a nice thought to contemplate; or she could endure this small detour into hell.

A second hand joined the first, easing up over Esther's ribs. "Instead of playing chambermaid to those ninnies in hair bows," he said, "you might consider more pleasant diversions with me, you know. I can be very considerate and quite discreet."

He could also manage a fair impression of ants crawling over Esther's skin. While he brushed his thumbs over the tops of her breasts and pushed his hips against her backside—thank God for her bustle— Esther sighed breathily.

"Lady Zephora has no patience, sir. To delay for even a moment will guarantee her enmity."

"I can placate Lady Zephora." His breath, reeking of the previous night's overindulgence, came hot against Esther's neck.

It was time to end this.

"Lady Morrisette has asked me to join her as soon as I've seen to the young ladies. If you'd get the door, sir. Please."

Esther suffused the last word with pleading, but knew a moment's real trepidation when Sir Jasper did not immediately do as she asked. He gave her breasts as much of a squeeze as her stomacher allowed, reached around her to lift the door latch, and stepped back.

"A man's protection would offer you a great deal more than this servile existence, Miss Himmelfarb." He stroked his crotch twice, his gaze on Esther's breasts. "A great deal more."

Gracious God. Esther did her best rendition of the flustered schoolgirl and ducked out of the stairway, kicking the door shut behind her with a shade too much force. Sir Jasper offered not marriage but ruin, and the cursed man no doubt honestly believed a few months of his favors were preferable to a respectable life with children.

Esther set the tray down on a sideboard and paused to consider her appearance in the mirror above it. Flushed, pale, *angry*.

Sir Jasper's offer, not the first of its kind, was not preferable to decades of respectable marriage and motherhood—but was it preferable to decades of impoverished spinsterhood? To being shuffled around her siblings' households as the poor relation? To growing old with her parents?

"I behold a vision, though not, I think, a happy one."

Behind her in the mirror, an unpowdered Percival Windham, golden hair loose about his shoulders, was smiling perplexedly at her reflection.

Now he chanced upon her? *Now*, when, on general principles, she wanted to cock back her arm and slap any man she saw?

She curtsied. "My lord. Good day."

"It is no such thing when you're consigned to carrying trays for the harpies populating this house party." He stepped a little closer and lowered his voice. "We've shared a moonlit posset, Miss Himmelfarb, though you seem determined to ignore the memory."

He was implying some question or other, while Esther wanted to…howl like a wolf, in part because they *had* shared a moonlit posset.

"Forgive me, my lord. I do not relish Lady Zephora's tongue-lashing when I appear belatedly with her tea tray."

He came around to stand between Esther and her

reflection, his lips pursed in study. "Hang Lady Zephora and the whole chorus. Something has you overset."

At that precise, benighted moment, Sir Jasper emerged from the stairway and sauntered along the corridor.

He nodded at Lord Percival. "My lord."

"Sir Jasper."

Jasper paused and ran an insolent gaze over Esther while she stood silently by the sideboard. Bad enough to be ogled, but it *hurt* to endure such treatment where Lord Percival could see it. Esther did not know whom to hate for that hurting—Jasper, Lord Percival, or herself.

Sir Jasper took himself off after a pointed look at the tea tray. Had she been alone, Esther might have ducked back into the maids' stairway and had a good cry.

Percival Windham turned an inscrutable gaze on her in the ensuing silence. "Esther Himmelfarb, was that weasel bothering you?"

The question held such quiet ferocity, Esther wanted to laugh and cry at the same time. She nodded, because whatever else was true about Percival Windham, he hadn't blamed her for Sir Jasper's weaseling. "I should have known better than to use the maids' stairs. He is a predictable nuisance."

"You will not blame yourself for his bad behavior. Come along." Lord Percival picked up the tea tray like it weighed nothing and winged an elbow at Esther. "You look tired, my dear, but I know you aren't lurking in gardens of a late hour."

Esther took his arm, recalling the muscles there only when she wrapped her fingers around them. "How could you know that?"

"I've made the kitchen garden my private retreat,

but I've also repaired there in hopes of continuing our previous conversation. One needs allies. Witness your encounter with Sir Weasel."

And because Percival Windham had dubbed himself Esther's ally, she had his escort right to the door of Lady Zephora's chambers. He even went so far as to take the tray into the sitting room, causing a flurry of billing and cooing among the ladies gathered there in morning attire.

Esther took a window seat, watching while Lord Percival dodged invitations to walk, to ride out, to share a *private archery lesson* with this young lady, or a meal alfresco with that one. As she contemplated a duke's son having to duck and leap his way through a series of morning greetings, it occurred to her that for him, there was risk lurking not just at the top of the maids' stairs but on every hand.

Which made the notion of him retreating to the kitchen garden, alone but for the moonlight, a very intriguing thought indeed.

❧

"These things grow more tedious each year." Lord Morrisette fastened his falls, missing a button on the left side. "The difficulty is the ladies make up the guest lists, and we gentlemen are left like orphaned pups, seeking any available titty, as it were."

Percival did not respond to his host's observation. The ladies had withdrawn, leaving the gentlemen to make use of the chamber pots and the decanters, in no particular order.

"Any titty is better than no titty," somebody observed from the opposite corner.

A philosophical discussion ensued as to the ideal shape for the female breast: large, small, soft, firm—all had their enthusiasts.

"The real quesh-tion." Lord Morrisette blinked at his glass. "The more pertinent in-quire-ree is what shape ought the ideal female orifice follow? The assembled company will be pleased to know I've made a study on this."

Spoons were rapped against glasses amid a round of cheers and jeers.

Percival hooked Tony by one elbow. "Let's get some air, shall we?"

They left the room—ostensibly to smoke, to pass gas out of doors, or to chase housemaids—as a vote was proposed regarding the advantages of the inverted wine glass shape over the champagne flute.

"I thought nothing could be as stupid as drunken soldiers far from home and in need of a sound swiving, but I must revise my opinions." As they headed away from the sound of male laughter, Tony sounded impatient, an odd circumstance for him.

"This is Kent," Percival reminded him, steering him toward the stairs. "There is no greater concentration of the wealthy and aimless on the entire planet than in this county at this time of year."

"So you're not enjoying all the married women, chaperones, lady's maids, and other offerings? I could swear Hector Bellamy was trying to entice me into bed the other night with a chambermaid thrown in as a sop to convention."

Tony clearly did not find this amusing—neither did Percival. "You're handsome, blond, and almost as tall as I am," Percival replied, then directed Tony toward the kitchens. "I know a place where we won't be disturbed, accosted, or propositioned."

"As long as it's not Canada."

They emerged into the moonlit kitchen garden, only to spy Esther Himmelfarb seated on the bench against the wall.

She rose immediately and bobbed a curtsy. "My lords, I'll bid you good night."

Before Percival could signal Tony to take himself off, before he could detain the lady with anything approaching a witticism, she hared away amid a cloud of fragrance and maidenly shyness.

"Pretty girl," Tony remarked, settling onto the bench. "She grows on one. Gladys said we ought to keep a lookout for her."

Percy took the place beside him, though he couldn't help cursing himself for bringing Tony along to this destination at this hour. "When did the fair Gladys pass along that sentiment?"

"We correspond, discreetly of course."

One tended to underestimate Anthony Windham. Tony offended no one, he invited confidences, and— perhaps his greatest attribute—he was also capable of keeping them.

"What would you think of acquiring Esther Himmelfarb as a sister-in-law?" Percival asked.

Tony was silent a long time, which was better than had he burst out laughing.

"Her Grace would make her life hell," he said eventually. "His Grace would accept her."

An accurate assessment, as far as it went. "And you?"

Another protracted silence broken by the serenades of crickets, who knew nothing of titles and sang for their true loves every night.

"She'd do, Perce. You aren't the frivolous younger son you were five years ago. Canada sorted you out, or something did. Miss Esther would follow the drum, did you ask it, and Her Grace would have to choose her battles with that one."

"No, she would not."

Tony's observation and Percival's own reply brought some order to the chaos of a man contemplating—seriously contemplating—holy matrimony for the first time. Percival sat forward on the bench, his elbows braced on his knees.

"At first, I merely thought myself smitten with Miss Himmelfarb's good looks and self-possession. She's so irreproachably Teutonic about the chin, you know. Stirs a man's instincts, that chin."

Tony maintained a politic silence, so Percy continued to work out his logic with words. "Esther Himmelfarb is lovely, but she's also canny, and she's resourceful. These are qualities to admire, qualities a lady with a title needs if she's to manage well."

And now it was time for an officer to gather his courage and confide in his little brother. "She said Starkweather had been judged by a court higher than the military, and I must not argue with its decision."

"You told her about him?"

Percy nodded. The crickets sang, the scent of rosemary wafted on the breeze, and what had been a hunch in Percy's mind, an instinct, solidified into an objective. "I came upon her after Layton had been pestering her on the stairs. Tony, I had all I could do not to flatten the man right then and there."

"Why didn't you?"

Insightful question. "Because until my ring is on her finger, such behavior would redound to Esther's discredit... I'm also not sure she'd accept me."

"And that," Tony said slowly, "is why she would make an excellent Duchess of Moreland, should the day ever come."

"Precisely. I must woo Esther, and I'm not entirely sure how to go about it." The admission lay between them, a puzzling anomaly in their long history of late-night conversations wherein Percival typically parsed Tony's confusions and blind turns.

"Bit of a puzzle," Tony said, "when a gal don't flirt, carry on, or cast any lures. You could try kissing her."

"I expect Jasper Layton has made the same attempt, and likely others have as well." She slept with a chair wedged under her door latch, considered all food and drink suspect, and trusted none of the ladies to guard her back, for God's sake. A frontal assault was not going to win the lady's heart.

"Sometimes answers come if we're patient," Tony said. "I'm waiting for Gladys to turn twenty-one."

"How much longer?"

"Another bloody year, and her mama is making noises about an excellent match in the offing. Makes it difficult to twiddle one's thumbs here in Kent when one's love is twiddling hers back in Town."

"So you write letters and twiddle and swill Morrisette's brandy."

"You'll expect me to keep an eye out for Miss Himmelfarb too."

The image of Jasper Layton eyeing the lady with undisguised lust rose in Percival's mind. "I'll keep an eye out for her as well, and as for the wooing part, maybe something inspired will come to me."

                        ∽

Percival Windham was the most aggravating specimen of an aggravating gender ever to attend an aggravating house party.

Why would he have brought Lord Tony to the kitchen garden, when he'd all but invited Esther to tryst with him there? Perhaps tryst was stretching it a bit—stretching it a lot—but a brother was a brother, and Lord Tony hadn't shown any signs of departing the garden.

Esther had had two more days to observe Lord Percival, though from a distance. Ever since she'd appeared in Zephora Needham's sitting room on Lord Percival's arm, a silent conspiracy had arisen among the eligible young ladies. They might plunge daggers into one another's backs in their attempts to win Lord Percy's notice, but they were united in their determination to keep Esther from his lordship's company.

"And when you're done replacing the flowers in the front hallway and the green parlor, then you can check on the bouquets in the library, conservatory, music room, and upstairs corridors." Lady Morrisette smiled broadly and folded beringed fingers on the blotter of her escritoire. "I do hope you're enjoying yourself, my dear. These little tasks taken from my shoulders are such a help, and your mama was most insistent that I add you to the guest list."

Like blazes. Mama had consented to send Esther only because Michael had already been invited and Lady Pott's maid was nominally available to tend to Esther's clothing.

"The company is wonderful, my lady, and I have always enjoyed working with flowers."

Particularly when it would mean Esther had a sharp pair of shears in her hand. Sir Jasper was proving persistent, and the house party had two more weeks yet to run. She curtsied and collected a footman to accompany her to the conservatory, only to encounter Michael lounging on a bench under the potted palms.

"Michael, are you hiding?"

He got to his feet and aimed a pointed look at the footman.

"If you'd start on the roses?" Esther asked, passing the fellow the shears. He bowed and withdrew, though first he perused Michael in a manner not quite respectful.

"I am enjoying a moment of solitude. I've never met such a pack of females for dancing and hiking and promenading until all hours."

Esther regarded her cousin with a female relation's pitiless scrutiny. "You're up until all hours playing cards, Michael. The young ladies have complained to this effect. And you're losing."

He sank back down on the bench. "You can't know that. A gentleman expects a few losses when he's wagering socially."

That he would admit that much was not good. Esther

took the place beside him. "If you socialized more and wagered less, I would not have such cause to worry."

"I always come right sooner or later, Esther." He assayed a smile that would not have fooled their nearly blind grandmama. "Are you enjoying yourself?"

She could lambaste him, she could lecture him, or she could accept the olive branch he was holding out. "I have found some interesting poetry in the Morrisette library, and Quimbey is a wonderfully down-to-earth fellow."

"Also a confirmed bachelor."

"One more thing to like about him. Promise me you won't play too deeply, Michael. You cannot afford the losses, and I cannot afford the scandal."

"We are not widely known as cousins by this august assemblage, so cease carping, Esther Louise." He rose and extended a hand to her. "I've seen Lord Tony Windham on your arm from time to time. Any chance you could reel him in?"

Like a carp? "He's friendly, nothing more." And he'd appeared more than once when Jasper Layton had come sidling about, a coincidence Esther was not going to examine too closely.

"You could try being friendly, Cousin."

This went beyond bad advice to something approaching interfamilial treason. Esther propped her fists on her hips and glared at her cousin. "As far as these people are concerned, I have no dowry, my come-out was two years ago, and I'm too tall. Do you know what friendliness would merit me in this company?"

Michael's handsome features shuttered as Esther's meaning sank in.

A banging of the conservatory door spared Esther whatever protest Michael would have made.

"There you are!" Lord Tony Windham covered the length of the conservatory in double time. "Miss Himmelfarb, I have need of your company this instant. Sir, you will excuse the lady. She has promised to walk the gardens with me immediately."

He nodded at Michael, who offered Esther the merest glance to ascertain her consent before stepping back. "Miss Himmelfarb, good day. Lord Anthony."

"Right, good day, good afternoon, good morning." Lord Anthony linked his arm through Esther's and lowered his voice. "Time is of the essence, my dear. You must attend to the flowers in the rose salon immediately."

This was not the affable, smiling Lord Tony whom Esther had come to know in recent days. This was a fellow with urgent business on his mind.

"I must?"

"Indeed. It is of utmost importance that you do." He hustled her along, not stopping until they were outside the door of the parlor in question.

The closed door.

"Lord Anthony, what's afoot here?"

He opened the door and gave Esther a gently muscular shove. "My thanks for your company."

The tableau that greeted Esther spoke for itself. In a dress far too low cut for daylight hours, Charlotte Pankhurst reclined on a chaise, while Lord Percival stood over her, looking exasperated.

"Miss Himmelfarb." He bowed to her very low, his expression one of banked relief. "A *pleasure* to see you. Miss Pankhurst is feeling unwell, and I was just about to—"

The door from the blue salon next door opened abruptly, revealing Lady Morrisette and several of the other older women in attendance.

"I knew I heard voices!" Lady Morrisette's shrill observation rang out over the room while her cronies crowded in behind her.

"It's well you're here, my lady," Esther said before Charlotte could open her fool mouth. "I came in to check on the flowers and found Miss Pankhurst feeling poorly. Lord Percival stopped by and offered his aid when he perceived the lady was in distress. Perhaps the physician should be summoned?"

The distressed lady—for she clearly was distressed *now*—bolted to a sitting position. "That will not be necessary."

Lady Morrisette rose to the challenge after the merest blink of frustrated disbelief. "Perhaps it was the kippers at breakfast, my dear. They don't always agree with one. How fortunate his lordship and Miss Himmelfarb were here to render you aid."

Charlotte's expression turned from mulish to murderous as Lord Tony came sauntering in. "Greetings, all. Percy, the horses are being saddled as we speak, and you're not yet in riding attire. Miss Himmelfarb, I believe you were to join us?"

This was farce, but from the look in Charlotte's eyes, deadly farce.

Esther turned a dazzling smile on Lord Tony. "Just let me change into my habit, your lordship. Miss Pankhurst, I wish you a swift recovery."

She curtsied to all and sundry, spared a dozen wilted

bouquets half a thought, and sidled past Lord Tony into the hallway.

"Oh, Miss Himmelfarb!" Lady Morrisette's voice jerked Esther to a stop as effectively as if Esther were a spaniel upon whose leash the woman had tramped.

"My lady?"

Esther's hostess approached, glancing to the left and right as she did. "Charlotte is my goddaughter, and one can't blame her for trying. I'll understand if you have to depart early."

What was the woman saying? "Are you asking me to leave?"

"Oh, good Lord, no." Lady Morrisette's smile was feral. "What ensues now should be very interesting indeed. I'm simply saying if you do decide your mother has an ague, for example, or your younger sister should come down with lung fever, then I will be happy to make your excuses to the company. I know my goddaughter, and she does not deal well with disappointment."

A warning, then. "I appreciate your understanding. If you'll excuse me, I must change into my riding habit."

Lady Morrisette gave Esther a little salute. "Go down fighting, I always say. Enjoy your *ride*."

The innuendo was cheerful, vulgar, and snide. Contemplating that Parthian shot, Esther felt as if she'd been the one to consume a quantity of bad kippers—and in the next two weeks, the feeling could only get worse.

❧

Percival Windham did not believe in shirking his responsibilities. He boosted Esther Himmelfarb into the saddle, arranged her skirts over her boots, and remained standing by her stirrup.

"I am in your never-ending, eternal, perpetual debt, Miss Himmelfarb. I cannot thank you enough for your timely appearance in that salon. I'd received a note, you see, ostensibly from Lady Morrisette."

Several yards away, Tony was fussing with his horse's girth, no doubt sensible that the moment called for groveling.

"You should thank your brother, my lord, though I cannot think why he didn't simply intervene himself."

The lady's words bore a slight chill, something more than politesse but less than indignation. This did not bode well for a fellow who'd reached the inescapable conclusion that he'd met his one true love.

"Had Tony come upon us alone in that room, he would have been honor bound to relate what he saw to our mother, Her Grace, and she would have been delighted to accept Miss Pankhurst as a prospective daughter-in-law. You see before you a man in receipt of nothing less than a divine pardon, Miss Himmelfarb, and you the angel of its deliverance."

"That's laying it on a bit thick, your lordship."

Had her lips quirked? Was humor alight in her lovely green eyes?

"It is the God's honest truth, madam. You will consider what boon I might grant you in repayment."

He left her with that offer to consider—a stroke of genius if he did say so himself—and swung up onto his bay gelding. Two grooms mounted up on cobs, while Tony climbed onto a leggy gray.

"Would you like to see Morelands, Miss Himmelfarb? It's not five miles east cross-country."

"Lead on, your lordship. Any hour out of doors on such a lovely day is time well spent."

Esther Himmelfarb rode with the casual grace of one who'd been put in the saddle early and often, and while her habit was several years out of fashion, her sidesaddle was in excellent repair and superbly fitted to her seat.

Five miles passed quickly, with Tony falling behind a dozen yards to confer with the grooms.

"Let's take the next turning," Percival said. "There's somebody I'd like you to meet."

At his suggestion, Miss Himmelfarb nudged her mare to the left, down a bridle path that ran between two high hedges.

They hadn't gone twenty yards before she drew her horse up. "You wanted me to meet somebody in a graveyard?"

"I did, in fact." Percival swung down, handed the horse off to a groom, and assisted the lady to dismount. She put her hands on his shoulders and slid to the ground, the closest they'd stood in days, close enough that his good intentions could be assailed by the scent of lavender and the feel of a slender female waist under his very hands.

"Come." Percy grasped her gloved fingers in his. "Mrs. Wood bides here. This is the Windham family plot. All the best people are to be found in its confines."

She gave him a look suggesting he'd gone barmy, but kept pace as he circled the small plot. Tony, may the Almighty bless and keep him, had signaled that he'd assist the grooms to water the horses at a small burn a furlong away on the other side of the hedges.

"When I was a small boy and periodically suffused with indignation, I'd come here to seek consolation. Peter always knew where to find me."

He led her to a bench under an enormous oak.

"Peter would be the Marquess of Pembroke?"

"Tony still calls him Petey, if you can credit that." He drew her down to the bench and kept her hand in his. He was not going to part with that pretty feminine appendage until Doomsday or something of equal magnitude required it.

"Who is the cherub? Eustace Penhaligon Drysdale Fortinbras Windham? That's a lot of names for somebody who lived only…five years."

"My older brother, though I never knew him. He fell from his pony, and that was that. Peter says Eustace was a daredevil but always laughing. My mother adored him, or so my father says."

"It would break my heart to lose a child, and how your mother must have prayed for you and Lord Anthony, joining the cavalry and crossing the seas."

In the quiet, pretty graveyard, their hands joined, he wanted to tell her that being with her was comfortable in a way he hadn't experienced in all his varied undertakings with the fair sex. Esther Himmelfarb's company gave him a sense of coming home to a place he'd never been but always hoped existed.

"You would pray for your children, Esther. May I call you Esther?"

She did not withdraw her hand, but she pulled away somehow in silence. "When we are private, you may."

"Are you going to remind me that we're of different stations, *Esther*? Your grandfather was an earl. I'm a commoner, and I associate with whom I please."

"I will pay for that scene in the rose parlor, your lordship. You will not. Commoner you might be, but I am to all appearances undowered. I did not take, I am plain, and I have not ingratiated myself to the people who matter."

She was utterly convinced of her words, also utterly wrong.

"You are lovely. I'm glad you did not take, or some other fellow would have long since snatched you up, and I respect mightily that you have not ingratiated yourself with people who think they matter."

She straightened, and Percival realized his tone was nearly argumentative.

"You mentioned a boon, your lordship."

The female mind was not to be underestimated. "Don't ask me to ignore you, my dear. You've proven that you're a loyal friend, and don't tell me you can't use a friend too."

Friendship was progress, wasn't it? The exact dimensions of friendship with a female would be new territory for him, but the term seemed appropriate for the circumstances, and to Percival Windham, all females were deserving of beneficent regard, at least initially.

His new, reluctant friend was clutching his hand rather snugly too. "I want you to teach me how to kiss."

While Percival calculated whether he could peel off her glove and press his lips to her knuckles, Esther withdrew her hand and rose, pacing down a raked gravel walk to little Eustace's headstone. To pursue, or to sit on the hard bench and drink in how lovely, how right, she looked among the Windhams of days past?

And how blessedly convenient her request was to Percival's own plans for the lady.

He stuffed his gloves in his pocket and let himself stand behind her, close enough to drink in her lavender scent and to appreciate that, in riding attire, a woman was a more approachable creature indeed.

"You want me to teach you to kiss?"

She turned, the headstone at her back, which meant a marble angel's outstretched wings protected them from view. "I want you to teach me much more than that, Percival Windham, but there's a limit to my presumption—and to my folly. You are reputed to be proficient at kissing, and I would avail myself of your expertise."

Kissing was wonderful folly, though when undertaken with this woman, it was also going to be in absolute earnest.

"Esther, if folly and presumption and those other obfuscations were not a consideration, what boon would you ask of me?"

She stared at a point several inches above his heart for a long, lavender-scented moment.

"I am a poor relation in training."

Which made no sense, because upon inquiry, it turned out that Herr Jacob Himmelfarb was rumored to be quite well fixed. "And you're a veritable hag, and children run from you when the moon is full." He caught a strand of golden hair fluttering around her chin and tucked it back over her ear. "Ask me, Esther. I can deny you nothing."

She stared at his chest so hard, she was perhaps trying to see his heart beat as it thundered between his ribs.

"Teach me to kiss, and I shall be content."

No, she would not. If he had anything to say to it, she'd be burning with frustration and unspent lust.

Or perhaps, if God were generous and the lady willing, spent lust.

"We have an agreement." He brushed his lips over her cheek, not touching her anywhere else. "I shall teach you to kiss in exchange for your having spared me a lifetime of marital misery. I do not regard this as an adequate boon to compensate you for your kindness and quick thinking, but it's where we shall start."

Blond brows drew down as she tugged off a riding glove and touched two fingers to the spot on her cheek where his lips had wanted badly to linger. "That's it? You kiss my cheek and announce we have a bargain?"

"Your first lesson: anticipation or surprise should be part of any kiss that seeks to leave an impression. And rest assured, my dear, when it comes to kissing you, I shall be impressive indeed."

He bussed her other cheek and drew away.

This did not appear to mollify the lady, nor was it intended to. "You have only two weeks, my lord. I hope the entire course of your pedagogy is not limited to lectures."

Oh, how starchy she sounded. How determined.

"There will be practical instruction as well, Esther my dear." *And lots of it.*

Three

PERCIVAL FELL SILENT FOR A MOMENT, AND THEN Esther felt warm male fingers closing around her hand. He brought her knuckles to his lips and pressed a kiss there, then did not let go of her hand.

"How would you describe that kiss, Miss Himmelfarb?"

He wanted to *talk* about kissing? With *Miss Himmelfarb*? "I'd describe it as brief and uninteresting. Proper."

She put as much disgust into her description as she dared, and the dratted man chuckled. When Esther would have wrenched her hand free, he tightened his grip on her fingers. "Tell me about the kisses you'd like to receive, Esther. I must have some sense of my goal, for I am very intent on reaching it."

He had an odd way of showing his intentions.

"I want kisses I'll never forget," Esther began, speaking slowly because this topic—the exact nature of the kisses she sought—was not one she'd considered.

Not one she'd been bold enough to consider, and certainly not one she'd ever been encouraged to consider.

"I want kisses that I can feel through my whole body, through my heart and soul. I want kisses that render me speechless and helpless with longing for more kisses just like them. From you, I want kisses so…*profound* that every time I catch the scent of cedar and spices, my knees go a little weak and I smile in a way that makes all the gentlemen around me, even the old men, take notice and smile a little too."

He was rubbing his thumb slowly across her knuckles, as if waiting for her to go on.

"More than that," Esther said, "I suppose I want kisses that defy description."

"Passionate kisses?" Oh, how casual he sounded.

"Not only passion. I've been mauled and slobbered over. A man's passion strikes me as an undignified, selfish thing."

"Then you want kisses to inspire your own passion?"

She had the sense he was toying with her, trying to verbally back her into some corner where her dignity and her wits could not join her. Before common sense or some equally inconvenient virtue could stop her, Esther pushed him back so he sat on the headstone, and situated herself with a knee on either side of his hips—a somewhat athletic undertaking, given her riding skirts.

"Enough talk, Percival Windham." She fisted a hand in the hair at his nape. "I'm tired of talk, and you promised, and I will not be put off by your lectures and interrogations. All day long I step and fetch and smile and pretend, and just this once, I want somebody to attend me. The other girls know how to make the men toady to them, but all I get is—"

He kissed her, a fleeting press of warm, soft lips to her mouth. "Do hush, love. You'll bring Tony with the grooms, and at the very least, for such kisses as you describe, we deserve privacy."

Esther felt his arm encircle her waist, snugging her to his larger frame, and then a series of little tugs to her scalp.

"You are destroying my coiffure, Percival. Do you know how long I must work to arrange a coronet just so?"

"About five minutes, I'd guess. The rosebuds are a nice touch, but I want to see how long your braid is."

Esther dropped her forehead to his shoulder and let him have his way with her hair. Maybe he thought that little nothing of a buss qualified as a kiss; maybe he kissed ladies only with their hair in complete disarray. "This cannot have anything to do with kissing lessons."

"Tell me about your day, Esther. What did you have for breakfast?"

Her braid came slithering down her shoulders to rest along her spine, a kind of hair sigh to go with the soul weariness weighting her limbs and the frustration weighting her heart. More questions, though this question she could answer. "I like chocolate first thing in the morning, and warm scones with butter and strawberry jam."

Something brushed her ear—his nose? "My mother prefers strawberry jam. Do you like raisins in your scones?"

"I do not. They taste foul when they burn. You are plundering my hair."

"Just loosening a few pins."

She cuddled closer, purely enjoying the feel of his

hands in her hair. "I haven't a lady's maid, though Matilda Pott's maid is looking after my clothes."

"Hah. You're helping her look after Lady Pott's gowns. You smell even better up close, Esther Himmelfarb. You taste good too." His tongue, soft, damp, and unhurried, had slipped along the place where her neck and shoulder joined.

The sensation was both warm and shivery. "Do that again."

"As my lady wishes." He lingered over it this time, caressing her flesh with his tongue. It wasn't kissing, exactly; it was more than kissing and made her want to taste him in return.

"Your hair is like moon glow in my hands. I want to see it spread over a pillow by candlelight." He spoke very softly, the words tickling her ear, until he closed his mouth around her earlobe. "I want to see you naked but for this glorious, silky hair, Esther, and a smile of welcome for me."

This was love talk, silly nonsense men concocted to make ladies want to shed their clothes—and it was working. Esther squirmed and realized that Percival Windham's talk was having an effect on certain parts of his anatomy as well.

How…lovely. How intriguing. "What else?"

He laughed quietly. "Now who has the inconvenient questions? I want to make love to you, of course, endlessly, all night, until you are limp with pleasure and neither of us can move."

Esther lifted her face from his shoulder, needing to see his eyes. "All I sought were kisses, Percival. You need not flatter and dissemble."

His expression in the shadow of the angel's wings was hard to read, but he wasn't smiling. "Give me your hand, love."

She obliged, and he brought their joined hands down between their bodies.

"Feel that. A man can't fake desire. A kiss between a man and a woman should always have a little desire in it."

If this thick column of flesh was his idea of a *little* desire… Esther withdrew her hand and felt her cheeks flush. "You haven't even kissed me yet."

"Nor shall I."

For a devastated instant, she thought he was reneging, except his hand fisted on her braid, gently but implacably, and Esther understood in the next second what he was about.

He was hers to kiss. Here in this small, secluded graveyard, peace filling the air and cherubs and angels looking on with eternal smiles, Lord Percival Windham was hers.

"Esther?"

Not so casual now, and how she loved hearing her name on his lips. "I'm thinking."

Marveling at the possibilities. She made him wait for a few heady moments while she reveled in the feel of *his* hair in *her* hands, while she traced the shape of *his* ear with *her* nose, and she settled herself on the ridge of his erection. The luxury of time he gave her was a sumptuous gift, one she indulged in shamelessly.

"How does it feel when I do this?" She shifted her weight on him minutely, bringing on all manner of pleasurable sensations.

"It does not hurt. Will you kiss me, Esther?"

There was a "but" in his "it does not hurt," one Esther could not fathom. She hitched closer and wished she were in her nightclothes, or in nothing at all.

"Esther, *please…*"

Ah, the glory of hearing that hoarse, pleading whisper, of feeling it against her bare skin. Gently, slowly, Esther settled her mouth on his, treasuring everything about the moment.

The sound of their clothing rustling when she shifted, and his arm tightened around her.

The feel of his clean-shaven cheek against her palm as she cradled his jaw.

The scrape of his riding boots as he spread his legs and closed his fingers in her hair.

The sweet lemony taste of his tongue seaming her lips.

He keeps lemon drops in his snuffbox.

For long, long moments, that was Esther's last coherent thought. She became nothing more than the female half of a passionate, unforgettable, indescribable, *profound* kiss, and how long she existed in that blissful state she could not have said, though for the duration of their kiss, Percival Windham was both storm and refuge, both the inspiration for her desire and the frustration of it.

When Esther at last subsided against his shoulder, she was panting and wishing her clothing to Hades—she was also wishing *his* clothing to Hades—and enjoying the feel of his hand stroking slowly, slowly over her hair.

"Can you describe that kiss, Esther Himmelfarb? I surely cannot." There was wonder in his voice, awe even.

"My first kiss?" A modest description, also a confession of sorts. She wanted him never to stop touching her hair in that soothing caress and yet, as long as he touched her in that way, she would have no means of reassembling her scattered wits.

"Our third kiss, my love."

"Fourth, if we're to be precise."

"Third—the little nothing before was just the appetizer. Let me hold you."

He was counting their kisses. Esther hoarded up that realization and did indeed let him hold her, and hold her, and hold her. At some point, he shifted and rose with her cradled against his chest, and still she did not stir. He carried her—her, Esther Himmelfarb, whom the dainty, petite Charlotte had described as Amazonian—down the walkway to the wooden bench, then took a seat directly beside her.

Esther retrieved her riding gloves from a skirt pocket and slipped them on, the better to control the impulse to touch Percival Windham's hair, to cradle his palm once more against her cheek.

When Anthony came up the walk, whistling a jaunty version of "God Save the King," Esther was still sitting beside Percival Windham, not touching him but wondering how—how on earth—she would describe the kisses that just passed between them.

❦

Esther had regrets. She regretted not packing more of her best gowns; she regretted her family's assumption that she could be any kind of aid to Michael in his marital machinations and any kind of check on his wagering impulses. She regretted bitterly that there hadn't been time to devise some other plan for rescuing Lord Percival from Charlotte Pankhurst's infernal schemes.

More than any of that, Esther regretted that she'd asked Percival Windham only for mere kissing lessons.

"He didn't even blink," she informed an enormous white cat curled at the foot of her bed. "Desperate spinsters must importune him for kissing lessons the livelong day."

The cat squeezed its eyes closed, eyes that sported the same startling, lovely, rosemary-in-bloom blue boasted by Percival Windham's eyes.

Esther paced the confines of her small chamber. "I have been accosted, you see. I have been groped and slobbered over, I have been propositioned, and I have even been proposed to."

She shuddered at the memory of Baron Bagshot's proposal. She'd had to help him up from his genuflection, and given the baron's fondness for his victuals and the unreliability of his septuagenarian knees, the undertaking had been ungainly.

And he'd been so unabashedly *hopeful*.

"I was supposed to consider myself fortunate, for he assured me I'd quickly be a widow and well-fixed. What sort of bride wishes her husband into the grave?"

The cat rearranged itself to a sitting position.

"Percival isn't the least bit conceited." Esther regarded the cat, a creature born with a full complement of conceit. "He's easy to talk to, and he smells good, and when he lifts one from a horse, one feels…dainty."

Dainty was a novelty and precious. No other man

had conjured this feeling in Esther's breast, as if she might shelter in his arms, lean upon him, and enjoy conversing with his chin instead of enduring his conversation with the tops of her breasts.

"He has a determined chin, nothing retiring about it. I am in a sad case when I am besotted with a man's chin… The way he uses his hands is equally enchanting, firm and…firm."

Esther sat on the bed and picked up the cat, who had commenced to groom itself and looked none too pleased to be interrupted.

"My mama still berates us in wonderfully precise German when we transgress. She's very practical, and I know exactly what is meant when a man and woman become lovers, cat."

Because Esther was scratching the nape of the beast's neck, a comforting vibration began to rumble forth from her confidante.

Esther whispered, her lips close to the cat's elegant fur, "I should have asked him to become my lover. This is a house party, we're sophisticated people, and even a poor relation in training is entitled to a few lovely memories."

The cat began to knead Esther's shoulder through her nightclothes.

"Naughty kitty." She cuddled the cat closer, mentally assuring herself, for the thousandth time, that asking Lord Percival for his kisses had not been foolish and she would not regret it.

She would, however, regret not asking him for more.

❧

The Marquess of Pembroke was a blond, shambling giant with genial features and a heartwarming devotion to his wife and daughters. As his father studied him, Pembroke sat by a mullioned window and pretended to read some thick tome, though no doubt a pamphlet on grafting roses or distilling perfumes lay between the pages of Pembroke's book.

Pembroke pushed his glasses up his nose then rubbed the heel of his right hand absently against his sternum. The gesture belonged on an old man, but in recent years had become alarmingly characteristic of the Moreland heir.

His Grace launched himself into the room, lest he be found spying on his oldest surviving son. "Is your indigestion acting up?"

Pembroke blinked, set the book aside, and rose slowly. "Not particularly. Good day, Your Grace."

"And the same to you. I trust your lady fares well?"

Bella had been present for last night's meal, it being Her Grace's decree that the family dine together in the evening, though formality had always characterized His Grace's dealings with his sons.

"She's out riding with the girls. It's a fine day for a hack. Was there something I might do for you, Your Grace?"

His Grace did not remark the infrequency of Pembroke's own ventures on horseback. As a younger man, Peter, like his brothers, had ridden like a demon—when his mother would not get wind of it—but marriage, or that ache in the man's chest, had sobered the marquess considerably.

His Grace gestured to the settee. "May I sit?"

"Of course. Shall I ring for tea?"

God's holy, everlasting balls… Their dinner conversation was the same. A parody of dialogue.

His Grace flipped out the tails of his coat and appropriated the middle of the sofa while Pembroke subsided into his reading chair. "Tea won't be necessary. Her Grace would like us to attend the last week of the Morrisette house party. The children needn't come, of course, though I'm sure Lady Morrisette will make accommodation if you insist."

He rather hoped the children would come, for both of his granddaughters were delightful young ladies who liked for their grandpapa to read to them and tell them tales of life at court.

Pembroke took off his glasses and fished a handkerchief out of his pocket, no doubt mentally fashioning a response while polishing spotless lenses.

"You never refer to her as 'my mother,' as 'our mother.' Did you know that?" Pembroke's tone was not accusing, it was merely curious, perhaps carefully curious.

From parody to farce—or tragedy? "The duchess is rather attached to the privileges of her station. Is there a point you would make, Pembroke?"

"I love my wife." Pembroke's chin came up a bit as he said this.

"Your sentiments do you credit." The duke's answer was swift and sincere.

Also, apparently, surprising to them both.

Pembroke rose and stood facing the window, which looked out over the stables and nearer paddocks. "I have wondered how my parents contrived to have four children, given what I know of my progenitors now. She's set the dogs on Percy and Tony."

She being Her Grace, of course, and the implied criticism being that His Grace had done nothing to stop her matchmaking—which he had not.

"Percival and Anthony are of an age to be taking spouses. You were younger, and your union has been blessed."

Pembroke shot a look over his shoulder. "I believe you mean that."

"I most assuredly do, and with your brothers married, perhaps you and your marchioness will finally have some peace. Ten years is long enough to bear the entire brunt of ducal expectations."

Blond brows rose, as if Pembroke's circumstances could not possibly have figured into the duke's thinking where Percival and Tony were concerned.

"I'll tell Bella we're to join the house party."

A change of subject, but in Pembroke's tone, the duke divined the truth: Pembroke would ask Arabella if she would mind very much spending just a few days placating Her Grace with a social outing. Bella would turn up stubborn, convinced if she agreed and they attended, then Pembroke would be even more miserable than she. Much fuming and many portentous looks would be served up with dinner for the remainder of the week.

And in the end, they'd both go, and both hate it. Perhaps they'd even slide a hair closer to hating Her Grace.

Managing a large and prosperous duchy was simple compared to dealing with one small, relatively civil family. His Grace rose to stand beside his son.

"Anthony is in clandestine pursuit of the Holsopple heiress, who is not trying very hard to elude capture. She's had several seasons to lark about, and refused any number of offers. Her Grace is making overtures to the girl's mother, and thus the entire idea will be Her—*your mother's* invention, provided Anthony and his love do not elope first, and provided I can manage to communicate as much to your baby brother."

Pembroke folded his glasses and stuffed them into a pocket. "And Percy?"

"Percival is acquitting himself cordially to all and sundry. I predict that when he falls, he'll fall hard and without respect to where Her—your mother would like him to fall. Do I take it you are not inclined to join the house party?"

"Bella despises those gatherings."

"As do I."

This bit of honesty proved too much for Pembroke's reserve. The marquess aimed a rare, sympathetic smile at his father. "Is it time for your lungs to act up?"

"My lungs—? Oh, I think not. Twombly has defected from his post as Her Grace's favorite gallant, and I am afforded a rare opportunity to escort my wife. I will make your excuses to her regarding your attendance, yours and Lady Bella's."

"My thanks, Your Grace." The relief in his son's eyes was hard to look on.

"For God's sake, Pembroke, Her Grace behaves as she does only because she cannot abide the idea that any of her children should be unhappy. She's neither evil nor unreasonable, just very determined."

"If you say so, sir."

His Grace took his leave, and Pembroke's nose was back in the book before the duke had left the parlor. The duchess was determined, mortally determined, but her ends were perfectly justified. Nonetheless, it was Pembroke's lady wife who'd carried the burden of the duchess's disappointment for nearly a decade. The duke held his daughter-in-law in great affection, and enough was enough.

As His Grace sought the duchess to relay word that Pembroke and his marchioness would not be joining the house party, an uncomfortable thought occurred to him:

Unlike Pembroke, Percival would not have needed his papa to serve as a go-between with the duchess. Percival would have told his mother he wasn't inclined to attend, and no matter how Her Grace fumed, pouted, and twisted the thumbscrews of maternal guilt, Percival would not have yielded.

Given the way Pembroke rubbed at his chest and kept company with books and rosebushes, the day might come when the dukedom fell into Percival's hands.

And that would not be an entirely bad thing—for the dukedom.

❧

"My full name is Percival St. Stephens Tiberius Joachim Windham. I am very thankful His Grace could contain my mother's excesses and limit her to four names for each child. Quimbey has eight baptismal names of at least three syllables each. What about you?"

Esther gave herself a moment to memorize his lordship's entire name—Percival St. Stephens Tiberius

Joachim Windham. "I am Esther Louise Himmelfarb, plain and simple."

"You have told two falsehoods, my dear. You are neither plain nor simple. When is your natal day?"

Esther answered that question, just as she'd answered so many others, and all during his lordship's polite interrogation she was aware of a chorus of crickets chirping in the moon-shadowed garden. She was aware of Percival Windham sitting so close to her, the heat of his muscular thigh along hers was evident through the fabric of her nightgown and wrapper. She was aware of his scent and aware of the way his voice in the darkness felt like an aural caress.

Most of all, though, she was aware that two days after promising to teach her how to kiss—and two long, restless nights—he most assuredly had not kissed her again.

"I have a question for you, your lordship."

"Percy will do, madam. You are quite forgetful about my request that you abandon the formalities."

He sounded amused, while Esther wanted to grind her teeth. "I named a boon to you when we visited your family plot, and you agreed to grant it. Do you consider the obligation discharged, or have you forgotten my request?"

Without any change in his lordship's posture, the quality of his presence beside her shifted, as did the nature of the darkness surrounding them. The moon was a thin crescent in the sky, and the night was mild. From beyond the walls of the kitchen garden, an owl hooted, making Esther think of all the mama mice grateful their children were safe in bed.

Bed, where she ought to be.

Though not alone. For once in her sensible, lonely, pragmatic existence, Esther Himmelfarb did not want to go to bed alone. This realization had come to her as she'd sat in Lady Pott's tiny dressing room, mending a hem at Zephora Needham's request. Lady Pott had been snoring off her brandied tea in the next room, and the billowing ball gowns on their respective hooks had felt like so many cobwebs clinging to Esther's life.

Percival's fingers, strong and warm, closed over Esther's hand. "If you think for one instant I could forget either kissing you or the prospect of kissing you again, Esther Louise, you are much mistaken."

I want to see you naked but for this glorious, silky hair, Esther, and a smile of welcome for me. She recalled his words, and they made her brave—or reckless.

"I want to see you naked, sir."

He went still beside her then drew her to her feet. "Not here."

If not here, then somewhere—anywhere. She did not care, provided he granted her this wish, because a man in want of his clothing was often a man in want of his wits—her grandmother had told her that, and with a wink and a laugh too.

"Where are we going?"

He tugged her along a path that led away from the house. "Somewhere private, safe from prying eyes and gossiping tongues. If you're to make free with my person—and I with yours—I want there to be no hurry about it."

And yet *he* was hurrying. Hurrying Esther toward the dark expanse of the home wood, a tangled, over-grown place she'd ridden through with Lord Tony just yesterday. A nightingale started caroling, or maybe Esther was simply noticing the birdsong as they traveled into deeper shadows.

"How can you possibly see where we're going?"

"I have excellent night vision, and I scouted the terrain last week."

He'd been thinking of trysting places even a week ago? The notion brought a serpent into the garden of Esther's anticipation. She shook her hand loose from his. "Have you—?"

He rounded on her and linked his arms over her shoulders. "Of course not, not with anybody else, nor will I."

She prepared to launch into a lecture, a stern description of what she expected of him during the remaining days of the house party, but he drew her into his embrace. "Do you think I could share a kiss such as you bestowed upon me two days past and then casually dally with another? Do you think I'd wait in the garden, night after night, hoping for another quarter hour's conversation with you, then turn easily to the likes of the Harpies and Hair Bows lurking in the alcoves?"

He sounded a touch incredulous, maybe even exasperated. Esther tried to tell herself his sentiments were superficial gallantries.

Herself wasn't inclined to listen. She leaned into him. "I want to make love with you."

His hand on her back went still, and Esther felt his chin resting on her crown. "My dear, there are consequences to such decisions, potentially grave consequences."

She might conceive, though the timing made that very unlikely. "I am prepared to accept those consequences."

"Are you?" Had his embrace become more snug?

Was he *arguing* with her? The darkness prevented Esther from reading his expression, so she gave in to an impulse—one that would inspire him to put his lovely mouth to ends better suited to her plans than arguing.

She slid her hand down the muscular plane of his chest, over his flat belly, down to the gratifyingly firm—dauntingly sizable—bulge behind his falls. "Enough talk, Percy. Make love with me."

He pushed into her hand for a moment, once, twice, then led her farther into the woods, to a moonlit clearing. In moments, his cloak was spread on the soft grass and Esther was flat on her back, while he loomed over her, blocking out the stars.

"You must be sure, Esther. There can be no undoing what happens now, no regretting it."

So earnest, so unlike the shallow cavalier she'd seen across the room not two weeks ago.

He would not be earnest and careful like this with other women. As he untied the bows of her dressing gown, Esther knew the relief of certainty. He would be charming and lighthearted, tender even, and generous, but he would not be so…serious. For that, she loved him—loved him a little more.

She trapped his hands in hers. "You first."

He sat back on their makeshift blanket and had his waistcoat unbuttoned in seconds. "You want to see the goods, do you? Ought I to be flattered or nervous?"

His shirt followed, drawn right over his head.

"You ought to be neither. You ought to be naked."

"*We* ought to be naked. I would never have taken you for pagan, my dear. It's a fine quality in a woman, a latent streak of paganism." He sat back to tug off his boots. Esther hiked herself to her elbows and wished she hadn't wasted the full moon on proprieties and insecurities.

"I'm nervous, if you must know."

He left off unbuttoning his falls to peer over at her. "You will enjoy this. You'll enjoy *me*. That's a vow, my lady. You may say good-bye to your maidenly vapors. They have overstayed their welcome."

He sat back and worked his breeches over his hips, moving without a hint of self-doubt. Moving as if… he might be concerned she'd change her mind.

What a cheering thought. When he prowled over to her side, naked as the day he came into the world, Esther had cause to regret that she hadn't scheduled this coupling for the broad light of day.

"You are a beautiful man." She ran a finger down one muscled bicep. "Beautifully strong, beautifully smooth and warm to the touch, beautifully brave…"

He caught her hand and wrapped it around a part of him Esther hadn't had the courage to examine yet. "Beautifully aching for you."

And for all his swaggering and social nimbleness, Percival Windham was also a man capable of patience. He let her explore with her fingertips, with her palms, with eyes and nose. Let her consume him with her senses, until Esther was again flat on her back, this time with a naked Percy Windham crouched over her and her nightclothes frothed around her in the moonlight.

"We either turn back to our separate paths now, Esther, or we forge ahead together. The choice is exclusively yours." He laced his fingers with hers where her hands lay amid her unbound hair on the cloak. The feel of that, of his hands linked to hers, was both a portent and a reassurance.

"Together," she said. "Now, let us be together."

She braced herself to feel him probing at her body, but he surprised her with lazy, sweet kisses, teasing kisses and big, manly sighs, until she was a mindless puddle of female wanting beneath him.

"Percival, please."

"Soon."

His idea of soon was *maddening*. "Now."

He nudged about, in no hurry at all. Purely at her wit's end, Esther lunged up with her hips and found herself…found herself a lover. The sensation was wonderful and strange, and yet when several moments of silence and immobility went by… "Percival, will you move?"

His hand came around to cradle the back her head. "You're all right?"

Only a few words, but so tender.

"I am mad for wanting you," she began. "You have no sense of dispatch, and I am relying on you entirely to know how to go on, as difficult as relying on anybody for anything is for such as I, but I take leave to doubt whether—"

He laughed—a low, happy chuckle signaling both affection and approval—and he *moved*, a lovely, sinuous undulation that soothed as it aroused, as it fascinated.

"You can move too, love. Move with me."

Esther's body had a sense of dispatch, a sense of soaring, galloping pleasure in the man she'd chosen for her first intimate encounter. She moved as he'd suggested, and found he knew things, marvelous, subtle things about how to leave a woman breathless with wonder and panting with ecstasy.

Percival Windham knew that a woman's ears were marvelously sensitive. He knew that patience on a man's part was an aphrodisiac. He knew exactly when to increase the tempo and depth of his thrusts, when to cradle Esther's head so she could cry out softly against his throat. He knew to hold her just as closely as her pleasure ebbed, and to hold her more closely still when an urge to weep tugged at her happiness.

For the rest of her life, Esther would treasure—and miss—Percival Windham and the things he knew.

And yet… Percival braced himself over her, giving her just enough of his weight that the night breezes cooled her skin without leaving a chill. She took a whiff of cedar and spices and stroked her hand through his unbound hair.

"What about you, Percival? Are you to have no pleasure for yourself?"

"If I endured any more pleasure, my love…"

She stopped his inchoate blather with her fingers over his mouth. "No flatteries, no prevarications, Percival. I have withheld nothing from you. Nothing. I only wish…"

He snuggled closer, a large, fit man to whom Esther was sure the term "sexual athlete" might be accurately applied, and yet he'd been so careful with her.

He shifted so his lips grazed her neck. "What do you wish?"

His hair was so marvelously soft, as soft as moonlight.

"I wish I knew how to render you as witless and befuddled as I am, as…" *In love.* That would be trespassing against common sense, so she compromised. "As helpless."

A beat of silence went by, while Esther feared her limited disclosures had overstepped whatever the rules of dalliance permitted, but then Percival began to move, slowly, powerfully.

Intimately. "My love, you already have."

Hours later, when the crickets had gone quiet and the nightingale no longer stirred, Percival retied the bows on Esther's nightclothes, wrapped her in his cloak, and put himself to rights while Esther watched through slumberous eyes. He carried her— effortlessly—through the gardens and up three flights of steps to deposit her onto the cot in the garret.

He sat at her hip then leaned down to kiss her on the forehead.

"I will see you in my dreams, my lady, and they will be sweet dreams indeed."

She murmured something about cracking the window—she was already half dreaming herself—felt a cool, sweet breeze waft into the room, and heard the door latch click shut in the darkness.

When she rose in the morning and went down to breakfast, eager to see by daylight the man with whom she'd shared such wondrous intimacies by moonlight, she learned that Percival Windham, along with his brother Anthony, had quit the premises entirely.

Four

"Do I take it you're jaunting into Town with me to ride chaperone on any trysts I might stumble into?"

Anthony sounded put out as only a younger brother could when saddled with the unwanted company of an elder sibling. Percival tossed a coin to the coaching inn's stable lad and swung up onto Reveille before answering.

"I have pressing errands in Town, and the last thing I want is to be a party to your amorous endeavors."

Anthony considered him from Anthem's back. "Are you perchance going to pay a call on the O'Donnell creature? Get the manly humors back in balance?"

The very idea had Percival aiming his horse away from the inn yard at a brisk trot. "The O'Donnell creature and I are not now nor were we ever an item of significant interest, I'll have you know."

Anthony's gelding easily kept pace. "You were of interest to her, or it certainly seemed that way last month."

"My coin was of interest to her, until some general offered her a more lucrative arrangement. I wish her well." He also spared a thought for the general, because the poor fellow was taking up with the most mercenary female Percival had ever made the mistake of allowing into his bed.

"I rather like Mrs. St. Just." Anthony rather liked everybody, including attractive, friendly Dublin-born redheads of easy virtue.

"You are trying to get rid of me, Anthony, but you need not bother. I will not be your duenna for any passionate interludes you have planned with Miss Holsopple, nor will I be calling on the fair Mrs. St. Just. She departed for Ireland prior to the Heckenbaum house party, and while her charms were considerable, our liaison is at an end."

And what an odd relief that it was so. Both Mrs. St. Just and Cecily O'Donnell were beautiful, intelligent, sexually experienced, and worldly wise—also interested only in exploiting a man's base urges for financial gain, though the St. Just woman seemed to genuinely enjoy Percival's company. No matter how generously Percival reimbursed them, neither lady would ever demand kissing lessons from him; they would never listen to his memories of service in Canada; they would never understand—he, himself had not understood—that for Her Grace to send sons into the cavalry had to have been particularly difficult.

"I'm going to ask Gladys to elope with me."

Percival brought his horse back to the walk. "Why in blazes would you tell me such a thing? Am I supposed to stop you or abet you?"

"Both. Neither. I got a note from Gladys, you see, and it's confounded complicated."

Anthony was cheerful by nature, but this plan of his had him sounding morose.

"Are you sure she's the one, Anthony?"

"Yes."

Anthony was also not decisive by nature, and yet Gladys Holsopple had his unequivocal allegiance. What was it going to be like, to know Esther Himmelfarb had granted to Percival the same immediate, unquestioning devotion? To know she accepted it from him?

"Why not honor your Gladys with the usual approach? You ask her papa for permission to court, you ask her, you set a date, the ladies make a great fuss, you wait…"

"That waiting business can be problematic."

Percival digested that for about a quarter mile. "How far along is she?"

Anthony heaved the sigh of unmarried prospective fathers the world over. "That's part of the confounded problem. She isn't sure she is, she isn't sure she…isn't. Not all fillies are the same, and we only had three occasions, so to speak."

Three? "Fast work, Brother, and once is enough."

Though if Anthony's situation with Gladys bore any resemblance to Percival's with Esther, once would never, ever be enough.

"She's all up in the bows over this, and it tears at a man to know his lady is upset and he can do nothing to comfort her."

It tore at a man simply to be parted from his lady. "So you will comfort her now and hatch up desperate plots. I hope you do not have need of them, but I will do all

in my power to aid you." The words should not have
been necessary—Tony was his *brother*—but the relief on
Tony's face suggested the assurances were appreciated.

"And you too, Perce. If you and the Himmelfarb
girl need reinforcements, we're here for you, Gladys
and myself."

"My thanks."

Except Gladys was under her mother's watchful eye
in Town, an elopement would see both parties haring
off to Scotland, and winning the Himmelfarb girl's
heart was an uncertain undertaking, regardless of how
passionately she'd shared her body.

❧

"You look as tired as I feel." Michael tugged on
Esther's sleeve and led her to a dusty little room full
of guns, game bags, and other hunting accoutrements.
"Are you getting any rest at all?"

Esther glanced around, her gaze landing on a stag's
head mounted on the opposite wall. The animal's glass
eyes stared at a preserved hare crouching on a set of
quarter shelves in a corner.

"House parties are fatiguing," Esther said. "In your
case, I'd say they're impoverishing as well."

Michael's gaze narrowed as he pushed the door
closed with a booted foot. "I'm trying to express
concern for you and your response is to nag? Even a
cousin finds that tiresome behavior in a female."

Was he concerned? Esther gave herself leave to doubt
that. "Lady Morrisette remarked last night after dinner
that she will make it a point to oppose you at whist
because she's sure to increase her pin money that way."

"Women's gossip. She opposes me at whist so she might make free with her hands on my person under the table, while our partners likely do the same across the table."

Esther thought back to the previous evening, when Sir Jasper and Charlotte Pankhurst had completed the foursome at Michael's table.

"You might well be right, but, Michael, I am worried for you. These people are above our strata. We're tolerated here to make up the numbers, and they are not our friends. Your folly would provoke their amused scorn, not their sympathy."

He crossed his arms while his expression became superior. "And what of you, Esther Himmelfarb? Lurking in gardens with a ducal spare? That's more than a bit ambitious, I'd say, even for an earl's granddaughter."

An arrangement of silver hunting flasks sat on the quarter shelf below the hare. The flasks were going a bit tarnished, but they'd make satisfying missiles fired at Michael's head.

"Were you spying on me, Michael?"

"I was taking a bit of air, Cousin, and heard voices on the other side of the garden wall. *Percival St. Stephens Joachim Windham* was getting quite friendly with you."

He'd forgotten a name—Tiberius. Thank God the wall had been high and solid.

"I can visit with whom I please, Michael, and regardless of how I'm spending what little spare time I have here, you are supposed to be courting ladies, not financial ruin."

Michael apparently decided on a tactical retreat. "What can you tell me about Herodia Bellamy?"

And this was likely the point of Michael's "concern." He was losing badly at cards, and instead of browsing the available brides himself, he expected Esther to do his scouting for him.

"Marriage is intended to resolve a lack of companionship, Michael, not a lack of coin."

His smile was quick and genuine. "You sound exactly like Uncle Jacob. Marriage can solve both. The best families have known this for generations and prosper as a result. Tell me about the Bellamy girl."

There was no reason not to, though Esther eyed the flasks with longing. They would make such a loud, satisfying crash pitched against the old speckled mirror above the mantel.

"Herodia is a trifle too smart for her own good. She's bored silly but knows better than to get tangled up in anything truly disgraceful. Engage her mind, and she'll notice you."

"I'd rather engage her mind than spend my days complimenting hair bows." Michael looked thoughtful. "I'm also hoping I might make progress with the Needmore heiress now that the Windhams have gone larking into Town."

Esther barely refrained from clutching her cousin's arm to wring further details from him, though she manufactured an indifferent expression rather than pique Michael's curiosity. "I wasn't aware they'd departed from the gathering. And her name is Needham."

Michael began a perambulation of the room, inspecting the hunting paraphernalia and trophies as he wandered. "Lord Percy is partial to mistresses with flaming red hair and lush proportions. At last report, he had at least two of that description meeting his needs in Town. Lord Tony probably went along for similar entertainments, or perhaps they share—though I ought not to offer such speculation in your company. Where do you suppose Lord Morrisette killed this thing?"

A man would do that—leap in conversation from mistresses to hunting trophies and be oblivious to the non sequitur, or maybe not even grasp that there might be one. "It's a skunk. Perhaps he purchased it from somebody who's hunted in the New World."

The animal was probably very pretty when alive. Lush black-and-white fur ended in a graceful plume of a tail, and yet in death, the beast's eyes bore the same blank stare as every other prize in the room.

"Well, I'm off to hunt a bride or perhaps some sport more entertaining than dodging Lady Morrisette's overtures." He paused by the door and regarded Esther for a moment. "You're too decent for a gathering like this. I'm surprised Aunt and Uncle let you attend."

"I'm nominally under Lady Pott's wing, when she's awake. You'd best be going lest somebody remark our tête-à-tête, but I truly wish you'd limit yourself to farthing points." Esther wished as well she could tell her numbskull cousin she'd been "permitted" to attend mostly to keep an eye on him.

Michael pursed his lips in a sulky pout. "Schoolboys play for farthing points."

When the door clicked softly closed behind him, Esther informed the hare, the skunk, the stag's head, and a four-foot-long silver-and-black snake twined around a limb above the mantel, "Even schoolboys know their debts of honor must be paid."

And Esther knew that Lady Morrisette had endless tasks waiting, and yet this dusty, ghoulish closet-shrine to idle masculinity was probably the closest thing to a refuge Esther might find. She took a seat on a worn leather hassock and tried to absorb that Percy Windham had made passionate love with her, tucked her up in bed—*left her there*—and gone off a few hours later to disport with not one but two beautiful mistresses.

Her parents' marriage had been a love match, but Esther knew such unions were unusual in the better families—the titled families.

The world certainly expected her to be celibate, but what right had she to expect *Percival* would be celibate?

"Every right," she assured the skunk. For the duration of one brief house party, he might have at least limited his attentions to her. She remained on her hassock, mentally lecturing herself for treasuring memories that clearly were of no moment to her lover.

The feel of his hands in her hair.

The sound of his voice in the darkness.

The feel of his body joined carefully and intimately with hers...

"Miss Himmelfarb." Sir Jasper had opened the door so quietly, he was inside the room and had the door closed again before Esther noticed him standing under the stag. "Of all the ladies to find being private with the impecunious Mr. Adelman."

Esther remained seated. If the only rank she could assert was that of lady, then assert it, she would. "Is he impecunious, or unlucky in his choice of games?"

"Touché, my lady." He slouched closer, the dusty light making his face powder appear another artifact of zoological preservation. "Though it appears I'm the one in luck at the moment. I don't hear Lady Zephora whining for her tea, and the word at breakfast was that the Lords Windham had gone off to revive themselves with some sophisticated sport in Town. Quimbey is out shooting hares, and here you are"—he came to a halt beside Esther's hassock, which had the disagreeable result of putting his falls at her nose level—"all by yourself, at your leisure at last."

His fingers brushed her chin, a hint of threat in his touch. Esther tried hard not to move, not to flinch. He wasn't hurting her; he wasn't even groping her.

But he was *insulting* her. For all Percival Windham might at that very moment be bathing with both of his mistresses, Lord Percy had not offered Esther insult, nor had he taken liberties beyond what she'd willingly shared.

Esther batted Sir Jasper's hand aside so stoutly, she had the gratification of seeing surprise on his face as she rose, brushed past him, and left him to the company of creatures already dead, stuffed, mounted, and gathering dust.

❧

Five years of making war on colonials had impressed upon Sir Jasper several important lessons—lessons not taught on the hallowed playing fields of Eton.

First, what counted was neither who had better form, nor who charmed the spectators, nor who looked better on a horse. What counted in any contest was who won.

Second, marching about in straight lines, forming up

into squares, and keeping a bright red uniform spotless was so much lunacy when the enemy soldiers respected no rules, could melt into the woods like wraiths, and used any weapon at hand to advance their cause.

Third, a baronet's succession was as important to the baronet as a duke's might be to the duke.

With those verities in mind, Sir Jasper waited in the conservatory at teatime, knowing it to be Mr. Michael Adelman's favorite place to avoid company.

"Are you considering a career in botany, Mr. Adelman?"

The younger fellow startled as Sir Jasper emerged from behind a thriving stand of some enormous cane plant.

"Sir Jasper. I enjoy the quiet here. I assume you do as well, so I'll leave you to it."

Not so fast, pup. "Before you scamper off to the charms of our fair companions, might I inquire as to when you'll be redeeming your vowels?"

Mr. Adelman was dark haired, handsome by any standard, and smooth cheeked. Not a scar to be seen on his physiognomy, which Sir Jasper told himself he did not hold against the fellow. That such a one should be welcome to share closets and whispered confidences with Esther Windham, however, was not to be borne.

Adelman drew himself up, though he was no taller than Sir Jasper. "One doesn't typically carry large sums about to social gatherings, sir."

"Precisely." Sir Jasper withdrew a gold watch and flipped it open. "But when said entertainments are of several weeks' duration, one can certainly send to his man of business for a bank draft." He glanced up from the watch, flicking it shut and dropping it back into his pocket. "You do have a man of business?"

Adelman positively flushed with indignation. "Had I known you were so precipitous in collecting social debts, I would have already notified him." Adelman brushed back the skirt of his coat and hooked a thumb in his waistcoat pocket, a lovely pose—casual, cocky, and designed to flaunt excellent tailoring. "Do you rule out the possibility that I will regain my losses?"

"Indeed, I do." Sir Jasper offered his snuffbox, an elegant accessory of gold and onyx. "The play to be had in such genteel surrounds has palled. Name a date, Mr. Adelman, and I'll have my man of business attend yours at the location of your choice."

Adelman had no natural talent for dissembling. This was what made him a bad card player, but also what caused Sir Jasper an unwanted stirring of pity. Dueling was good sport when a man was a crack shot, but Adelman was only a couple of years down from university, a plain mister, and apparently of some value to Esther Himmelfarb.

While resistance from a worthy female was all part of the game, her outright antipathy would be a nuisance under intimate circumstances.

"I will offer you a compromise, Mr. Adelman. Either produce the coin you owe me by the first of the week, or I will appropriate from you something I consider to be of equal or greater value." Sir Jasper whiffed a pinch of snuff into his left nostril, while Adelman looked away.

"The first of the week is too soon."

"The first of the week is three days from now. You

have all the time in the world to procure the means. I would, however, advise you to avoid the gambling offered by our hostess."

"I am not unlucky—" Adelman puffed up like a peacock.

"No, you are unaware, which can be remedied. The ladies cheat, you see, and the gentlemen—your charming self included—overimbibe, and thus the odds are not at all what you think they are. I bid you a pleasant day and will expect remuneration within seventy-two hours."

Sir Jasper sauntered off, content with the exchange. Watching Adelman fidget away the next two days, then hare away at the crack of dawn three mornings hence would be entertaining—and God knew entertainment was in short supply at this gathering—and it would leave Esther Himmelfarb without her preferred swain.

All in all, a productive little chat.

❧

His Grace the Duke of Quimbey was tall, rangy, had kind blue eyes and a nice laugh, and was not one for standing on ceremony. That he was twice Charlotte's age was of no moment. No unmarried duke was too old, too stout, too much given to the company of opera dancers, or even too impoverished for an ambitious, well-dowered girl to discount as a marital prospect.

As Charlotte let herself into the small chamber under the eaves, she assured herself Quimbey was also not too enamored of Esther Himmelfarb. His Grace had attached himself to the lady's side since the Windham menfolk had departed the day before, and no amount of flirting, teasing, or scheming had dislodged him.

But one well-placed billet-doux ought to shine a very different light on the perfect Miss Esther Himmelfarb.

At the very least, such a note, when made public, would get the girl sent home in disgrace, leaving her betters with a clearer field upon which to pursue and divide up the marital spoils in the final week of the house party. Since appropriating the note from its intended means of delivery, Charlotte had spent a day weighing options and making plans, and those plans, oddly enough, brought her to a chamber so unprepossessing as to rouse a niggling sense of guilt regarding her schemes.

Esther Himmelfarb's room was plain to the point of insult. The mirror over the vanity had a small crack near the base, the carpet was frayed where it met the bed skirt, and the single small window was clouded with age and grime. The only point of elegance was a white cat, enthroned on a chair upholstered in faded pink brocade.

The cat took one look at Charlotte and quit the premises, leaving Charlotte to consider where a letter might lie in plain sight without being immediately noticed—a delicate decision.

"Why, Miss Pankhurst, what a delight."

Sir Jasper lounged in the doorway, for once free of wig and powder. His blue eyes traveled over her figure, up, down, pause, down farther. The expression in them as he sauntered into the room was not kind.

That expression gave Charlotte a salacious little thrill, truth be known. Sir Jasper's bearing had the casual elegance of the career soldier, his manners were exquisite, he did not suffer fools, and neither did he cheat at cards or make life difficult for those who did.

He also had wonderfully muscular thighs.

"Sir Jasper."

He came closer, his gaze thoughtful. "Am I to believe that my good fortune in finding you here results from your desire to spend time with your dear friend, Miss Himmelfarb? When last I saw her, she was instructing Quimbey on the proper approach to fouling another's ball at croquet. His Grace was listening attentively."

Sir Jasper had prowled closer, bringing a faint whiff of roses to Charlotte's nose. Too late, she realized that she was alone in a bedroom with a single male, and the door barely open behind him.

"I suppose I'd best go join Miss Himmelfarb at the croquet game."

He snatched the letter from Charlotte's hand so quickly, indignation took a moment to battle its way through her surprise. "Give that back, sir."

Sir Jasper stepped away, unfolded the note, and took it over to the little window.

"'My dearest and most precious Esther—' A sincere if unimaginative beginning. 'After such pleasure as I have known in your company, any parting from you is torture. Rest assured I will return to your tender embrace as soon as I am able. Until we kiss again, my love, you will remain ever uppermost in my thoughts, and I shall remain exclusively and eternally yours. Percival.'"

Sir Jasper refolded the note but did not return it, even when Charlotte held out her hand for it. "The signature is not in the same hand. It isn't even in the same ink."

Drat all men with keen eyesight. "It's close enough."

"Windham would not have been stupid enough to sign such a note. No one will believe it's from him." Sir Jasper didn't believe it was from Percy Windham; that much was obvious.

Charlotte crossed the room and plopped down on the bed. "Some fellow left that note on her sidesaddle. A groom found it and gave it to my maid to leave in Miss Himmelfarb's room. I chose to assign authorship to Lord Percival, because he's highborn enough that the scandal won't matter to him, and enough of a rascal that everyone will believe he'd dally like this. Quimbey is so decent, he'd just marry her, and that entirely defeats the point of the exercise."

Sir Jasper considered the note again and set it on the vanity. He joined Charlotte on the bed, making the mattress dip to the extent that she fetched up against him, hip to hip. "You are a naughty woman, Miss Pankhurst. I may, to a minor degree, have underestimated you—or possibly your determination in matrimonial matters."

He sounded not exactly admiring, but neither was he criticizing her.

"Miss Himmelfarb has to be got rid of," Charlotte said, in case the idea was too subtle for the baronet's masculine brain. "She's ruining all of our chances, at Quimbey, at Lord Tony, Lord Percival, *at you.*" The last was an afterthought added at the prodding of feminine intuition.

Sir Jasper took the bait—he also took Charlotte's

hand. "I do not flatter myself a mere baronet would be worthy of one of your station, my lady, but with a small exercise in forgery—the signature really should match the body of the note, my dear—there's a way I might be of service to you."

His hand was surprisingly warm, his grasp firm. A baronet was no prize, of course, but that didn't mean a lady couldn't enjoy spending some time with him.

"Close the door, Sir Jasper. If we're to discuss forgery, then privacy is in order."

❧

"Why a fellow has to racket about Town for two days, and then hop on his destrier in the teeming rain, ruin his boots, his lungs, *and* his disposition in a headlong dash for the hinterlands is beyond my feeble powers of divination." Tony emphasized his harangue with a cough.

Percival handed off his cape and gloves—both sopping wet—to a footman. "Our boots will dry out. I could not leave Miss Himmelfarb here undefended save for Quimbey's dubious protection any longer than necessary."

"Necessary is a relative term."

Tony was entitled to grumble. Thrashing their way back to the Morrisette estate on the muddy tracks that passed for the King's highways had been an ordeal; waiting another day to rejoin his intended would have been torture.

"Why, my lords!" Hippolyta Morrisette paused in the entrance to the high-ceilinged foyer to join her hands at her breastbone. "Riding about in this weather will give you an ague, and then your dear mother will ring a peal over my head for a certainty—not that we aren't glad to see you again!"

There was something sly in her greeting, for all its effusiveness. Percy bowed without taking her hand. "My lady, greetings. If I might be so bold as to ask the whereabouts of Miss Himmelfarb?"

The gleam in Lady Morrisette's eye became calculating. "Surely you don't intend to greet a young lady in all your dirt, my lord?"

"Yes," Tony said, an edge to his tone, "he most certainly does. He about killed the horses for that very purpose. Best oblige him, my lady."

She glanced from one young lord to the other, and apparently decided to heed Tony's advice. "This way."

She swept toward the back of the house, and Percival followed, Tony bringing up the rear with boots squeaking and squishing.

The guests were assembled in the largest informal parlor, which was fortunate. It meant as he wound his way through the east wing, Percival had a few moments to organize his thoughts despite the screaming need to see Esther again, to make sure she'd weathered his absence without mischief befalling her.

The same instincts that had warned Percival when his superiors had sent him off on doomed errands were urging him to shove Lady Morrisette aside and ransack the house, bellowing Esther's name until she was again in his arms.

Which would not do. Her Grace would have an apoplexy if word of such behavior reached her.

Lady Morrisette paused while a footman opened the parlor doors, and too late, Percival understood the ambush he'd charged into: Her Grace *and* His Grace sat reading a newspaper at the same table by the window where Esther Himmelfarb had been playing cards more than two weeks ago.

"Possible hostiles near the window," Tony muttered, coming up on Percy's shoulder.

Nothing possible about it, and yet there was Esther, embroidering in a corner on a settee, Quimbey sitting beside her and looking entirely too content, while the rest of the room looked askance at the recent arrivals.

"Look who I found in the foyer!" Lady Morrisette's cheerful announcement had all heads turning, but where Percival had expected to see welcome in Esther's eyes, he saw guardedness.

She said something to Quimbey, who smiled like a man besotted, then went back to her embroidery.

Percy could not take his eyes off Esther—though she was *ignoring* him. "My apologies to the company for the state of my attire, but my errands in Town were urgent."

The Pankhurst girl rose, as if she'd leave the room or say something, but her gaze went swiveling from Percy to Esther and back to Percy.

"Percival, what can you be about?" His mother's tone was dry as dust. "Disgracing yourself and tracking mud all over Lady Morrisette's carpets. Take your brother and see to your wardrobe."

She turned a page of the newspaper laid out before her, paying no more heed to her sons than if they had been footmen caught in an indecorous exchange. His Grace neither followed up with a ducal rebuke nor interceded for his sons—of course.

"I beg your pardon, Your Grace." Percival bowed to his mother. "Before I take my leave, I would address Miss Himmelfarb in private."

Sir Jasper Lay-About cleared his throat. "Perhaps Miss Himmelfarb isn't interested in what you have to say."

The supercilious ass offered his suggestion from a pose by the fireplace, one leg bent, an elbow propped on the mantel. In full morning finery, he was the picture of gentlemanly grace. The urge to knock the presuming idiot on his backside was nigh unbearable.

"Not now, Perce," Tony whispered. "Get the girl, then deal with the buffoon."

Esther was watching him, but there was no welcome in her eyes. Quimbey would not have trespassed, and Esther would never have yielded to Sir Jasper's importuning...and yet...

As Percy watched her, unease curled more tightly in the part of a man's gut that could save his life if he listened to it. "Then I'll say my piece to her here."

Like a marionette whose strings had been jerked, Charlotte Pankhurst came to life. "Esther Himmelfarb, how could I have forgotten! I have been remiss, and I do beg your pardon. I promised to give you back the correspondence you gave me for safekeeping, and it completely slipped my mind."

As the girl withdrew a folded piece of paper from her workbasket, Esther turned to regard her. "I gave you no correspondence, Charlotte."

"Oh, now don't be coy!" With a flourish and an odd glance at Sir Jasper, Miss Pankhurst started to read. "It's signed by Sir Jasper. 'My dearest and most precious Esther.'" She paused long enough to take visual inventory of her rapt audience, while Percival's hand went to the place at his side where his sword hilt would have been.

"Silence, woman!"

He'd bellowed indoors, an infraction guaranteed to give his mother the vapors, but over by the window, the duke had placed a hand on his duchess's wrist.

Charlotte Pankhurst clearly had a longing for death, for she *smirked* at Percival. "Sir Jasper isn't taking exception to having his billet-doux read in company. It's just a note, my lord. Sophisticated company such as this would never take such a thing seriously."

Esther had risen, her fists clenched at her side. "It's not a note I ever received, Charlotte, nor would I have given you anything for safekeeping."

She hadn't received it?

She hadn't received it?

For three days she'd been left wondering, alone, thinking all manner of untoward things? The very notion was…

It wasn't to be borne.

Percival regarded the woman he loved, willing her to meet his gaze. "Then my dearest and most precious Esther, you must allow me to recite it for you—and I am remiss for not signing my love letter. In future, I will remedy the oversight, and you may be certain all my love letters will be addressed to you."

The room went silent, and for the first time, Esther's eyes held something besides self-possession. She looked at him with hope, with a wary, wounded variety of the emotion, one that cut Percy to the heart.

He took a breath, gathering his courage, and prepared to offer his heart. "My dearest and most precious Esther, after such pleasures as I have known in your company, any parting from you is torture. Rest assured I will return to your tender embrace as soon as I am able. Until we kiss again, my love, you will remain ever uppermost in my thoughts, and I shall remain exclusively and eternally yours."

After an interminable beat of silence, Esther's eyes began to sparkle. "Say it again, my lord. Please. More slowly this time, for surely if such a note had found its way to me, I would have read it a thousand times by now."

Behind him, Tony was shifting from one squeaky boot to the other. Charlotte Pankhurst was looking like a little girl who'd forgotten her lines at the church play, while Percy's heart starting dancing a jig.

"My dearest and *most* precious Esther." He declaimed the words, hoping every servant in the corridor and every gossipmonger in the room was committing them to memory. "After such pleasures as I have known in your company—"

"Cease this nonsense at once!" Her Grace did not rise, likely because His Grace still had her by the wrist. "Percival Windham, you will not be publicly making love to a mere earl's granddaughter. I know not what spell she has cast, nor do I care. Pack your effects, and take yourself back to Morelands."

The joy in Esther's gaze winked out. Without moving, she wilted where she stood, and nobody, not one person in the entire room, remonstrated with the duchess for her rudeness.

Percival crossed the room and linked his fingers with his intended, turning a glower on his mother. "I apologize for the abrupt and public manner of my declaration, but Your Grace will apologize to Miss Himmelfarb."

"I will do no such thing. I permit you to socialize in hopes you'll attach a suitable prospect, and this is the thanks I get? You may go back to the Canadian wilderness if you think to comport yourself thus."

The duke cleared his throat. Tony groaned.

Percival tucked an arm around Esther's waist. "I have resigned my commission, Your Grace. I have no doubt my intended would follow the drum cheerfully did I ask it of her, but I have no wish to subject her to such hardships."

The duchess sniffed. "Your intended—"

"My beloved intended," Percival shot back. "Whose father has given me permission to court her, and whose finger will soon be wearing this modest token of my esteem, if she'll have me."

Ringing declarations were all well and good, but a man ought to be judged by his actions too. Percival withdrew a small parcel from his pocket, fished the ring out of the cloth he'd wrapped it in, and took his beloved by the hand.

"Esther Louise Himmelfarb, will you—"

She put a finger to his lips, and his heart stopped. "No, I will not." She caressed his lip fleetingly then dropped her hand. "Not without your mother's blessing."

What the hell?

Across the room, His Grace finally bestirred himself to speak. "Hear your lady out, Percival, for I think she has the right of it."

The duchess speared Moreland with a look that pronounced him daft or possessed of three heads, but she held her tongue too.

"I love you as well, Percival Windham," Esther said. She wasn't offering a performance for the assemblage, though; she was speaking straight to Percival's heart. "Nothing would please me more than to be your wife and the mother of your children. You saw me when I was supposed to be invisible. You treated me like a person, not a fixture in service. Your manners were those of a gentleman in the best sense of the word. You listened—"

He did not interrupt her. He let her gather her dignity, because in part she was offering a reproach worthy of a Dissenting minister to her supposed betters.

"You *listened* to me and took my welfare seriously. Of course, I would be honored to be your wife, but your mother loves you too."

A soft gasp from the direction of the duchess suggested Esther had scored a hit, but she went on speaking. "Her Grace is protective of those she loves, as a mother should be. I don't give that"—Esther snapped her fingers crisply before his nose—"for permission from a duchess to wed the man I love, but I care very much for a mother's blessing."

Somebody sighed. Not the duchess. She sniffed again, but it wasn't a sniff of disapproval.

Quimbey offered his handkerchief to Lady Zephora. Sir Jasper led a distraught Miss Pankhurst from the room. Tony's boots had gone silent.

The duchess rose and opened her mouth, then shut it. Esther turned to face the older woman, though

Percival did not for an instant think of turning his most precious, dearest, most *stubborn* beloved loose.

"Please, Your Grace." Esther swallowed, and it felt to Percival as if she might have tucked herself more closely to him. "Your Graces. I love your son. My affection for him is as fierce as it is sudden—and as it is surprising even to me. I know he would bring consequence, wealth, and comfort to the union, but I care not for the gifts he can give me with his hands. I seek only the gifts he promises me with his eyes."

Another silence stretched while the duchess groped for her husband's hand, and Percival tried to will his mother to see reason.

"But you're not..." Her Grace's expression went from glowering to puzzled to bewildered. "George? She's not... She hasn't..." Like the sails of a ship drifting into the eye of the wind, her indignation luffed, slowed, then died away. "Moreland? What are we to make of this?"

Had he not heard the words himself, Percival would not have believed them. Agatha, Duchess of Moreland, had *in public* turned to her spouse for reassurances. The expression on Moreland's face was far from incredulous. The duke was smiling faintly at his duchess and stroking her hand with his fingers.

"Young people today," Moreland said in dismissive tones. "All is high drama with them, though given these passionate declarations, one can hope Percival and his lady will at least be enthusiastic about providing us grandchildren."

His Grace emphasized the point by kissing his wife's knuckles and keeping her hand in his.

Grandchildren. Oh, of course. Moreland had

dangled before the duchess the ultimate prize, the trophy awarded on behalf of duty that would serve so wonderfully in the name of love.

"We can assure you of that," Percival said. "If we have your blessing."

Esther, in a gesture that boded well for their marital union, held her silence—and his hand.

The duchess drew herself up and laced her arm though the duke's. "Come along, Moreland. If we're to have a prayer of seeing the ceremony properly planned, there is much to be done."

But the duke didn't immediately lead his wife from the room. He instead tucked her hand over his arm and paused, giving her a look that was positively doting. "And if I am to have a prayer of arranging the settlements adequately, I must of course consult with my duchess. And remind me, my dear, was it the Holsopple girl you had in mind for Anthony?"

They processed from the room, dignity very much in evidence.

When the door had closed behind them, Tony squished across the room and clapped Percival soundly on the shoulder. "Well done, you lot. Madam, my lady hostess, regardless of the hour, we'll be having your best champagne, as it appears congratulations are very much in order."

Quimbey started the applause, Lady Pott thumped her cane repeatedly on the floor, Lady Zephora and Miss Needham wept openly in the arms of whatever swain had presented himself at the convenient moment.

While Percival kissed his ladylove.

⚓

"Come along, you." Percival looped his arm through Esther's, and before she could start in with the lectures Her Grace had assured her were necessary for the proper training of a prospective husband, she was being escorted down the garden path.

"Percival, you must stop kidnapping me like this."

"No, I must not. I must become accomplished at it, so that even when we are knee-deep in little Windhams, I can still steal you away on a moment's notice."

Esther stopped walking and tried to glower at him. "Which will only ensure the parade of little Windhams continues without ceasing."

His smile was blissful. "Precisely. I had a letter from your cousin Michael. He finds life as a colonel in the cavalry very much to his liking."

"Have I thanked you for that?"

"No, you have not, not as a properly grateful fiancée ought to. I will accept your thanks on our wedding night, along with any other generosities you feel inclined to bestow on me. Tony says Sir Jasper and Lady Lay-About have departed on a wedding journey to Rome. No doubt there will be war on the Continent within the sennight."

He was incorrigible, also very passionate. Two fine qualities in a man destined to raise up a large brood of children. Esther couldn't help but smile as they resumed walking. "Sir Jasper claimed he would have offered me marriage."

"You would not have suffered that buffoon for an instant—would you?"

"Of course not." Though the hint of belligerence in the question—and uncertainty behind it—was gratifying. "There's something I've been meaning to ask you, Percival."

He held back a branch of an encroaching lilac bush for her, reminding her of a spring night in the darkened wood weeks ago.

"I adore your interrogations, Esther."

He particularly liked it when she interviewed various parts of his male anatomy, an undertaking at which she'd grown increasingly bold.

"My question is this: Have you thought of names?"

"Names? I rather enjoy it when you use the German endearments. I've never been anybody's dearest handsome treasure before." He'd dropped into a German accent, imitating Esther's papa, with whom Percival spent many hours arguing politics.

He'd also brought Esther's hand to his lips, there to kiss and nuzzle at her knuckles, her palm, her wrist...

"Percival, the wedding is still two weeks off, and we must exercise some restraint."

The Moreland gardens were lovely, giving way to a landscaped park that eventually led to the home wood. For today's outing, Percival had captured her from the duchess's company and taken her straight through the French doors and down across the terraces, leaving Her Grace to fume and pace and ring for Lady Arabella's soothing presence.

"Restraint, indeed. Were I not exercising restraint, Esther Louise, you'd be tossed over my shoulder."

He could do it, too, and had on more than one occasion.

"I was not referring to endearments such as you might imagine you hear when my wits go begging. I was referring to names you might like for these little Windhams you're so enthusiastic about."

He fell silent, which was something Esther also loved about him. He could bluster and tease and even—when he and her papa were enjoying their after-dinner drinks—shout, but he was also capable of contemplative silence.

"What are you trying to tell me, Esther?"

"I am trying to tell you that our frequent and enthusiastic bouts of passion have led to their natural consequence. I will be lucky to fit into my wedding dress."

He dropped her hand, subjecting Esther to an unwelcome bout of uncertainty.

"You're sure?"

She nodded, finding the bed of red roses of interest. They had thorns, of course, but they were beautiful and hardy, and their scent was incomparable.

"When, Esther?"

His question was quiet, his expression unreadable.

"The first time, I think. I haven't had my... I haven't bled since that first time."

He stepped closer and enfolded her in a gentle embrace. For a long moment he said nothing. Her bellowing, blustering, teasing, beloved fiancé said not one word.

And then, very softly, his lips at her ear, he said, "Bartholomew, I think. Uncle Bart is Her Grace's favorite brother, though she'd never say so. He put me on my first pony and supported my decision to buy my colors."

"It's a good name." Though on a daughter, it might be a trifle awkward.

The moment didn't call for pragmatism, though. Percival remained silent, holding her, until Esther realized—budding wifely instinct, perhaps—that he was *moved* beyond words. In her arms, he felt particularly warm, and there was a huskiness to his voice suggesting strong emotion.

She remained in his embrace a long while, the scent of the roses rising around them, the soft summer air stirring a lock of Percival's unbound hair against her cheek.

"Are you all right, Esther? Carrying a child can be hard on some women."

"I have never felt a greater sense of well-being than I have since accepting your proposal, Percival Windham."

In the sigh that went out of him, Esther realized he'd needed to hear her say that. He would probably need to hear her say that many times in the ensuing months, years, and—God willing—decades. Fortunately, it was the simple truth.

He kissed her ear and nuzzled her temple. "I will take such good care of you, my dear, that short of the benevolent intercession of the Almighty Himself, nobody could take better care of you."

"I know. I'll take care of you too."

"And of our children."

Another sweet moment passed, and then Esther took her Percival by the hand—he seemed to have lost some of his customary boldness—and led him into the home wood. When they emerged in time for tea some hours later, not even Her Grace remarked the grass stains Percival had acquired on the knees of his breeches.

The Duke and His Duchess

To couples who've hit rough patches, which is to say, all couples, eventually.

One

"YOU'RE YOUNG AND HAVE ALL YOUR TEETH." GEORGE, His Grace the Duke of Moreland, made this state of affairs sound as if Percival had committed a double hanging felony. "If you swive this wife to death, you can always get another."

Lord Percival Windham's brothers reacted to the duke's observation predictably. Tony shot Percy a look of commiseration while Peter—more properly the Marquess of Pembroke—pushed back from the card table.

"I find myself ready to retire," Peter announced. He rose and bowed to the duke. "Your Grace, pleasant dreams."

Peter's younger brothers merited a nod, one conveying more than a touch of sympathy. On this topic at least, the heir to a dukedom could delegate dealing with an irascible old peer to the spares.

"You two are sorry company for an old man," His Grace spat. "Fetch me a footman that I might preserve myself from the tedium to be endured when you won't allow me so much as a finger of decent libation."

Tony and Percy each got a hand under one of His Grace's elbows and boosted the duke to his feet. Tony pushed the chair away, and then—only then—His Grace shook off his sons' hold. "Think of me as you're getting drunk yet again." He glowered at each son in turn. "And I meant what I said, Percival. Your lady wife has dropped four bull calves in little more than five years of marriage. In my day, a gentleman didn't trouble his wife beyond the necessary, and certainly not when he could afford to take his rutting elsewhere. Her Grace would have agreed with me."

Percival didn't dignify that scold with a response, though Tony—brave man—murmured, "Good night, Papa," as they handed the duke off to a stout, blank-faced footman.

When the door was closed and a thick silence had taken root, Percival went back to the table and started organizing the cards.

"He's wrong, Perce." Tony's path took him to the decanter. "Her Grace would not agree. She'd say Esther's duty was to provide as many sons as you and the good Lord saw fit to get on her. Her Grace was a terror when it came to the succession."

In Percival's hands, the queen of diamonds turned up first. "The old boy may have a point. Esther has done her duty to the succession."

And at what cost? She fell into bed exhausted each evening, though never once had Percival heard her complain.

With decanter in hand, Tony took himself and a glass of brandy to the side of the game room where darts were played. A stout surface of Portuguese cork surrounded the scarred circular target, the pits and gashes growing fewer closer to the center.

"I would better prosecute a game of darts were I in my cups," Tony muttered, taking aim. "You will not be the death of your wife, Perce. His Grace is mourning, is all, and not going about it very well."

Percival kept his hands busy organizing the cards, all the pips going in the same direction, from highest to lowest, suit by suit. "He's not only mourning, he's dying. Can a man mourn his own incipient passing?"

Tony shot him a look. "You're sounding ducal again. Incipient passing? I say it's Peter we have to worry about most. His Grace has enough spleen left to live to be a hundred. He and Her Grace had a few cordial years there toward the end—largely as a function of your success populating the nursery, if you ask me."

When Percival had the deck stacked in perfect order, he cut and shuffled, then shuffled again. The snap and riffle of the cards soothed him, putting him in mind of years spent soldiering—and shivering—in Canada. "How long has it been since Peter ventured outside?"

A dart went sailing toward the wall only to land several inches from the target. "Damn. He sits out on the terrace when the weather's fair. Once a man turns forty, he's entitled to a more sedentary schedule."

Sedentary? In his youth, Peter had been a robust, blond giant. Heir to a dukedom, he'd been the biggest prize on the marriage mart in every sense. When he'd departed on his Grand Tour, half the ladies in London had gone into a decline. And now…Peter's blond hair was going silver, and his complexion suggested he abused arsenic when he never touched the stuff. Worst of all, Peter looked at his half-grown daughters like a man who'd reconciled himself to heartbreak.

Percival reorganized the cards, this time starting with hearts. "Maybe it's Peter's incipient death His Grace is mourning."

"This is maudlin talk, Perce, and you've hardly touched a drop all night." Tony fired a second dart toward the wall, only to have it bounce off the edge of the target. "Rotten, bloody luck."

"Rotten, bloody aim. You need to focus, Anthony."

And Percival might well need a mistress. The notion that his father could be right was loathsome.

"You need to get drunk and go swive your lady," Anthony countered. "Moreland's carping because Her Grace booted him out of her bedroom once I came along. He doesn't want to see you and Esther come to the same sorry pass."

The things Tony knew—and the things he let come flying out of his fool mouth. "Esther has given us an heir, a spare, and a pair of Tonys," Percival observed. "Perhaps there's been enough swiving in my marriage."

A Tony. In Moreland family parlance, any son younger than the spare was a Tony, a hedge against bad luck, and a prudent course every titled family with sense followed. Some were blessed with an abundance of Tonys.

For the third dart, Tony set his drink aside, toed an invisible line on the oak parquet floor, and narrowed his gaze at the target. "You love your wife, Percival. You fell arse over teakettle for her the moment you laid eyes on her. You'd break Esther's heart if you took your favors elsewhere, and I don't give a hang what Polite Society, senile dukes, or their departed wives have to say on the matter."

The dart flew true, hitting the bull's-eye with a decisive thunk.

People tended to underestimate blond, amiable Tony, and Percival had a hunch Tony liked it that way. "Is Gladys carrying again?"

Tony pulled two darts from the cork and picked the third up from the floor. "One suspects she is." His smile was bashful, pleased, and a trifle scared.

"Can't one simply ask his wife? The girl is forth-right to a fault, Anthony." Something Percival adored about Gladys, especially when the rest of the family shied away from difficult truths like a royal court flee-ing the plague.

"One cannot." Tony put the darts on the mantel and set his half-full glass beside them. "One, as you well know, waits patiently for that happy day when one's wife reposes her trust in one with news of an inchoate miracle, and then one prays incessantly for months, until said miracle is squalling in one's nursery."

In this, Tony was not the hail-fellow-well-met, he was wise.

The ace of hearts was missing, which wasn't pos-sible, because the damned thing had been present and accounted for moments ago. Percival began at the top of the deck, thumbing through card by card. "Canada was good training for marriage, wasn't it? Hazards on every hand, hardship, boredom…"

God in heaven, was that what his marriage had become?

"I get a decent complement of howling at the moon, or at my lady wife, so I'm content," Tony said. "Believe I'll give the girl my regards while the night is yet young."

With fatuous smile firmly in place, Tony saluted and took his leave.

While Percival hunted in vain for the damned ace of hearts.

⁓

"I love you," Esther Windham whispered to the fellow in her arms. "I will always love you, and love you better than any other lady loves you. I love my husband too." Also better than any other lady loved him, though lately, that love had taken on a heaviness.

Esther's regard for Percival had acquired an element of forbearance that troubled her, because it went beyond the patience any couple married five years endured with each other from time to time. Percival was a doting father, a dutiful son, a loving husband, and yet…

"Is he asleep?" Little Bart had crept to his mother's side on silent feet—a surprising accomplishment for a lad who could shriek down the rafters with his glee and his ire. "Can we go yet?"

"Hush." Esther leaned over and kissed the top of Bart's head. He already hated when she did that. "You'll wake the baby."

Impatience crossed Bart's cherubic features but he knew better than to commit the nursery equivalent of high treason. He was solid, stubborn, charming, and in line to become the Duke of Moreland. The charm and stubbornness would serve him well, though

Esther had learned to steel herself against both. She rose with the baby and put wee Valentine in his crib, gave the nursemaid a smile—for the next hour at least, there would be peace in the nursery, provided neither the baby nor two-year-old Victor woke up—and extended her other hand to Gayle.

Gayle was not charming in the same way his brother was. He was serious, curious, and sweet natured. He and Bart got on famously, thank a merciful God.

"Will we sail boats?" Bart asked, yanking on Esther's hand as they headed for the stairs. "We can do Viking burials again, can't we? Will Papa come too?"

"Papa is busy today, but yes, we can do Viking burials. Gayle, what would you like to do?"

This was her one afternoon a week to spend with the children, the one she and Percival had vowed and declared would be inviolate. The one the children looked forward to.

The one she used to look forward to, too.

"Pet the kitties."

"A lovely notion." Though Bart would scare most of the kitties away, all except the shameless old mamas who seemed to know a kitten favored by a child might find an easy life as a pantry mouser rather than the rigorous existence awaiting the barn cats.

When they reached the ground floor, Bart pelted off in the direction of the library, there to collect paper from the duke's desk. Esther paused long enough to tell a footman—old Thomas—to have a brazier and some spills prepared for the services to be held at the stream.

Outside the library door, Gayle dropped her hand and peered up at her. He had beautiful green eyes, the same as Bart. Victor's eyes were a slightly darker hue, and baby Valentine's eyes had lost nearly all traces of their newborn blue.

"Mama?"

Esther dropped to her knees. Gayle did not shout his sentiments, even in his most sanguine moods. "My dear?"

She pushed soft auburn curls away from his face. He'd been born blond, but his hair was darkening as he matured. He tolerated her affection silently, a little man more preoccupied with his inner world than most his age.

"If you could do anything you wanted to do this afternoon," Gayle asked, "what would you do?"

Esther turned, braced her back against the wall, and slid to a sitting position. "I'm not sure." This question, and her reply to it, caused a lump in her throat. Many things brought a lump to her throat. "I might take a nice long nap."

She was treated to a frown that put her much in mind of her husband. "A nap isn't fun. We're supposed to have fun for our outings. Petting the kitties is fun."

"You don't like the Viking burials, do you?"

The frown did not dissipate. "Was Grandmama a Viking?"

In the way of little minds, he'd skipped across several ideas to connect two disparate concepts. He did this a lot, which fascinated Esther as much as it worried her.

"Gayle, we did not put your grandmother's body on a ship, light the ship on fire, and send the ship out to sea. That was for great Viking warriors, for kings long ago and far away. Nobody does that anymore."

"Grandpapa won't go away on a ship?"

Ah.

Esther pulled him into her lap, a warm, sturdy bundle of little boy full of questions and fears a mother could only guess at. He bore the scent of hay, suggesting some obliging footman had already stood guard over a sortie to the haymow, where the boys played Highwaymen and Pirates and Damned Upstart Colonials.

Why did little boys never play Dukes and Earls?

"His Grace will go to heaven when God sees fit to call him home. Grandpapa has lived a long, honorable life, and St. Peter will throw a great fete when His Grace strolls through the pearly gates."

"Will Grandpapa need a footman to help him?"

Such worry in such a small body. "He will not. He will strut."

This caused a smile. "Like Papa?"

"Like all of my menfolk." Esther blew on the back of Gayle's neck, making the sort of rude sound boys delighted in.

She thought he'd squirm away then, but he sighed, little shoulders heaving up with momentous thoughts, then down. "Will Uncle Peter strut when he goes to heaven?"

Gracious God.

"He will strut, and he will shout to everybody that he has come home." Dear Peter probably hadn't shouted or strutted since Esther had met him five years ago.

Now Gayle did scramble to his feet. "Will I shout and strut when I go to heaven? Will I be as big as Bart?"

Esther rose, though it was an effort that left her a trifle light-headed. "You will carry on as loudly as anybody, and my guess is you will become very proficient at strutting. You are a Windham, after all. As for being as big as Bart, you are as big now as Bart was when he was your age."

This concept, that Bart was merely half a lap ahead in the race to adult height, always pleased Gayle. "I want to make birds with my paper, not ships that burn."

"We can do both." Though Bart would want to throw rocks at the birds when they became airborne, and Gayle—in a perfect imitation of His Grace—would point out that burning ships was a waste of paper.

Esther followed her son into the library, where Bart—appropriately enough—was already seated at the desk, sturdy legs kicking the air as he folded paper into some semblance of ships.

While the boys argued halfheartedly about which was more fun—birds or ships—Esther sank into a chair and tried not to think about whether she'd be capable of strutting into heaven when her turn came.

No, she would not, though in heaven, she would get a decent nap. She would get as long a nap as ever she wished for.

~

"Madam, you have a leaf in your hair."

Esther glanced over at Percival, her expression confirming that she'd misinterpreted her husband's attempt at friendly repartee as censorship. Percival reached forward to tease the little bit of brown from the curls at Esther's nape. That she had time to picnic and lounge about should please him, but had she really sat through dinner with a leaf in her hair?

The instant Percival's fingers were free of her hair, she moved away. "How was Squire Arbuthnot?"

A year ago, heavy with child, she would have moved into her husband's touch.

"Rather the worse for drink, as usual, but the man can ride better drunk than I can sober. And he understands drainage, whether we're talking about the contents of the wine cellar or boggy terrain." Boggy, stinky, insect-laden, unplowable, useless land, such as graced too many acres of Moreland property. "I was damned lucky Comet didn't come a cropper."

Percival's lady wife was already in a nightgown and robe, depriving him of the pleasure of undressing her. Something about her posture suggested that Percival—a man with five years of marital reconnaissance under his belt—had best wrestle off his own boots.

Esther sat at her vanity and pulled pins from the coronet of braids encircling her head. "Did you come to any conclusions in your time with Arbuthnot?"

"I concluded His Grace has spent many years establishing a presence at court, and more years railing against the buffoonery of the Whigs, but he has neglected his acres." Which surely counted as a greater offense than being comely and having all one's teeth. "Putting things to rights here will take years."

Esther rose from her vanity and approached him. He could see she was tired, see it in the shadows beneath her green eyes, in the tightness around her mouth. Even so, his body warmed and his heart sped up in anticipation of her touch. Was not the uxorial embrace a married man's greatest comfort at the end of a wearying day?

Her fingers went to his cravat. "Have we coin to put things to rights?"

Percival lifted his chin, while in his breeches, something else did not lift at all. "Coin is not a cheering topic, Esther. After dinner, I tried to bring up the need for improvements on the home farm and the tenant farms. Peter stared at his cards as if whist were some arcane Eastern invention. Tony took up a post by the sideboard, and His Grace started lecturing me on my shortcomings."

Though that lecture hadn't been half so objectionable as a single remark earlier in the week regarding a dead wife.

"Shall I approach His Grace?" Esther asked. She drew Percival's cravat from around his neck, draped it over his shoulder, and started on his shirt buttons.

She sounded quite serious. "You?"

"We are operating on the same allowance you were allotted upon our marriage, Husband, and yet we are also now blessed with four children."

Children did not eat much. Their clothes were small and passed down from one to another, and the boys were too young to need tutors. Still, there were aspects of raising a family that loomed as terra incognita to Percival, and his wife was tired.

He took Esther's hands in his, finding her fingers cool. "Esther, have you need of more coin?"

As he asked the question, he realized she was wearing a robe she'd had when they'd wed, more than five years previously. Then it had been a rich emerald velvet; now the elbows had gone shiny with wear.

"I have no need of coin beyond the pin money established in my settlements, but two nursery maids for four little boys is rather a strain."

A strain. He dimly perceived she might be telling him that strain devolved to her, and his father's crude barb came back to him. Because the topic was difficult, Percival took his wife in his arms, the better to read her reactions.

"What sort of strain?" Esther bore the scent of roses—she'd always borne the scent of roses—and that alone made some of his fatigue fall away.

"Valentine does not yet sleep through the night. Victor is also prone to wakefulness. Somebody is always cutting a new tooth or scraping an elbow. Winter is coming, and with it, illness is a given. Boys destroy clothes hourly—this is their God-given right, of course—and the house staff cannot be bothered sewing clothes for the children of a younger son. Boys also need toys, books, games, things to edify and distract. They need linens—Victor abhors sleeping in a crib when Bart and Gayle have their own beds, but I haven't the nerve to ask for another bedroom for Bart and Gayle. Bart wants a pony, but you well know what it will mean if you procure one for him."

She paused. He kissed her cheek. Perhaps her monthly approached, though it had been a rare visitor in their marriage. "Bart will share with his brothers?"

"He will *not* share, meaning Gayle must have a pony too, and somebody must teach the children to ride. Each boy must have proper attire, we must have pony saddles made or purchased, a groom must be detailed to care for their mounts and ride out with them, and there is no money for any of it."

Must, must, must. He knew better. He knew better than to launch into an explanation of how to solve those petty annoyances that loomed so large in her weary mind, and yet he spoke anyway.

"I spent several years in His Majesty's cavalry. I can teach the boys to ride, I can instruct them on grooming, saddling, and so forth. I'll speak to the housekeeper about making a room available for Bart and Gayle. We've space enough." Endless leaking corridors of space, in fact.

Esther dropped her forehead to his shoulder. This was not a gesture of relief or thanks. In fact, it dawned on Percival that she was standing in his embrace, meek and obliging, but her arms were not around her husband. They remained at her sides.

"You can speak to the housekeeper all you like, Percival. Nothing will change."

A frisson of alarm snaked down from Percival's throat to his vitals. The resignation in his wife's tone was complete. She'd given up on this issue, and Esther Himmelfarb Windham was not a woman to give up, ever.

"Why does nothing change? Does she expect the boys to be crammed four to a room until they're off to university?"

He hadn't meant to speak sharply, God help him. He'd meant to tease.

Esther moved off, toward the enormous bed in which they'd made four noisy, boisterous children. Well, three—Bart's conception had been a rustic antenuptial interlude that would forever give Percival pleasant associations with alfresco meals.

"The housekeeper took orders only from Her Grace. For the past year, Mrs. Helstead has maintained that she'll answer only to His Grace or Almighty God. Lady Arabella is the logical intercessor, but Peter's wife is too preoccupied with her own concerns to intervene, and I haven't wanted to trouble His Grace without your permission."

Percival shrugged out of his shirt and shucked his breeches. On the bed, his darling wife wasn't even watching, which was fortunate, because nothing noteworthy had been revealed.

Surely, her monthly was looming. Had to be, though he would not dare ask her.

"Speak to His Grace, Wife. He dotes on the boys." And who wouldn't? A more charming, dear band of rapscallions had never graced any man's nursery.

On the bed, Esther heaved up a sigh like a dying queen reclining on her funeral barge.

He hated this, hated decoding every nod and nuance. "What?"

"I will speak to His Grace, but he will forget, Percival. He will agree to see to the matter, and then lose sight of it altogether." The bed creaked on its ropes as she sat up and punched the pillows into her preferred contour. "He's failing. His energy, his memory, his will. When Her Grace died, she took a part of him with her, maybe the best part."

And what was that supposed to mean?

Percival tended to his ablutions, torn between the impulse to state his own list of woes and worries, and the desire to kiss his wife's miseries into oblivion.

Though where would that lead? They'd never resumed relations after a birth without Esther finding herself again in an interesting condition within a few months. At least one thing was clear: if he wanted to keep a mistress—and he was not at all sure that course held appeal—he'd have to find more coin first.

From the bed, Esther's voice was a sleepy murmur. "The boys said to tell you they missed you."

Why would his sons miss him? He stopped by the nursery every morning before he rode out. There, he listened to Bart and Gayle's mighty plans for the day, dandled Victor for long enough to make the boy giggle and laugh, and cuddled Valentine for at least a moment—providing the dear little fellow was not in need of a change of nappies.

Sometimes, Percival even stayed for a few moments because…just because.

"Do you know whom I missed today, madam?" He tossed the flannel in the general direction of the privacy screen and climbed onto the bed naked. "I missed my wife."

She was on her side, facing away, so he couldn't measure her reaction to this announcement.

"I missed the mother of my children, and I missed the boys too. What say we plan a picnic before the weather turns up nasty again? This mild spell cannot last. We'll bury a few Vikings at sea—"

He stopped mid-crawl toward his wife and subsided against the mattress.

Bloody, bedamned hell. Today was Thursday.

Thursday was their day to spend time with the children en famille, though lately Percival had been absent at those gatherings more than he'd attended them. The dead leaf in Esther's hair took on particular significance.

"Esther? I'm sorry. I hadn't meant to dine with Arbuthnot, but the man is a font of information, and if I can get the high meadow drained, it's excellent pasture. We need more pasture… I am sorry, though. I'll tell the boys tomorrow morning."

He rolled over and slipped an arm around her waist. Was she losing flesh, or had he just forgotten what she felt like when she wasn't carrying?

"Esther?"

She twitched. In sleep, his composed, poised wife twitched a fair amount. She also sometimes talked in her sleep, little nonsense phrases that always made him smile. He kissed her cheek and rolled onto his back.

"I miss my wife." Lying naked in the same bed with her, Percival missed his wife with an ache that was only partly sexual.

He considered pleasuring himself and discarded the notion. The flesh was willing—the flesh was perpetually willing—but the spirit was weary and bewildered. He'd blundered today, as a husband and a father. He'd blundered as a son too, in his father's estimation, and very likely he was blundering as a brother in some manner he'd yet to perceive.

Beside him, Esther's feet twitched. She'd told him once she often dreamed of their courtship, a brief, passionate, fraught undertaking that now seemed as distant as Canada.

Percival rolled away from his wife and let her dream in peace.

⚜

Esther felt a wall rising in the middle of the Windham family, for all they appeared to be placidly consuming a hearty English breakfast.

His Grace commandeered the head of the table, of course. Esther tried to picture quiet, soft-spoken Peter in that location and couldn't. Opposite His Grace, at the foot, the chair remained empty, though as the senior lady of rank and next duchess, the position belonged to Peter's wife, Lady Arabella.

Peter sat at his father's right hand, Arabella next to her husband, and Esther below Arabella. Across the table, Percival hid behind a newspaper on the duke's left, Tony inhaled beefsteak and kippers next to his brother, and across from Esther, Tony's wife, Gladys, took dainty nibbles of her eggs.

Had Esther wanted to, there was no way she could have nudged her husband's foot under the table, casually touched his hand, or murmured an aside to him. When had they decided to sit as far apart from each other as possible? When had she decided to sit on the side of the invalided heir?

"You'll be going up to London, Pembroke." His Grace glowered at a buttered toast point while the rest of the table exchanged glances at this news. "I've been asked to sit on a commission to study the provisioning of the army overseas. Damned lot of nonsense, but one doesn't refuse such a request."

He bit off a corner of the toast while a pained

silence spread. Peter hadn't been off the property even to go to services for at least two years. A trip to the stables left him exhausted, and if he missed an afternoon nap, he had to absent himself from dinner.

Esther lifted the teapot. "More tea, Your Grace?"

"I don't want any damned tea. If you bothered to familiarize yourself with the indignities of old age, you'd never offer such a thing."

Gladys shot Esther a sympathetic look. Percival slowly, deliberately, folded his newspaper down and stared at his father.

Please, Percival, I beg you do not—

"I'll thank you not to rebuke my lady wife for a proper display of table manners, sir."

Lady Arabella laid her hand on Peter's sleeve; Tony paused in the demolition of his breakfast.

"Perhaps I might serve on this committee?" Tony suggested. "Been to Canada, after all, and it's not as if I'm needed here."

"You?" Tony might have been old Thomas the footman for all the incredulity in the Duke's tone. "It's time you took a damned wife and stopped frolicking about under every skirt to catch your eye."

This time the sympathetic look went from Esther to Gladys.

"Tony and I will both go," Percival said, passing his newspaper to Peter and rising. "Scout the terrain, get a sense of what's afoot. Pembroke can come up to Town when the decisions are to be made, and of course we'll keep you informed, Your Grace. Ladies, I bid you good day. I'm off to wish my offspring a pleasant morning."

For just a moment, bewilderment clouded the duke's faded blue eyes. Before anyone else could speak, though, he rallied. "Daily reports, if you please, and don't stint on the details. I know not which is worse: the Whigs, the colonials, Wales's ridiculous flights, or the dear king's poor health. Madam"—he turned his glower on Esther—"you will stop hoarding that teapot. A man needs to wash down his breakfast, such as it is."

Esther passed the teapot to Arabella, and nobody looked at anybody. The King had recovered from his difficult spell more than a year ago, while Esther feared the duke's was only beginning.

Percival squeezed his father's shoulder. "We'll keep you informed regarding all of it." He bowed and withdrew, while Esther tried to puzzle out what expression had been on her husband's face during that last exchange.

Compassion for the old duke, whose confusion was becoming daily more evident, had been the predominant sentiment. Percival was pragmatic, also capable of clear-eyed understanding. That he neither judged his father nor ridiculed him warmed Esther's heart.

Good sons turned into good fathers.

Another emotion had lurked behind the compassion, though. Esther pushed her eggs around rather than watch as Tony tucked into yet another portion of rare steak.

Percival had been *relieved* at the prospect of leaving Kent and biding in London with his brother over the coming winter. Esther was not relieved, not relieved at all to think of her husband decamping for the vice and venery of the capital, while she remained behind to deal with teething babies and ailing lords.

Two

"WHY IS IT," PERCIVAL ASKED HIS FIVE-YEAR-OLD SON, "every woman I behold these days seems exhausted?"

Bart grinned up at his father and capered away. "Because they have to chase me!"

For a ducal heir, that answer would serve nicely for at least the next thirty years. Percival caught the nursery maid's eye. "Go have a cup of tea, miss. I'll tarry a moment here."

She bobbed her thanks, paused in the next room to speak with the nurse supervising the babies, and closed the nursery-suite door with a soft click of the latch. Percival did likewise with the door dividing the play-room from the babies' room, wanting privacy with his older sons and some defense against the olfactory assault of Valentine's predictably dirty nappies.

"I swear that child should be turned loose on any colonial upstarts. He'd soon put them to rout."

Gayle glanced up from the rug. "He's a baby, Papa. Nobody is scared of him."

"Such a literalist. Some day you'll learn about infantile tyrants. What are you reading?"

Gayle, being a man of few words, held up a book. Bart, by contrast, was garrulous enough for two boys.

"Shall I read to you?"

Bart came thundering back. "Read to me too!"

Percival glanced out the window. The morning was yet another late reprise of the mildness of summer, but to the south, in the direction of the Channel, a bank of thick, gray clouds was piling up on the horizon.

"I have to ride into the village today and meet with the aldermen, then stop by the vicarage and be regaled about the sorry state of the roof over the choir. When that task is complete, I'm expected to call on Rothgreb and catch him up on the Town gossip, which will be interesting, because I haven't any. My afternoon will commence with an inspection of—"

Two little faces regarded him with impatient consternation.

"Right." Percival folded himself down onto the rug, crossed his legs, and tucked a child close on each side. "First things first."

He embarked on a tale about a princess—didn't all fairy tales involve princesses?—and the brave hero who had to do great deeds to win her hand.

"Except," Percival summarized, "the blighted woman fell into an enchanted sleep."

"Then what happened?" Bart asked, budging closer.

"He…" According to the story, the fellow swived her silly—"got her with child," rather—which was what any brave hero would do after a rousing adventure. "He kissed her."

"Mama fell asleep."

That from Gayle, who wasn't the budging sort. The little fellow's brows were drawn down, the same sign his mother evinced when she was anxious.

"Keeping up with you lot would have anybody stealing naps," Percival said.

"Not a nap." Gayle sprang to his feet and went to the middle of the carpet like an actor assuming center stage. "She faded."

He collapsed to the rug with a dramatic thump, lying unmoving, with his eyes closed for a few instants before scrambling to his feet. "Old Thomas says the ladies do that when they're breeding. Bart wondered if we should bury her at sea."

"I did *not*. I said *if* she died, then we should bury her. She wasn't dead. She woke right up."

Gayle put his hands on his skinny hips. "You did too, and then she took a nap right there on the ship."

The ship being the picnic blanket, Percival supposed. "You saw her fall like that, both of you?"

Two solemn nods, which suggested this development was of more import to them than their inchoate argument. Percival set the book aside and held out one arm to Gayle while wrapping the other around Bart.

"Old Thomas is right." He tucked both boys close, as much for his own comfort as theirs. "Ladies sometimes fall asleep like that when they're peckish or their stays are too snug or they're breeding." Though Esther wore jumps, not stays, and never laced them too tightly.

"Mama breeds a lot," Bart observed.

"Your mother has fulfilled her obligation to the succession admirably."

"That means she does," Gayle translated. "She napped a lot too, when I wanted to fly my birds."

"Your birds are stupid," Bart observed.

Percival squeezed the ducal heir tightly and kissed the top of his head. "Rotten boy. Your little brothers will gang up on you if you keep that up. They'll leave Valentine's nappies under your bed."

Gayle smiled a diabolically innocent smile at this suggestion.

"Your mother likely needed to catch up on her rest, and she knew you two could be counted on to protect her while she did. I'm sorry I wasn't there to join you."

And he was sorrier still that by this time next week, he'd likely be in London, miles and miles away from his children, unless…

"Percival?"

Esther stood in the doorway, tall, slim, and elegant in a chemise gown of soft green and gold. The morning sun gave her a luminous quality, and with her standing above them, Percival was reminded that his wife was a beautiful woman.

Also quite pale.

"You've caught me out. I chased off the nursery maid to cadge a few moments with my first and second lieutenants. Won't you join us?"

Bart scooted free, and Gayle followed suit. "Good morning, Mama!" They pelted up to her, each boy taking her by the hand, Gayle waiting silently while Bart chattered on. "Papa was reading us a story, but he didn't finish. He said we can shoot Gayle's stupid birds on our next outing."

When Percival expected Gayle to enter the verbal melee with a ferocious contradiction, Gayle's gaze strayed to the door, behind which baby Valentine, King of the Dirty Nappies, held court.

Esther moved into the room, a boy on each side. "I'm sure your father said no such thing. I thought we might work on drawing tigers this morning though, and tigers might try to catch the birds as they flew away."

"Tigers!"

Why did Bart shout everything, and why did nobody correct him for it?

Percival unfolded himself from the floor. "You'd make a very poor tiger indeed if you can't be any quieter than that. Why don't you creep down to the library and have a footman fetch you some paper?"

More paper in addition to whatever they'd wasted making Gayle's birds. No wonder coin was in such short supply.

The boys crept away, growling and swiping their paws in the air, leaving Percival alone in daylight hours with his wife. His tired, lovely wife who had fainted the previous day and not told him about it. He slid his arms around her and drew her against his body.

He would not be a clodpate like he'd been the previous night.

He would ask her about her health. He would ask her how she felt about him going to London. He would compliment her on their children—a reliable strategy for ensuring happy marital relations.

The scent of roses came to him as she relaxed against him. "Madam, we can lock that door, you know."

She pushed away, smiling. "Only to scandalize all and sundry when the boys start pounding on the other side."

The interlude was unexpected, and Percival was glad for it. They so rarely had privacy when they weren't both tired and full of the tensions and trials of the day. "Will you sit with me for a bit, Wife?"

She gave him a curious look and let him lead her to the table near the window.

Which would not do. He changed course and took a seat in the largest reading chair the nursery had to offer, which was quite large indeed.

He gave a tug on her wrist, and she tumbled into his lap. "Percival!"

"Hush, madam. You and I have cuddled up in this chair when you were magnificently gravid. We fit nicely now."

She harrumphed and gracious God-ed once or twice under her breath, then settled easily enough.

"How are you, wife of mine? And I did not suggest Bart could stone Gayle's paper birds."

She relaxed against him. When had his wife gotten so lithe? So...skinny?

A practical, unappealing thought came to him: in London, a man did not have to pay for a mistress. Court was a very proper place, true, but outside of court, merry widows and straying wives were thick in the corridors. The idea of stepping into a dark alcove with some peer's well-fed, deep-bosomed spouse— all painted and powdered the better to display her wares—was vaguely nauseating.

Though Esther had fainted. A considerate husband did not overly tax his wife.

Said wife snuggled closer on a soft rustle of fabric. "Boys are bloodthirsty, especially in company with one another. You were kind to offer to go to London. How long do you think you'll be gone?"

Too long. Holding her like this, the quiet morning sunshine firing all the red and gold highlights in her hair, Percival felt two emotions well up and twine together.

He kissed her brow, yielding first to the tenderness assailing him so unexpectedly. "I don't know how long I'll be away. There's always warfare in some corner of the realm. We leave the Americans to their wilderness only to find some raja has taken the Crown into dislike. Colonials don't fight fair. Our boys line up in neat rows, muskets at the ready, while the natives fire at them from up in the trees or while dodging about in the underbrush. The wilderness ensures only the conniving and determined survive, and the colonials have been breeding those qualities for centuries."

She tucked herself against his chest. "If I haven't said it before, Percival, I'm saying it now: I am glad you resigned your commission. England expects much of her military, and I would not know how to go on were you lost to me."

The tenderness expanded as she lay against him, soft, pretty, rose-scented, and dear. He posed the next question quietly. "Esther, are you carrying again?"

Because if she were, it might explain the despair trying to choke its way past the tenderness.

"Thomas tattled on me?"

That was not a no. Percival closed his eyes and prayed. Not a prayer for wisdom or for guidance or for strength to know how to stretch their coin yet further, not even a prayer for strength to endure.

He sent up a prayer for his wife.

❦

How long had it been since Esther had enjoyed her husband's embrace? Between the baby being not quite weaned, the older boys climbing all over her, and Victor grabbing at her hands and skirts, Esther often felt her only privacy was in the bath, and then only if her husband did not walk into the room and offer his dear and dubious brand of "assistance."

Something he hadn't done in…quite some time.

And yet Percival still wore the cedary scent he'd used when they courted, and she still loved it. She still loved how his hands felt caressing her back in slow, smooth sweeps, still loved that he could tease about locked doors and broad daylight.

Loved *him.*

The realization brought relief, because it was also true she didn't always like the man she'd married, and often didn't agree with him.

"I don't know if I'm carrying. My monthly is not regular." Hadn't been regular since she'd started keeping company with her husband. Percival shifted beneath her while Esther tried to recall if they'd even had relations since last she'd bled.

His hand on her back went still. "Ah."

What did that mean? *Ah?*

"Do you want more children, Percival?" In the name of marital diplomacy and not shouting at Percival when anyone could hear, she refrained from bellowing: *You can't possibly want more children, can you, Percival? Not so soon…*

He was silent for a moment while his fingers resumed tracing the bumps of her spine. Esther strongly suspected he wanted some daughters. Once upon a time, they had both foolishly admitted to wanting a large family, equal cohorts of sons and daughters.

"I want my wife to be healthy and happy more than I want anything in the world."

He sounded like he meant it, also like he only realized he meant it as the words left his lips.

"I'm in good health. I'm just…tired."

"Tired to the point of fainting, Esther?" He kissed her brow again, something he did with breathtaking tenderness.

"Thomas should be pensioned. I swore him to secrecy, and I was light-headed only because I stood up too fast."

When she had been pregnant, she'd expected the occasional swoon, though none had befallen her. Ladies in the country, particularly women with a baby at the breast, wore front-lacing corsets without stiff reinforcement and were thus able to breathe easily.

Esther closed her eyes and let herself enjoy the languor her husband was weaving right there in the nursery.

"Come to London with me, Esther."

In his way, that was a question, an invitation phrased as an order. Put like that, the idea of leaving Morelands, with its confused duke, its ailing heir, and its upset household staff held a wistful sort of appeal.

"I'm still nursing Valentine every evening. He won't settle without it." And sometimes, the little mite woke up fretful in the night, and Esther indulged him again because nothing else consoled him. The man who snored the night away beside her might have known this. He might also have known that most midwives swore breast-feeding made it harder to conceive babies in close succession.

Percival was quiet in the manner that told Esther he was strategizing, weighing alternatives, considering angles. The military had lost a great general-in-the-making when Percival had sold his commission. Esther felt not the least twinge of guilt over their loss.

"I would miss you, were you to remain here," Percival said. This time he kissed her closed eyelids. "Keeping the army in decent boots and dry powder is important too. Lives depend on it."

Despair tried to push aside the sense of sanctuary Esther felt in her husband's arms. His Grace was failing, Peter's health was precarious, and in London, Percival would be assailed by all those seeking to curry the favor of the Moreland heir, which he could well be in a very few years.

"I will miss you, but the children need me, Husband." And her husband did not need her. Esther tucked closer rather than face the question of whether she needed him. "I never wanted to be a duchess."

Bad enough she was Lady Percival Windham.

"If God is merciful, we will dodge the title for many years, and Arabella is yet young enough she could have a son."

Arabella hadn't had intimate congress with Peter for years. To hear the lady tell it, her husband simply wasn't up to the exertion. Despair tightened its hold when Esther recalled that London boasted women aplenty willing to grace her husband's bed.

"I will miss you very much, Percival. Perhaps by the holidays I can wean Valentine, but to leave the children here, alone, in winter…"

"I know. A doughty old duke, a preoccupied, ineffectual heir, Arabella and Gladys absorbed with their daughters… I know."

His understanding was something new. Esther cared neither from whence it sprang nor whether it grasped the particulars of her concern. The idea of contending here without him, each meal a battleground, each day a trial…

She did need him, and perhaps in every way that counted, she was losing him. The thought made her want to cling and beg and weep, none of which would contribute meaningfully to the instant discussion.

And then her husband said something that put the urge to weep in a different light, a light of intense relief.

"Come to London with me, Esther. Pack up the children, the nursery maids, the whole kit, and come with me. In London, we'll have command of the entire house staff, none of this squabbling over whose job it is to fetch the coal to the nursery. His Grace won't bark at you one moment and forget who you are the next."

Five years ago, all Esther could see was that Percival Windham had been far above her touch, gorgeous, and possessed of blue eyes that seemed to understand much and give away little. She had adored him for his gallantry, charm, and forthright manner.

Over time, the forthright manner was proving his best quality, and Esther rose to the challenge before common sense could lodge a protest.

"I'll need some time to pack."

His hold on her became fierce. "I can give you three days, and then, by God, the lot of us are getting free of this place."

The way he kissed her suggested prisoners of war had never looked forward to escape with as much desperation as her husband felt about this trip to Town. Esther was just deciding she had the energy to kiss him back with equal fervor when the door burst open and Bart declared, "We found the paper, and we're ready to make tigers now!"

❧

"Why doesn't Gladys use a wet nurse?"

If Tony thought Percival's question absurd, too personal, or indicative of premature dementia, he didn't show it.

"No coin," Tony replied. "A wet nurse is something of a luxury, and I'm the impecunious youngest son. Then too, Gladys says children get attached to their wet nurses, and my lady wife is very particular about who gets attached to whom."

No coin, perhaps this, rather than the parenting biases of the mercantile class from which both Esther and Gladys sprang, was why Esther had also eschewed a wet nurse.

The horses walked along for another furlong before Percival comprehended that Tony was referring to his wife's opinion on mistresses. In Canada, he and his brother had spent hours on horseback like this, tramping through wilderness as yet ungraced with roads. The distances rather forced a man to parse his companion's silences.

"She told you as much, did she? No other attachments for you?"

Tony stared at his horse's mane, which lay on the left side of its neck—an oddity, that. "She said in so many words that he who goes a-Maying will come home to find his wife has gone a-straying."

"My sister-in-law is a poetess. What happened to your gray gelding?"

"Sold him. A man can ride only one horse at time."

The poetess was married to a philosopher, and this jaunt to London was looking to be a very long, cold trip indeed.

Percival stretched up in his stirrups then settled back into the saddle. "At least the roads are frozen. God help us if it warms up this afternoon."

"More likely to snow or sleet," Tony said, his gaze on the sky. "Even so…" He swiveled a glance over his shoulder at the traveling coaches lumbering along behind them.

"Even so, God have mercy on anybody trapped in a coach with my children," Percival finished the thought. And then, because he had no one else with whom to discuss the situation, and because, for all his impecunious-younger-son blather, Tony had always kept his confidences, Percival added, "There's something amiss with my wife."

Tony darted a glance at his brother then fiddled with his reins. "Esther Windham would no more go a-straying—"

Percival cut that nonsense off with a glower. "Your defense of the lady's honor does you credit, of course, but not everybody is preoccupied with straying,

Anthony." Intriguing topic though it might be. "Did you notice, when the coaches were being loaded, that Gladys had to direct the footmen and nursery maids and so forth?"

"Gladys likes to direct. It's one of her most endearing features, and has many interesting applications. She frequently directs me to disrobe in the middle of the day, for example, and ever her servant, I, with an alacrity that would astound—"

"*Must* you sound so besotted? Gladys is remaining at Morelands and had no cause to be involved in the packing. A woman normally likes to take charge of her own effects."

This silenced the besotted philosopher for nearly a quarter mile. "The Windham ladies are friends, I think. Being daughters-in-law to a difficult duchess did that for them, and Peter and Arabella were lonely before we sold our commissions."

"Arabella, certainly."

With Peter, it was harder to say, because he was frequently to be found in the intellectual company of that pontifical nincompoop, Marcus Aurelius, or others of his antique and gloomy ilk.

"What do you think is wrong with Esther, Perce? She seems hale enough to me, if a bit harried."

That was some encouragement. Tony noticed more than most gave him credit for—or he had, prior to his marriage.

"She fainted on her last outing with the boys, before the weather changed."

"She's breeding?"

Percival wanted to shout at his brother for leaping

to the obvious conclusion. Wanted to knock him off his damned horse and pound him flat. "Possibly."

"For God's sake, Perce, use a damned sheath. Better some sheep give up its life than you overtax your wife. The succession is assured four times over, and Gladys and I may yet bring up the rear with a few sons of our own."

"Sheaths can break." Did break, with alarming frequency.

"Bloody bad luck. Condolences then, or congratulations. Both, I suppose." Tony was studying the road ahead with diplomatic intensity. "Maybe you'll get a girl this time. Girls are"—his expression turned besotted, *again*—"they're magical. I can't describe what it's like when a daughter smiles up at her papa or takes his hand to drag him across the nursery."

Sweet suffering Christ.

"Esther claims she just stood up too quickly, but I asked Thomas about it. Damned old blighter had to think first—said he was sworn to secrecy and would not betray her ladyship's confidences."

Comet made a casual attempt to nip Tony's gelding, proof positive nobody was enjoying this journey.

Tony nudged his horse up onto the verge beside the wagon rut. "Good man, Thomas. When nobody else can reason with His Grace, Thomas can talk sense to him. Calls him Georgie, like they were mates."

Anthony seemed intent on providing one irritating rejoinder after another. Percival forged onward despite his brother's unhelpfulness.

"I told Thomas I knew Esther had fainted, and wanted him to confirm particulars only. It was a protracted exercise in yes-or-no questions. I swear I'm going to pension him come summer."

"You're not going to pension anybody, and neither is Peter. His Grace has the staff's complete loyalty, and well you know it."

"Anthony Tertullian Morehouse Windham, I am well aware of the strictures upon our household." The plaguey bastard smiled, and as much to knock him figuratively off his horse as anything else, Percival got to the heart of the matter. "My wife lied to me."

Tony grimaced. "Not good when the ladies dissemble, though in a small matter one can overlook it."

He was asking, delicately, if the matter had been small.

"She said she'd fainted because she stood up too quickly. Thomas had it that she'd stumbled twice on the way to the stream and had been waiting for the footmen to spread the blanket—just standing there—when she collapsed."

"That, Percy, is not good. Not the lying, not the collapsing, none of it. What did you do to provoke her into keeping such a thing from you? Are you having a spat, because if so, the best way to get past it is behind a closed door, fresh linens on the bed, and not a stitch of clothing between you."

Just as Percival would have spurred his horse to the canter in lieu of backhanding his brother, a coaching inn came into view.

Of course, they would have to stop. The coachy would want to water the horses and give them a chance to blow, the footmen would cadge a pint, the nursery maids would need the foot-bricks reheated, and the older children would need a trip to the jakes.

And Esther… Esther who'd been trapped in the coach all morning with their children? Percival turned his horse for the coaching yard and wished to Almighty God he knew what his wife needed.

⁘

"Look! Look right there!"

Maggie's head was forcibly shifted between her mother's hands, so she had to stare out the window of the coach.

"That's him! I knew it! That's your father, Magdalene! He's very handsome, isn't he?"

"Yes, Mama." Even at five years old, Maggie knew not to disagree with Mama. This so-called papa was all wrong though. He looked more serious than handsome. His horse was brown, not white. And he wasn't wearing a handsome wig like Mama's gentlemen friends did. Most telling of all, this papa fellow completely ignored his daughter when she was sitting in a closed carriage not ten yards away.

Her papa, her *real* papa, would never ignore her like this. He'd smile at her and have treats in his pocket for her and buy her a pony. He'd read stories to her and tell her she was pretty. He would not let Mama slap her so much—Mama was a great one for slapping. Mama slapped the maids, the potboy, her little dog.

Slapping wasn't so bad, not as bad as the yelling and breaking things, and the weeping that happened when Mama had a row with a gentleman friend.

A little part of Maggie wished the fellow on the wrong-colored horse was her papa—provided he didn't like slapping. Miss Anglethorpe said there were men who didn't.

Maggie knew there were also men who did.

This man must have caught sight of Maggie gaping at him from the carriage window, because he paused in the middle of his conversation with some other gentleman on horseback, raised his hat to Maggie, and winked at her.

At her.

Maggie's knuckles went to her mouth in astonishment. She'd raised her hand to wave at him, when her mother yanked her away from the window.

"He mustn't see you—yet. Not until the moment is right. The situation requires delicate handling if Lord Percival is to do his duty by you."

As the carriage rolled away, Maggie sat on her hand rather than reach out the window and wave to the man. When she got home, though, when Miss Anglethorpe had taken her medicine and gone to sleep, and Mama was off with the gentlemen, Maggie would creep from her bed to the mirror in the hall.

She was going to learn to wink. She would practice until she got it right.

Just like her…like that man.

~≪⌒≫~

"Please, let this child fall into a peaceful slumber and wake up healthy and happy in the morning."

Esther murmured her prayer quietly, because Valentine was not yet truly fussing. He was whimpering and fretting, sufficiently displeased with the remove to Town to be waking several times a night. The ties on

Esther's nightgown gave easily, and she put the child to her breast without having to think about it.

He latched on with the desperate purpose of a hungry infant, while Esther closed her eyes and wondered why even this—a mother's most fundamental nurturing of her baby—should provoke a sensation of despair so intense as to be physical.

While Valentine slurped and nursed, Esther examined the feeling suffusing her body. Despair was the prominent note, followed up by…desolation. A sense of being utterly isolated, though she was intimately connected to another human being.

"Esther?"

How long had Percival been standing in the shadows just inside the playroom door?

"You're home early."

She wasn't accusing him of anything—though it might have sounded like it.

"Wales overimbibed, and the footmen took him to his chambers, so the rest of us were free to leave." Percival crossed the room and threw himself into the other chair. He drew off his wig in a gesture redolent of weariness, and hung the thing over the top of the hearth stand like a dead pelt. "Have I mentioned lately that I hate court?"

He hated the pomp and powder, which was not the same thing.

"You enjoy the politics."

He also enjoyed watching Esther nurse their children. She'd thought that endearing, once upon a time.

Valentine having finished with the first breast, Esther put him to the second. Before she could tend to her clothes, Percival leaned over and twitched her shawl higher on her shoulders, covering up her damp nipple. He excelled at such casual intimacies, thought nothing of them, in fact. He touched her as if she thought nothing of them either.

Esther allowed it, though all that despair and desolation had been crowded back by a healthy tot of resentment borne on a rising tide of fatigue and a strong undercurrent of anger.

"I do enjoy politics," he said, sitting back and stretching out his legs toward the fire. "I've been approached about running for a seat in the Commons."

"I suppose that makes sense." Belatedly, Esther realized Percival was asking her opinion. She mustered her focus to consider the matter, despite her bad mood, because he was her husband, and he was a good husband. "We would have to be in Town more, and the stewards and tenants are looking to you for direction at Morelands."

"Yes."

He stared at the fire, which meant Esther had time to study him.

He looked...not old exactly, but mature. The last vestiges of the handsome young officer had been displaced by a gravity that wasn't at all unattractive. He was barely thirty, though she'd found a gray hair on him their first morning in Town.

She had said nothing about that.

"What are you thinking, Percival? Valentine and I will keep your confidences."

His smile was a mere sketch of what he was capable of when intent upon charming, but it had been real.

"We would have to entertain. You would have to go out and about. Tony can take on the duties at Morelands—he's better suited to cajolery and flattery than I'll ever be—and it isn't as if the succession has been neglected."

At that last observation, Percival ran a finger over Valentine's cheek. The child released the breast on a sigh of great proportions for such a small fellow.

"He's done carousing," Percival said, reaching for the baby. "Ready to sleep off a surfeit of motherly love."

Esther let him have the baby and was grateful for the assistance. Percival—veteran of many postprandial interludes with his sons—put a handkerchief on his shoulder, tucked Valentine against his chest, and patted the small back gently.

"You're not enjoying this remove to Town, are you, Esther?"

The question was unexpected, awkward, and brave. "The children are not settling in well. Babies like their routine, and Bart and Gayle were used to rambling in any direction at Morelands. Here, we must arrange outings to the park. Then too, the servants haven't sorted themselves out yet."

Percival sighed, sounding much like his young son, but nowhere near as content. "I suppose it's human nature for them to feud. I wasn't asking about the children or the servants, though. I was asking you, Esther. You're not happy here."

With the part of her that loved him, Esther knew he wasn't accusing her of anything. "I wasn't happy at Morelands."

For a long moment, the only sound was the hissing and popping of the fire. Percival had ordered that wood be burned in the nursery, claiming it was healthier for small lungs than the constant stink of coal smoke.

Valentine burped. A single, stentorian eructation followed by another contented-baby sigh.

"Your son enjoys healthy digestion, madam." She expected Percival to hand the baby back to her, but he kept the child tucked against his shoulder. "And as to that, I don't see how you could have been happy at Morelands. I doubt if anybody is happy at Morelands, save the livestock and the pantry mouser."

Percival had not been happy at Morelands. The realization struck Esther along with a pang of guilt. She was tired, lonely, and out of sorts, and her husband—in the same sorry condition himself—was offering her understanding. When he could have fallen exhausted into bed, he'd sought her out and extended this marital olive branch.

Another silence ensued, this one more thoughtful.

"We should go to bed, Percival. You don't often get in at a decent hour, and you need your rest too."

She was dodging behind the mundane realities, but her husband did not accommodate her.

"Esther, I am worried about you. Organizing this trip seems to have overtaxed you, and you fainted again yesterday morning. A moment earlier, and you would have fallen to this very carpet here with Valentine in your arms."

Esther closed her eyes against this unforeseen assault. She knew how to handle blustering and shouting. Percival's rages against this or that governmental excess or insult to the Crown were mere display, and his frustrations at Morelands resolved themselves with regular applications of hard work.

But this...*concern* devastated her. "You must not trifle over female vapors. I will recover my strength directly. If you want to stand for a seat, we can entertain, attend all the necessary functions, and flit about Town from now until Michaelmas."

Percival rose and crossed into the next room, Valentine in his arms. When he returned to the playroom, having cleared the field of noncombatants, he resumed his seat and advanced his forces again.

"I think you should consult a midwife, Esther, if not a physician."

She did not want a doctor or a midwife. She did not even want a nap. What Esther wanted, just then, was her husband's embrace. The impulse was surprising, but it did not fade as it ought. "I am not sickening, Percival, and as far as I know, I am not carrying."

He should know that too. They slept together and shared a bedroom. Some husbands might not notice a wife's bodily cycles, but Percival was in nowise some husbands. Reconnaissance came to him as easily as command.

"You'll think about it? A little bleeding can rebalance the humors."

He wasn't wrong, and yet Esther had parted with enough blood in her various lying-ins to feel rather possessive about the quantity yet flowing in her veins. "I'll think about it."

"That's all I ask."

And then, just when she thought the skirmish had played itself out, he took her prisoner. Scooped her up against his chest and carried her from the room, the spoils of an altercation Esther hadn't seen coming and certainly hadn't won.

❧

An officer could raise his voice when the situation warranted, could swear a bloody streak, drink himself into oblivion, and order some miscreant flogged for serious transgressions.

A husband and father had no such outlets, not with children sleeping in the next room and a wife who looked so lovely and sad nursing her infant that Percival wanted to tear his hair in panic.

In his arms, Esther felt light as a wraith, and her very docility scared him worse than the French, the Indians, or the wild creatures of the Canadian forest ever had. She offered not even a "Percival Windham, put me down" across the length of the entire house—and with such a precious burden, he did not hurry.

He deposited her beside their bed then divested her of her robe. "To bed, madam, and you will sleep in tomorrow. If you are fatigued, and you refuse to consult medical authority, then you will submit to *my* authority when I tell you to rest."

His authority was nonexistent with her. He'd known that before they married and had delighted in her independence. A man in love was a fool.

While he tried to glower at her—please God, let his glowers be more effective with the children than they were with his wife—she met his gaze. He knew that look, knew that obdurate, mulish expression, and felt a predictable response to the challenge it portended.

His blood quickened in anticipation of a great row—maybe their most rousing argument so far—when Esther slowly, deliberately, crossed her arms and inched her nightgown up over her head.

Sweet suffering Christ. Like a damned upstart colonial, she was launching a sneak attack.

"I've missed you, Percival. Perhaps you'd like to get into this bed with me."

She flung the words at him like a gauntlet, an accusation of intentional neglect that was not at all fair. Then the infernal woman plastered herself—her entire naked, warm, lithe self—against him and took his mouth in a kiss.

"Esther…"

Holy God, she felt wonderful. His hand, sliding down the elegant turn of her flank, gloried in the absence of flannel and propriety. Could a man's hands be hungry? For his surely were—for the feel of her, for the exact contours and shifts of her muscle and bone beneath his palms. Her nudity, so rare in recent months, topped any argument his reason might have put forth about their mutual need for rest, or a man not pestering his wife beyond the necessary.

This was *necessary*. It was necessary that Percival fling his clothes away between kisses; it was necessary that he heave his wife onto the bed like he hadn't since the early weeks of their marriage. It was as necessary as his next breath that he climb over her and trap her body beneath his, the better to plunder her mouth with his own.

And then—because he was not just a husband and father, but also a man still in love, it was necessary that he try to exercise some damned restraint.

"I should find a sheath, Esther." Though the sheaths were clear across the room, secreted somewhere in the wardrobe—halfway to Canada, according to the compass needle pointing directly at Percival's wife.

She got her mouth on him again, sank her teeth into his jawbone, not enough to hurt, but enough to distract. "Sheaths break. Love me." To emphasize her words, she traced his lower lip with her tongue, dipping inside his mouth then feinting back.

"Esther, I am concerned for—" Worried sick, he was. Somewhere beneath the tempest of passion she was evoking, he was worried for her, for their marriage, for his family. Nigh distraught with it.

His cock, however, was distraught in an entirely different and—just at that moment—more convincing manner.

"Love me."

"I do. I do love you, dammit, but for the love of God, if you don't stop—" He went on the offensive, covering her mouth with his own, trapping her hands beneath his against the pillow.

She went still, breasts heaving beneath him, a tease and retreat of puckered nipples against his chest. By the narrowing of her eyes, he realized she understood what even her *breathing* did to him.

"I love you," he said again, more softly. A plea this time. "Let me love you."

She closed her eyes, as much surrender as he would get from her in a duel he neither understood nor welcomed. When he kissed her cheek, the grip of her fingers in his shifted, became a joining of hands rather than a prelude to whatever sexual hostilities

she had in mind when she'd challenged him with
her nudity.

"I love you, Esther. I will always love you."

How to love her was becoming both increasingly
obscure and increasingly more important.

Joining with her, though, remained within his gift,
thank God. For a small eternity, he kissed her. He
reacquainted himself with the texture of each of her
features, used his lips and his nose—Esther had once
admitted to an affection for his nose—to map her
face. He used the tip of his tongue to trace her lips,
then paused to rest his chin, then his cheek, against
her hair.

He loved her hair, loved the golden abundance of
it spilling over her shoulders before she trussed it up
in thick, shiny braids.

When she began small, restless movements of her
hips, he settled between her legs and by lazy, comforting increments, threaded himself into her body.

How had he forgotten this? How had he lost the
memory of that first beautiful, soft sigh near his ear
when he pushed himself inside her?

Before they'd found a rhythm, before he'd given
her a hint of satisfaction, he damned near spent, so
startling was the depth of pleasure he found in his
wife's body. She flung herself against his thrusts,
strained against him, and made a solid bid to wrestle
Percival's control from his grasp. While Percival held
the balance between a ferocious determination to
please his wife and the equally ferocious effects of
sexual deprivation, he dimly perceived that something
besides desire had Esther in its grip.

The first shudder went through her; then she bucked against him, signaling that he could follow her into pleasure. He thrust hard, then harder as she clung and moaned, then harder still.

His last thought—a desperate flight of imagination, surely—was that Esther's passion was real, but as she shook and keened beneath him, she was wrestling not only with desire but also with despair.

Three

"ESTHER, THIS REMOVE TO TOWN HAS YOU LOOKING peaked and wan. Percival must be beside himself."

Gladys had sent word that another day cooped up at Morelands would give her a megrim, and Tony, apparently having a full complement of prudence and a mortal fear of his wife's megrims, had collected his family from the country accordingly.

Having rested for all of one night, nothing would do but that Gladys would muster the troops for an outing to the park, regardless of the cold, regardless of anything.

"I haven't bounced back from the upheaval," Esther replied slowly. She could be honest because the boys were in the next coach back, with the maids and Gladys's eldest daughter.

Gladys glanced over at her sharply. "From the move? You haven't bounced back from the move up here?"

"Not from that either." Dawning truth was not always a comfortable thing, but there was relief in it. "From Valentine's birth, I think."

The coach clattered along past the dormant trees and dead grass of Grosvenor Square. Gladys peered out the window then huffed a sigh.

"It was worse for me with Elizabeth. I thought I'd never stop weeping. Her Grace, of all people, was a comfort."

The idea that Her Grace could have been a comfort to anybody was intriguing. "How?"

"She'd lost Eustace, you'll recall, when he was only five. She said a mother must not give in to the melancholy, that your children will always be with you in some regard, despite that you must send them out into the world. I think she also cornered Tony and told him to cosset me within an inch of his life."

"As if he doesn't anyway?"

They shared a smile, though as conversation again lapsed, Esther marveled that she and Gladys hadn't had this discussion before. Perhaps, with six children between them under the age of six, they'd been too busy.

Melancholy was a serious word, a potentially dangerous word. "I don't weep, much. Hardly at all, but there's a sense…"

Gladys barged into the silence. "Your heart aches abominably after the baby arrives. When I was a girl, we used to go to Lyme in the summer. I'd stand on the beach in my bare feet and let the water swirl about my ankles. After Elizabeth was born, I felt like something was dragging at my ankles the same way, taking all my happiness and pulling it out to sea. I'd cry at anything and nothing."

In for a penny… "Did you faint?"

"Not until Charlotte came along."

Another shared smile, nowhere near as merry.

"I don't think I'm carrying again." Though after last night… Last night had been a mistake in some senses, and much needed in others. Esther hadn't completely sorted the whole business out, but she'd slept well, and she had not made arrangements to consult any physicians.

Nor had Percival brought it up again at breakfast.

"Esther, lower the shade." Gladys reached over and unrolled the leather that covered the window.

"Why are we shutting out the last sunshine we might see for days?"

"Because that beastly O'Donnell woman was sitting in her open carriage, flirting right there in the street with some poor man."

"She must earn her living too, Gladys." Esther could be charitable, because Percival had assured her early in their marriage—early and often—that he'd been ready to divest himself of the drama and greed of professional liaisons.

At the time, she'd believed him. Through a crack between the window and the shade, Esther studied Cecily O'Donnell, one of Percival's former mistresses—the tabbies had been all too happy to inform a new bride exactly where her competition might lie. The lady's coiffure was elaborate and well powdered, a green satin calash draped over it just so. Her white muff was enormous, her attire elegant to the point of ostentatious, and in her eyes there was a calculation Esther could see even from a distance of several yards.

The carriage rolled past Mrs. O'Donnell's flirting swain, and Esther thought of Percival's words from the previous night: *I do love you. I'll always love you.*

She'd believed him then. She still believed him in the harsh light of the winter day.

❧

"Good of you to receive me, Kathleen."

Percival bowed over the hand of a woman he had seen little of in the previous five years, and had seen every inch of prior to his marriage. Her hands were still soft, her smile gracious, and her modest house welcoming.

And yet she had aged. The life of a courtesan was a life of lies, of making the difficult look easy and amusing, when it was in truth dangerous and grueling. Percival knew that now, now that he was married.

Or maybe he'd always known it, only now he could afford to admit his part in it.

Kathleen St. Just rose from a graceful curtsy. "My lord, you look well. May I offer you refreshment?"

He loathed tea, and he did not want to consume anything under her roof for reasons having to do with Greek legends regarding trips through the underworld. He parted with her hand.

"Nothing for me, and I won't take up much of your time. I trust you are well?"

She glanced around the room, which, now that he studied it, was also showing a few signs of wear. By candlelight, the frayed edge of the Turkey carpet would not be obvious, nor would the lighter rectangle on the wall where a painting had hung.

In the harsh light of day, the decor had deteriorated significantly.

"I'm well enough. I hear you are a papa now." She led him to a sofa Percival recognized from his visits here more than five years ago. He sat as gingerly as he could, having taken his pleasure of the lady more than once upon its cushions.

This sortie was proving damned awkward, but sending a note would not do.

"I am blessed with four healthy sons, if you can believe it."

She considered him. Her hair was still a rich, dark auburn, her eyes a marvelous green. Even without her paint and powder—especially without it—she was a beautiful woman, and yet…the bloom was off her. She'd been, in cavalry parlance, ridden hard and put away wet too many times, and all the coin in the world could not compensate her for that.

"And your lady wife? How does she fare?"

The question was a polite reminder that Kathleen St. Just did not permit married men among her intimate admirers—or she hadn't five years ago. Percival had liked that about her—respected her for it.

"It's about my lady wife that I have presumed to come to you."

He rose, the damned sofa being no place to discuss Esther's problems.

"Are you sure you wouldn't like something to drink, my lord?"

My lord? She'd seldom my-lorded him in the past, but there was comfort in the use of the title now. Kathleen was a fundamentally considerate woman, something he hadn't appreciated enough as a younger man.

"Nothing, thank you." He paced away from her to peer out her back window. In spring, her tiny yard was a riot of flowers, but now it was a bleak patch of dead, tangled foliage and bare earth, with a streak of dirty snow by the back fence. "I need advice, Kathleen, and information, and I cannot seek them from the usual sources."

"I will not gossip with you, my lord. Not about anybody. I know how you lordly types like to revile one another by day then toast one another by night."

He turned and smiled at her. "You know, my wife frequently takes that same starchy tone with me. I have always admired a formidable woman."

He'd confused her with that compliment. Beautifully arched brows drew down. "Perci—my lord, what are you doing here?"

He admired women who could be direct too.

"My lady wife is sickening for something, and she won't consult a physician. She didn't refuse me outright when I suggested it, but she has a way of not refusing that *is* a refusal. Whatever's wrong with her, it's female. You always had a tisane or a plaster to recommend when I was under the weather, and your remedies usually worked."

Kathleen left the sofa too and went to the sideboard. None of the decanters were full—in fact, they each sported only a couple of inches of drink. Her hands on the glass were pale and elegant, though the image struck Percival as cold too. He swung his gaze to the bleak little back garden, where a small boy was now engaged in making snowballs out of the dirty snow.

"You love your wife, I take it?"

In the detachment of her tone, Percival understood that the question was painful for a woman who would likely never marry and never have any pretensions to respectability again.

He kept his gaze on the small boy pelting the back fence with dirty snowballs. The boy had good aim, leaving a neat row of white explosions against the stone wall at exactly the same height.

"I love my wife very much, else I would not be here."

Kathleen said nothing for a moment while the snowballs hit the wall, one after another. "Describe her symptoms."

He did as best he could while the boy ran out of ammunition and knelt in the snow and mud to make more.

"Is she enceinte?"

Percival shook his head, much more comfortable watching the busy little soldier in the back garden than meeting Kathleen's gaze. "She doesn't smell as if she's carrying."

Kathleen came to stand at his shoulder. "What on earth does that mean?" A touch of their old familiarity infused the question. Just a touch.

"My wife always bears the scent of roses. I don't know how she accomplishes this, because she doesn't use perfume. Maybe it's her soap or the sachets in her wardrobe. It's just...*her*, her fragrance. Blindfolded, I could pick her out from a hundred other women by scent alone. When she's carrying, there's more of a nutmeg undertone to the scent. Very pleasant, a little earthier. I realized it with the second child, and it was true with the third and fourth too."

He glanced over at her and saw she was watching the boy too. The look in her eyes reminded him of Esther—whose name he had managed not to utter in this house—when she was nursing Valentine. Sad, lovely, and far, far away.

"My guess is nothing ails your lady that time will not put to rights, my lord. She is likely weakened by successive births and weary in spirit. My sister has nine children, my brother's wife eight. You must be considerate of her and encourage her to rest, eat good red meat—organ meat, if she's inclined. Steak and kidney pie or liver would be best. Under no circumstances should she be bled; nor should she conceive again until her health and her spirits are recovered. You should get her out for light exercise for her spirits—hacking out or walking, nothing strenuous."

Esther loathed organ meat. He'd never once in five years seen her eat either liver or kidney.

"How long will it take her to recover?"

Kathleen crossed her arms and considered him. She was a tall woman and did not have to peer up more than a few inches to meet his gaze. "You might ask a midwife, or one of those man-midwives becoming so popular among the titled ladies."

"I've yet to meet a member of the medical profession not prone to gossip and quackery—unless you can suggest somebody?" This was what he'd come for—a reliable reference. The ladies of the demimonde could not afford to jeopardize their health, especially not in its female particulars.

"Let me think for a bit. If some names come to mind, I can send them to you."

"That would be appreciated." It would also let him end this very awkward interview. As Percival gave Kathleen his direction, the little boy had abandoned his play and disappeared from the back garden. Percival wondered vaguely to whom the child belonged, that he was allowed to play unsupervised on a day that was growing colder, for all it was sunny.

Kathleen showed him to the door, and in her eyes, Percival might have seen either disappointment or relief that he was going.

The entry hall was devoid of flowers—Kathleen had always loved flowers. That he knew this about her was both melancholy and dear in a sentimental sense that made him feel old.

He paused as he pulled on his gloves. "Kathleen, do you need anything? Is there something I might do for you?"

No servants, no flowers. Scant drink in the decanters, paintings likely pawned... She was succumbing to the fate of all in her profession who overstayed their dewiest youth.

She looked haunted, like she might have asked him for a small loan then loathed herself—and him—for sacrificing this last scrap of pride to practicalities. A door banged down the hallway, and the small boy came pelting against Kathleen's skirts.

The lad said nothing, but turned to face Percival with a glower worthy of many a general. The knees of his breeches were wet and muddy, his hair was an unkempt, dark mop, and his little hand—red with cold—clutched a fistful of his mother's skirt.

"Hello, sir," Percival said. This fellow looked to be about Bart's age, perhaps a bit older, and every bit as stubborn—which was good. Boys should be stubborn. "A pleasant day to you."

Kathleen smoothed her hand over the lad's hair and said something to him in Gaelic. The boy looked mutinous, but swept a bow and muttered "G'day, m'lord." The glower never faltered.

As Percival took his leave, he realized why he'd felt such an immediate affection for the pugnacious young man: Kathleen's son had the exact same shade of green eyes that Percival's own boys shared. The same stubborn chin Gayle sported, the same swooping eyebrows Victor had had since birth, the same tendency to muddy his knees Bart delighted in.

Amazing how small boys could come from such different stations and be so alike.

❧

Mama grabbed Maggie by her shoulders and turned her forcibly toward the water. "Those boys are your brothers."

There were two of them, scavenging the verge for rocks to throw at the ice forming along the edge of the Serpentine. One boy was blond, the other had hair several shades darker than Maggie's red hair, and both—like most boys—were good at throwing rocks.

"I would rather have sisters." Sisters would not be doing something as silly as breaking ice that was just going to form again.

Mama's fingers pinched uncomfortably on Maggie's shoulders. "Be glad at least one of them is male. Your papa's papa and your papa's older brother are in poor health and failing rapidly, but should one of them outlive your father, that blond boy will become the next duke."

Mama sounded fiercely glad about this. Maggie had no idea why. From what little she knew, being a duke was also silly.

"Who is that lady?"

"That pale Viking creature is your papa's wife, and may he have the joy of her." Mama fairly snarled this information. Maggie would have bruises from the way Mama gripped her shoulders now.

"And the other lady?"

"Lord Tony's wife, your papa's sister-by-marriage. Why Lord Tony married a horse-faced Valkyrie when he could have had his pick of heiresses escapes me. Windham men are headstrong. Remember that."

Remember it for when? Unease shivered down Maggie's limbs along with the cold. "I need the necessary."

Mama shook her. "No, you do not. I told you to go before we got in the coach."

Which had been ages ago, because Mama had taken to lurking in the park and rolling around Mayfair by the hour, hoping to catch another glimpse of Maggie's papa.

And yet Maggie wanted desperately to get away from those laughing, rock-throwing boys and the pretty blond lady smiling at her red-haired friend. Their very joy and ease made Maggie anxious.

"I really do have to go, Mama. I'm sorry."

Of course, Mama slapped her. A slap against a cold cheek had a particular pain to it, a sting and a burn made worse for the frigid air. Maggie would remember *that*, and she would not cry—crying was for babies.

"You vile little rat," Mama hissed. "Everything I do, every single thing, is for your benefit, and yet you must whine and carry on and foil all my plans. I should have left you as a foundling on the steps of the lowest church in the meanest slum—"

Maggie cringed away, expecting the inevitable backhanded blow, but down by the water, the boys were no longer throwing rocks. They were staring at her and at Mama. They weren't laughing anymore.

"They're watching you, Mama."

All of them, the boys, the two ladies, a nursemaid who had a tiny girl by the hand, a footman near the boys, and a second nursemaid. All of them had gone still, watching Mama raise her hand to strike Maggie again.

That hand lowered slowly and straightened the collar of Maggie's cape. "Let them watch. The performance is just beginning. Come along."

Maggie had to run to keep up with Mama on the way back to the coach, run or be dragged. She glanced over her shoulder and saw the boys were still watching, and so was the tall blond lady.

Papa's wife was pretty, and she looked worried—for Maggie. The lady kept watching until Mama bundled Maggie into the coach, and even as the coach pulled away, Maggie peered out the window and saw her watching still.

When I grow up, I want to be a Viking creature too.

~∾~

Esther regarded her husband over a glass of hearty red wine—she preferred white, but somebody had mixed up the menus, so a roast of beef had been served instead of fowl.

"Have another bite, my dear." She obligingly nibbled from the fork he proffered. "Did you enjoy the outing to the park today?"

"I did, and I think the boys did too, very much." She had enjoyed most of it, despite the chill. She was also enjoying her husband's attentions, which had been marked throughout the meal. "Is there a reason we're dining in our chambers, Percival?"

"Tony and Gladys sought some privacy."

This had the ring of an improvised untruth. Tony and Gladys found privacy throughout the day, and sometimes didn't bother to find privacy when they ought. Esther munched another bite of perfectly prepared beef and cast around for a way to brace her husband on the day's events.

"And what did you find to do with yourself today, Percival?"

He studied the next bite of beef skewered on the silver fork. "This and that. Have you given any more thought to consulting a physician?"

"I have not." Nor would she, not when all that ailed her was a crushing fatigue and a passing touch of maternal melancholia. "You're neglecting your meal, sir."

He studied braised carrots swimming in beef juices. "Peter has not left his chambers since we departed for Town. He doesn't come down for meals."

Esther's ire at Percival's mention of a physician faded. She spoke as gently as she could. "Hectoring me to see a doctor will not restore your brother's good health, Husband."

He sat back, his expression unreadable. "Will you come riding with me tomorrow? Take a short turn in the park at midday?"

He was up to something, though Esther had no idea what. Percival worried about Peter, about the duke, about the infantry in the colonies, and about the King's health.

And her husband worried about her.

"Of course I'll ride with you, weather permitting." She'd be in the saddle by midday if she had to be carried to the mews. "Have you given any more thought to a seat in the Commons?"

That was a stab in the dark, because no matter how she studied him and reviewed the day's events, Esther could not fathom what burr had got under Percival's saddle. Peter had taken to his bed before, and Arabella jollied him out of it eventually.

They finished the meal in silence, and when the dishes had been removed, Percival confirmed Esther's suspicion that he was pursuing some objective known only to him—for now.

"I'm for bed, Wife. You will join me?"

She'd like nothing better, unless it was to have an honest answer from him regarding his present preoccupation. Not until they were in bed, side by side and not touching, did it occur to Esther that her husband might be feeling guilty.

Last night might have resulted in conception—it probably had, in fact. They were that fertile—that blessed—as a couple.

"Percival?"

"My dear?"

"Do you regret last night?" She could ask that in the dark. She could not ask him what was wrong and what she could do to help him with it. Beneath the covers, she felt his fingers close around her hand.

"I could never regret making love to my wife."

Another prevarication, though not exactly an untruth. Esther rolled against his side, hiked a leg over his thighs, and felt his arms encircle her. She remained silent, and that was a form of prevarication too.

What Esther wanted to say, the words that were burning to fill the darkness of that bedroom, had to do with a single, sharp moment etched into her memory from their visit to the park.

Cecily O'Donnell had emerged from her coach when the boys had vanquished a patch of ice along the Serpentine bank. She had towed a small child with her. A girl sporting hair as red as Mrs. O'Donnell's was revealed to be beneath her striking green calash.

Esther had been helpless not to watch as the solemn child had regarded Bart and Gayle hurling their rocks, laughing and carrying on like boys who'd been cooped up too long.

The girl was stoic, not succumbing to tears even when slapped stoutly by her mother—for she had to be Mrs. O'Donnell's child. She had her mother's generous mouth, had her mother's red hair. If Esther had to guess the girl's age, she'd place her a year older than Bartholomew at least, based on height and also on a certain gravity of bearing. She was pretty now and destined for greater beauty in a few years.

A year before Bart had been conceived, Percival would have been in Canada. The realization was no little comfort.

~∞~

"I cannot fathom why any man of sense would argue for the purchase of more ammunition without also advocating for more uniforms. Muskets won't fire if the fellows holding them are perishing from cold. Men can't march if the jungle has rotted their boots."

Tony rarely became agitated, though his fussing was welcome.

Percival steered Comet around a pile of pungent horse droppings steaming in the middle of the path. "Their argument is, we should outfit our fellows in something other than scarlet regimentals. Our boys might as well have targets painted on their backs."

"But in the smoke and noise of battle, when the cannon have been belching shot in every direction, those scarlet uniforms are all that keep a man from being killed by his own troops."

This was also true, and morale was somehow bound up in the traditional uniforms too.

"There are no good solutions to some problems," Percival replied, "and in any case, cannonballs are easier to requisition than new uniforms. If I asked you to return to Morelands, would you go?"

Tony's horse was not as fastidious as Comet. At the next evidence of another horse's recent passing, the gelding plodded right through, landing his off hind foot in the middle of the rank pile.

"You are going to be head of the family soon, Perce. I don't think you're facing this as squarely as you ought. If you want to dispatch me to Morelands, to Morelands I will go. Gladys understands."

Esther understood too, about some things. "Peter is bedridden again. Because Arabella is preoccupied with her spouse, His Grace is no longer coming down for meals either."

Tony's lips pursed. Around them, few others had braved the park's chill this early. Sunlight bounced off the Serpentine in brittle shards, and Percival wondered if he ought to cancel his outing later in the day with Esther.

"His Grace isn't one for pouting," Tony observed. "What does old Thomas say?"

"Old Thomas is posting me regular reports. Says His Grace is off his feed too."

Which was alarming. The duke Percival recalled from boyhood had been a hale, articulate, supremely self-possessed man, the equal of any occasion. The elderly, confused fellow at Morelands bore only the saddest resemblance to Percival's sire.

"I'll go, Perce. Gladys will want a day or so to shop and organize, but I'll go."

"My thanks."

They both fell silent as they came around a bend in the path. A woman sat perched on an elegant bay mare several yards ahead, the lady's unpowdered hair nearly matching the horse's gleaming coat.

And not a groom to be seen.

Percival's every instinct told him this was an ambush. Seeing Kathleen St. Just had brought the past to mind, and for Percival, that past included Cecily O'Donnell. Their paths had not yet crossed this trip, and Percival had been hoping to avoid the woman altogether.

While Percival liked Kathleen, respected her and wished her well, his association with Cecily O'Donnell was a small collection of expensive, rancid memories and uncomfortable regrets.

"Your lordships, good morning!"

The O'Donnell had always been abominably forward. Percival nodded coolly and urged Comet along the path.

She turned her horse to more completely block the way, which was bloody stupid when she was on a mare and Percival was on a frisky young stallion.

"Oh come now, Percy! Can't you greet an old friend? And, Tony, you never used to be unfriendly."

Percival had the odd thought that even Cecily O'Donnell would not have approached him had he been with his lady wife. Would to God that he were.

"Madam, good day." He did not so much as touch his hat brim.

"Tony, you'll run along now. Dear Percy and I have things to discuss in private."

She'd drenched herself in some musky, sweet scent redolent of patchouli, and she used singsong tones another, much younger and sillier man might have taken for flirtation.

Tony, bless him, stayed right where he was and uttered not a word of greeting.

Percival let Comet toss his head restively. "I have nothing to discuss with you, madam. Unless you want to provoke my stallion to an unseemly display, you'll move aside."

Though in truth, it was the mare who might deliver a stout kick to the stallion if she were crowded.

"You are in error, dear man, and I am partly responsible. My apologies." The devil himself could not have offered less sincere regrets to St. Peter.

Percival shot a look at his brother. Tony would ride around and haul the woman's horse off the path by the bridle at the first indication from Percival, but then the damned female would only pop out from behind another bush at some more public moment.

"Anthony, if you would oblige the…woman." For she wasn't a lady.

Without acknowledging Mrs. O'Donnell in any way, Tony steered his gelding back a few yards on the path. A little privacy, no more, which was exactly what Percival intended.

"What can you possibly have to discuss with me, ma'am? When you threw me over for some general five years ago, I withdrew from the field without protest. I am happily married"—he *delighted* in telling her that—"and your circumstances now are of no interest to me whatsoever."

And yet…the morning sun was not kind to a woman who'd been plying a strumpet's trade practically since girlhood. Kathleen St. Just had looked tired, sad, and worried, while Cecily O'Donnell appeared as brittle and cold as the ice on the nearby water. Her hair, once her crowning glory, looked as if it had been dulled by regular applications of henna, and her skin, once toasted as flawless, looked sallow.

Pity was a damned nuisance when coupled with a man's regrets.

Percival waited until Cecily had turned her horse then allowed Comet to walk forward. "What do you want?"

"I'm a reasonable woman, Percy. What I want is reasonable too."

Part of what she wanted was dramatics. This aspect of her personality was one reason ending their casual association had been such a relief.

"You'd best spit it out. Both my father and brother are ailing. I may well be leaving for Morelands this afternoon." *Forgive me, Papa and Peter.*

"I know."

She let the echo of that broadside fade. She'd been spying on him, or at least keeping up with gossip. Neither was encouraging.

"Anybody who's been to the theater would know. Get to the point."

"I've missed you, Percy."

Oh, for the love of God. "I cannot find that notion flattering—or sincere. If that's all you had to say, I'll just be going." Comet, ever a sensitive lad, began to pull on the reins. Percival smoothed a hand down the stallion's crest.

"Damn you," she hissed. "I might have been ami-cable, but you're determined on your arrogance. You are the Moreland spare, and if you don't want scandal the like of which will disgrace your family and destroy your welcome in polite circles, you'll attend me at my home tomorrow promptly at ten of the clock."

Having made her threat, she whacked the mare stoutly with her whip and cantered off in high dudgeon, while Percival reined in and waited for Tony to catch up.

"So?" Tony asked.

"I am to attend her tomorrow morning at ten of the clock." Late enough that any guest from the previous evening would be gone, early enough that decent folk would not yet be calling on one another.

"I can't like it, Perce. She's a trollop in a way that has nothing to do with trading her favors for coin."

"I loathe it, but I'll go. She's plotting something, probably some form of blackmail. The woman has not aged well."

"Will I go with you?"

"You'll go back to Morelands." Leaving Percival's flank unprotected but guarding the home front.

"Did you breed Comet overmuch this autumn?"

Percival stared at his brother. "I did not. Why?"

"He hardly noticed there was a female present, not in the sense a swain notices a damsel."

"Neither did I." Which, thank a merciful Deity, was nothing less than the complete truth.

❧

"Did you enjoy your meal, Esther?"

Esther paused in setting up the white pieces on the chessboard—Percival insisted she have the opening advantage—and regarded her husband. "We're having rather a lot of beef lately. Cook must have misplaced the menus I gave her."

Percival regarded one of her exquisitely carved ivory knights then passed it across to her. "Perhaps Cook is trying to turn the butcher's boy up sweet. The shires can do with one or two fewer cows."

Several fewer cows. Percival had taken to passing her at least half his beefsteak at breakfast with a muttered, "Finish it for me? Mustn't let good food go to waste."

A kiss to her cheek, and he'd be off for his morning hack or to a levee or one of his "never-ending, blighted, bedamned committee meetings."

In moments, they had the pieces arranged on the chessboard between them. Percival sat back and passed her his brandy. "A toast to a well-fought match."

He was up to something—still, yet, again. Esther took a sip and passed the drink back. "To a well-fought match."

She regarded the board with a relish she hadn't felt since... "Percival, when was the last time we played chess?"

His frown probably matched her own. "Not since...you were carrying Victor? Or was it Gayle?"

They measured their lives in pregnancies and births, which had an intimacy to it. "Gayle. We played a lot of chess when I carried Gayle. You said the child would be professorial as a result, and he is."

"Then perhaps we should get into the habit of laughing, in the event you're carrying again. A merry little girl would liven up Morelands considerably."

How was a woman to concentrate on chess when her husband came out with such observations? Did he want to try for a daughter, or was he saying Morelands lacked cheerful females?

"My love, I am atremble in anticipation of your opening salvo."

Teasing, then. She was inclined to give as good as she got. "You should be atremble to contemplate your sons as grown men. If the mother's behavior in gestation influences the child's disposition, we're likely to see a number of grandchildren at an early age."

Percival's smile was sweet and naughty. "I suppose we are, at that."

Esther opened with a feint toward the King's Gambit, but whatever was distracting her husband of late, he was not completely oblivious to the pieces in play. She settled into a thoughtful game, sensing after about two dozen moves that Percival's lack of focus would cost him the game.

"Percival, you are not putting up enough of a fight." And the chessboard was practically the only place Esther could challenge him and enjoy it.

"I do apologize. More brandy?" He held up his drink, which he'd replenished at some point.

"A sip. Maybe you are trying to addle my wits."

"Spirits fortify the blood. It's *my* wits that are wanting. Shall I concede?"

Three years ago, he would have fought to the last move, teasing and taunting her, vowing retribution behind closed doors for wives presuming to trounce their husbands on the field of battle.

Three years ago, she had fought hard to provoke such nonsense.

"You're going to lose in about eight moves. I won't be offended if you'd rather we retire."

He knocked over the black king with one finger. "I married a woman who can be gracious in victory. It shall be my privilege to escort that woman upstairs."

In fact, he escorted her to the nursery, taking the second rocking chair when she sent Valentine off to sleep with his final snack of the day. The way her husband watched this bedtime ritual—his expression wistful to the point of tenderness—sent unease curling up from Esther's middle.

When Percival had tucked "his favorite little tyrant" in for the night and Esther herself was abed beside her husband, she reached for his hand. "Percival, I would not want to intrude into spheres beyond what is proper, but is something troubling you?"

His sigh in the darkness was answer enough, and when he rolled over and spooned himself around her, Esther's unease spiked higher.

"I received another communication from Peter today."

She'd been expecting him to put her off, or worse, explain to her that it was time their marriage took a more dignified turn. The little girl in the park came to mind, the one with the pretty features and the horrid mother.

Though at one time, Percival had apparently thought the mother the very opposite of horrid.

"This letter troubles you?"

"Exceedingly." Percival's hand traced along Esther's arm, a caress that let her know, for all his quiet, her husband was mentally galloping about at a great rate. She did not allow her mind to wander into thickets such as: Did my dear husband touch Mrs. O'Donnell like this? Did he lie beside her and tell her his worries when the candles were doused? *Does he long to again?*

Esther felt a brush of warm lips against her shoulder, and then Percival went on speaking, his mouth against her skin. "I have been telling myself that surely Peter and Arabella will be blessed with a son. Their affection for each other is beyond doubt."

"Far beyond doubt. One has only to see how Peter watches Arabella from across the room."

"Or how she watches him." Another silence, another kiss, then, "Peter sent a substantial bank draft."

Esther's first reaction was that they were badly in need of a substantial bank draft. Then another reality sank in: "This saddens you." She could hear it in his voice. Hear the grief and the dread.

"He's getting his affairs in order. He said as much in the letter, as if Peter's affairs could ever be anything else. He's preparing documents for the duke that will do likewise, and His Grace will sign those documents if Peter is the one asking him to."

The post came in the morning, and all day, the entire day, Percival had been carrying this burden alone. Esther rolled over and wrapped her arms around her husband. "Peter may yet rally. His Grace still has good days."

Percival submitted to Esther's embrace like the inherently affectionate man he was, also like a man who had too few safe havens. "Peter assured me there was no possibility Arabella could conceive."

Esther stroked a hand from Percival's forehead to his nape. Early in the marriage, she'd realized this particular touch soothed them both. "Peter and Arabella haven't enjoyed marital intimacy for at least two years. Her sense is that he's unable. Whatever ails him, it affects him in that regard as well."

She felt Percival's eyes close with the sweep of his lashes against the slope of her breast.

"For two years?"

"I did not want to add to your burdens." Though in hindsight, she wished she hadn't kept this intelligence from her husband. "Bartholomew truly is going to be a duke."

"He'll make a fine duke—you will see to it, if nothing else. It isn't Bart I'm worried about."

Esther continued stroking her husband's hair, taking some comfort from the idea that as reluctant as she was to contemplate becoming a duchess, her husband was equally reluctant to become a duke.

"You already are the duke, you know."

He shifted up and nuzzled her breast. "I am no such thing. I'm only the spare by an unfortunate act of providence."

Just as Esther did not ponder at any length whether her husband was resuming relations with a dashing mistress, Percival apparently did not want to examine too closely the prospect of a strawberry-leaf coronet.

"You are Moreland, Percival. You're tending to matters of state, you're running the estates, and you've secured the succession. For all relevant purposes, you are the duke—and you're making a fine job of it."

The conversation was intimate in a way that felt different from their previous intimacies. This was intimacy of the body, of course, but it was also intimacy of the woes and worries, and it bred desire as well.

If she initiated lovemaking with her weary, unhappy spouse, would he reciprocate, or would he withdraw, leaving Esther physically and emotionally empty?

She settled for taking his hand and resting it over her breast, then kissing his temple. Her last thought as she succumbed to slumber was a question: Would Percival use some of Peter's largesse to set up a mistress? For a duke was entitled to his comforts.

He probably would, and tell himself he was being considerate of his wife when he did.

Four

"HE'S A GOOD MAN, YOUR PAPA. AN IMPORTANT MAN."

Devlin did not meet his mother's gaze as they walked along. She was pleading with him somehow, and he didn't like it. He also didn't like this neighborhood, where the streets were wide and the walkways all swept and he didn't know the way home.

"Devlin, he was in the cavalry."

Devlin forgot about the list of things he didn't like.

"I'm going to be in the cavalry. I'm going to have my own horse, and I'm going to protect everybody for the King."

Now Mama stopped walking, and right there with people hurrying by, crouched before Devlin. "Your papa can make that dream come true, Devlin. I cannot."

Which was why they were going to his papa's house, he supposed. They'd been to visit other men's houses. Mama would wait in the stables and mews, and Devlin liked that just fine. Those places smelled of horses, and the grooms were usually friendly to a small boy who thought horses were God's best creation.

"Will you talk to him in the stables?"

Mama kissed the top of his head—he hated when she did that—and rose, taking his hand again. "If I have to." Her tone was grim, determined. She said Devlin got his determination from her.

She talked to men in the stables lately, sometimes telling Devlin to be good when she went into the saddle rooms or carriage houses with them. She was never gone long, and they could always get some food on the way home when she'd had one of her visits with the men.

Then too, stables were warm, and they smelled good. Home was not warm these days.

You could tell a lot about a man from his stables. Sir Richard Harrowsham was a friendly man who laughed a lot. His horses were content and well fed, his stables clean without being spotless.

Mr. Pelham's horses were nervous, the grooms always rushing about, and the aisles never swept until somebody stepped in something that ought to have been pitched on the muck heap as soon as it hit the ground. Mama had been crying when she'd come back from her little meeting with Mr. Pelham.

Devlin's papa's stables were large. There were riding horses, coach horses, and even a draft team, which was unusual in Town for the nobs, though not for the brewers and such.

Devlin did not think his papa was a brewer. The grooms were friendly, the tack was spotless and tidy, and the horses... Devlin peered down the aisle at the equine heads hanging over half doors.

The horses were magical. They were huge, glossy, and glorious even in their winter coats. Their expressions were alert and confident, somehow regal. If horses could be generals and colonels, then these horses would be.

"You wait here," Mama said, sitting Devlin on a trunk. "Be quiet and don't get in the way."

"Yes, Mama."

She said something else, very quietly, in Gaelic. Mama never spoke the Gaelic in public. "I love you."

Devlin smiled up at her, trying not to show how pleased he was. "Love you too!"

He watched her cross the stable yard and take up a position near somebody's back gate. All the houses here had back gardens; their kitchens didn't simply open onto a smelly alleyway. The grooms went about their business, mucking, scrubbing out water buckets and refilling them, cursing jovially at each other—but never at the horses.

When a groom asked Devlin if he'd like to help brush a horse, Devlin decided his papa must be a good man indeed.

❧

Esther knew who the pretty red-haired woman was and wondered if this remove to Town was intended by the Almighty as some sort of wifely penance.

"Mrs. St. Just, is there a reason why you're lurking at my back gate in the broad light of day?" *My husband's back gate, in point of fact.*

Upon closer inspection, Percival's former mistress was thin, she wore no gloves, and her hair bore not a hint of powder or styling. She wore it in a simple knot, like a serving woman might. Esther hadn't been

able to put any condescension into the question—
Percival recalled this lady fondly, drat her.

Drat him.

"All I seek is a word with you, my lady."

Here, where any neighbor, Percival, or the children
might happen along? Not likely. "Come with me."

Esther's footman looked uncertain, while Mrs.
St. Just looked…frightened. She glanced toward the
stables, as if she'd steal a horse and ride away rather
than enter the ducal household.

"I must tell my son where I've gone. He's just a
boy, a little boy, and he worries."

What Esther needed, desperately, was to hate this
woman who'd had intimate knowledge of her husband, to loathe her and all her kind, and yet Mrs. St.
Just worried for her son and apparently had no one
with whom she could leave the child safely.

"Bring him along."

Relief flashed in the woman's eyes. She scurried
across the alley and reemerged from the mews, towing
a dark-haired boy.

"Devlin, make your bow."

The lad gave Esther a good day and a far more
decorous bow than Bart usually managed.

"Pleased to make your acquaintance, Master St. Just."

He was thin, and his green eyes were too serious
for a boy his age. Esther was not at all pleased to make
his acquaintance, wondering with more than a little
irritation which swaggering young lordling had turned
his back on this blameless child.

The next thought that tried to crowd into Esther's
mind she sent fleeing like a bat up the chimney.

Esther took her guests—what else was she to call them?—in through the big, warm kitchen. Mrs. St. Just looked uncomfortable, while the boy was wide-eyed with curiosity.

"Perhaps your son would like some chocolate while we visit, Mrs. St. Just?"

If the help recognized the woman's name, they were too well-bred to give any sign. The scullery maid remained bent over her pots, the boot boy didn't look up from his work at the hearth, and the undercook kept up a steady rhythm chop, chop, chopping a pungent onion.

"Devlin?" Mrs. St. Just knelt to her son's eye level. "You be good, mind? Don't spill, and be quiet. I won't be long."

"Yes, Mama."

Esther did not tarry to study the curve of the boy's chin or the swoop of his eyebrows. He was a hungry boy, and any mother knew exactly what to do with a hungry boy. She caught the undercook's eye and made sure the lad would be stuffed like a goose before he left.

The next issue was where to serve tea to her husband's former mistress—for Esther would offer the woman sustenance as well. That was simple Christian charity.

Esther addressed the undercook, who'd gotten out bread and butter and was reaching for a hanging ham. "I'm feeling a bit peckish, so please bring the tray to Mrs. Slade's parlor."

The choice was practical: the housekeeper's parlor would be warm and would spare Mrs. St. Just a tour past the upstairs servants. It would also mean mother and son were not separated by more than a closed door.

When that door had been latched, Esther turned, crossed her arms, and regarded Mrs. St. Just where she stood, red hands extended toward the fire.

For her sons, Esther would cheerfully kill. She'd walk naked through the streets, denounce her king, sing blasphemous songs in Westminster Abbey, and dance with the devil.

What Kathleen St. Just had done for her child was arguably harder than all of that put together. Esther took a place next to the woman facing the fire, their cloaks touching.

It occurred to her that they were both frightened. This realization neither comforted nor amused. Esther grabbed her courage with both hands, sent up a prayer for wisdom, and made her curtsy before the devil.

"Two questions, Mrs. St. Just. First, does his lordship know that boy is his son, and second, how much do you need?"

❧

Kathleen St. Just's household had shown signs of wear and want. In Cecily O'Donnell's, the floors gleamed with polish, the rugs were beaten clean, and a liveried and bewigged porter still manned the door.

And yet, as Percival followed the woman into a warm, elegant little parlor, his footsteps echoed, suggesting every other room in the place was empty of furniture. Fortunately, this parlor held no memories of intimacy, for Cecily entertained only above stairs on an enormous carved bed sporting a troop of misbehaving Cupids.

"Shall I ring for tea?" she asked as she closed the door behind him.

"You shall state your business. One is expected to attend the morning's levee."

Her lips curved up in merriment. "How it gratifies me to know you'd rather spend this time with me than with our dear sovereign."

She went to the door and rang for tea—of course. When the door was again closed and he was assured of privacy, Percival speared his hostess with a look that had quelled riots among recruits culled from the lowest gin houses.

"State your business, woman, or you will be drinking your tea in solitude."

To emphasize his point, he moved toward the door. She stopped him with a hand clamped around his wrist. "You will regret your haste, my lord."

There was desperation in her grip...which could work to his favor. Percival aimed his glower at her fingers—her ringless fingers—and she eased away.

His next glower was at the clock on her mantel. "You have five minutes."

A tap on the door interrupted whatever venom she might have spewed next. "Come in."

A maidservant entered, accompanied by a little girl with red hair and a stubborn chin. He'd seen the child before somewhere, but couldn't place her for the unease coursing through him.

The girl was not attired in a short dress as befit one of her tender years, nor was her striking hair tamed into a pair of tidy braids. She was dressed in a miniature chemise gown of gold with a burgundy underskirt, her pale little shoulders puckered with gooseflesh. Her hair was pinned up on her head in a style appropriate to a woman twenty years her senior, and—Percival's stomach lurched to behold this—the child's lips were rouged.

"Magdalene, make your curtsy to the gentleman."

A perfectly—ghoulishly—graceful curtsy followed, suggesting the girl had been thoroughly grilled on even so minute a display. "Good day, kind sir."

Percival manufactured a smile, because the child's voice had quavered. "Good day, miss."

And *Magdalene*—a singularly unkind name for a courtesan's daughter.

Cecily grabbed the girl by the chin and pointed toward the sideboard, across the room from the fire's heat. "Be quiet. You"—she waved a hand at the nursemaid—"out."

Was everyone in this household terrified of the woman?

"You have three minutes, Mrs. O'Donnell, and then I shall do all in my power to ensure our paths never cross again." He meant those words, though his gaze was drawn back to the child, who stood stockstill, staring at the carpet in all her terrible finery.

"Three minutes, Percival? I say our paths have become joined for the rest of our days on earth. Whatever else I know to be true about you—and I have kept up, you may be assured of that—I doubt your vanity would allow your only daughter to be put to work in her mother's trade, would it?"

While the child remained motionless and mute, Percival felt his world turn on its axis. A hollow ache opened up in the pit of his stomach, a sense of regret so intense as to crowd any other emotion from his body.

The child *could* be his.

His dear, tired, dutiful wife would not kill him—that would be too easy a penance for a young man's folly—but she'd likely remove herself from his household, and not a soul would blame her. The rules of marital combat in Polite Society allowed a wife to discreetly distance herself from an errant husband once heirs were in place.

Percival picked up the child, who cuddled onto his shoulder with a sigh. She weighed too little for her height, which looked to exceed Bart's only slightly. Percival brought his burden—his daughter?—to the door and found the nursemaid, as expected, shivering in the corridor. "You will take miss back to the nursery, keep her there for the duration of my interview with your mistress, remove the damned paint from her face, and dress her appropriately to her station—and warmly. Is that understood?"

The maid cast a glance past Percival to Cecily, who nodded.

"Understood, my lord."

Without another word, the child was taken from the room. Percival remained in the doorway, watching as she was towed by the hand toward the stairs. On the bottom step, the girl turned and met Percival's gaze, surprising the daylights out of him by sending him a slow, careful wink.

Despite the tumult and despair rocketing through

him, he winked back, recalling in that moment where he'd seen her before: in the park, peering out of a coach window. She'd struck him as a lonely little princess being dragged about on some adult's errand, an accurate if understated assessment.

With a pointed glance at the clock, Percival turned and faced the woman who had in the last moments become the enemy of all he held dear. "What do you want?"

Her smile was the embodiment of evil, but she at least seemed to know enough not to approach him. "What I want is simple, my lord. I want you. Unless you can live with the fate of any girl born to Magdalene's circumstances and live with the knowledge that all and sundry will become aware of her patrimony, then I suggest you accede to my wishes."

He didn't believe for one minute she meant he'd have to accommodate her in bed. She'd have to be daft to think him capable of such a thing. She wanted his escort, his protection, his wealth. Cecily O'Donnell was nothing if not shrewd.

She would understand shrewdness in another.

"Hear me, woman: You will ensure no harm comes to that child, lest the repercussions redound to your eternal detriment. You will produce baptismal records, a midwife's sworn statement, and an affidavit from the man of the cloth who presided at the child's christening before I even entertain the notion that girl might be my get. And you may be assured, should misfortune befall Miss Magdalene, I am threatening your very life, just as you are threatening my welfare. Make no mistake about that."

She blinked, the only sign of intimidation he was likely to see from her.

"My arrangement with you was exclusive, my lord."

Percival moved toward the door, pausing with his hand on the latch. "Your arrangement with me was brief and long ago. Our encounters were meaningless and few, and between them, I did not trouble myself with what you got up to or with whom. You did not quibble over the compensation made to you at the time, and you know well the risks of your profession. I will see proof the child could be mine and then decide what's to be done about her."

A final glance at the clock—five minutes on the nose—and Percival walked out, feeling like a man given a reprieve from a date with the gallows. And yet, as he retrieved his stallion from the mews and turned the beast for home—there would be no attending any levees today—his mind circled around one question:

What would this cost him?

There would be a cost in coin, of course, and in convenience, because no child of his was going to grow up without her father's protection. Those costs were entirely bearable and the responsibility of any man who took his pleasures outside of marriage.

The greater cost was going to come in the distance this would create between Percival and his wife. Sooner or later, Esther would become aware Percival was supporting Mrs. O'Donnell again. Polite Society, having all the kindness of a troop of rabid wolverines, would make sure Esther knew of the child as well.

As he turned for home, the true price of his interview with Cecily O'Donnell settled into Percival's awareness next to the grief he felt at his father's senescence and at his brother's decline: the only way Percival could protect his wife from all the sorrows looming as a result of the morning's revelations was by sending her away and keeping her far from the reach of gossip.

⤝⤞

"I fear for the bovine population in the Home Counties," Esther muttered as her husband seated her for an evening meal that once again featured beef.

His smooth gallantry faltered, something only a wife of several years' duration would notice. Percival leaned closer to Esther's ear. "I care not what is served when the company at table is my lovely wife, whom I once again have all to myself."

Esther smiled, but Percival's flattery rang hollow. Everything had rung hollow since Esther had found Kathleen St. Just shivering at the gate.

Percival took his seat at Esther's elbow and poured them each a glass of wine. "What did my dear wife find to occupy herself today?"

Esther sampled her wine, needing the time to fashion a fabrication. "I saw Gladys and Tony off, settled a dispute between warring tribes of Hottentots in the nursery, penned a disgustingly cheery epistle to Arabella, reviewed the household accounts with Mrs. Slade, discussed with her several candidates for the upstairs maid's position, and then made a half-dozen morning calls. Devonshire sends his regards and despairs of your politics."

His Grace had sent a few looks Esther's way too, the rascal.

Percival seized on the one aspect of Esther's day with financial consequences. "We're hiring another maid?"

Esther watched while he served her a portion of soup that savored strongly of—but of course—beef broth.

"I'm replacing the one who found herself in an interesting condition. Surely you noticed?"

Percival's expression was hard to read, suggesting he truly hadn't noticed the girl's expanding belly. "Do we know who's responsible?"

"I have not inquired. I suspect one of the footmen."

The unreadable expression became one of distaste. "Shall I have a talk with the man?"

Esther had not considered this option, so she spoke slowly. "He's young, Percival, and probably fears if we know he's been taking liberties, he'll lose his position. Then he won't have even his wages to offer as support for the child."

An image of Kathleen St. Just came to mind, her dark-haired, watchful son at her side. Esther's fingers traced around her wrist. When she'd dressed this morning, she'd fastened on a pearl bracelet her grandmother had given her upon leaving the schoolroom. The jewelry wasn't fancy enough to raise eyebrows on Ludgate Hill, but it would feed the child for quite some time. She hoped it would feed the child.

"Let young Romeo keep his wages," Percival said, "provided he takes a wife. Are you enjoying your soup?"

Esther glanced at her nearly empty bowl. "It appears I am. You'd allow a footman to marry?"

"I will not allow a child to go hungry merely because her parents were young and foolish. The mother will have to find lodging elsewhere, lest Moreland take offense at my interference. Is she a village girl?"

"From Dorset, though she speaks well enough and is clever with a needle. I could send her some mending if she finds lodging nearby."

"Excellent notion." Percival moved the soup dishes to the side and began carving Esther a serving of roasted beef that would have fed Tony for several days of forced march. "How are my little Hottentots, and what could they possibly be waging war over?"

The topic of tribal warfare in the nursery was much safer, though why the exchange regarding a straying chambermaid and her swain should be upsetting, Esther did not know.

Not exactly upsetting, but Percival's reaction to it gave Esther pause.

He deserved to know about the boy, Devlin St. Just. Esther admitted this to herself as she and her husband wandered up to the jungle on the third floor, and tucked sleepy, well-fed, happy little warriors into their cozy beds.

As Esther settled Valentine into his crib, and Percival waited patiently in a rocking chair by the fire, Esther realized the decision was not truly about Percival's deserts, or about Mrs. St. Just's, or even about Esther's.

A boy needed to know who his father was and to have the protection that man could afford him in this precarious and difficult life. One pearl bracelet was no substitute for a father's protection, much less a father's love.

Coming to this conclusion and broaching the matter with her spouse were two separate acts of courage.

In a silence that should have been companionable, Esther accepted her husband's assistance undressing. His hands lingered in seductive locations, on her nape when he unfastened a necklace, at the base of her spine when he unhooked her dress. His lips strayed to the spot beneath her ear that sent shivers over her skin.

Of all nights, why was he seducing her now?

When she was wearing only a chemise, Esther turned, intending to unknot Percival's neckcloth. She was willing to be seduced, willing to accept some marital comfort and to forget for a few moments what—whom—the day had brought to her back gate.

Had Percival not built up the fire while Esther had removed her remaining jewelry, Esther might have missed the little glint of red on his sleeve. She drew his neckcloth from him slowly and turned to toss it over the open door of the wardrobe, when a hint of coppery fire caught her eye.

Two red hairs lay on his coat at the shoulder, two brilliant, gracefully curving commas of evidence that Percival had been close to somebody other than his wife. Mrs. St. Just had hair that shade, but she would hardly have come calling at the home of a man who was paying her for her favors, would she?

Gladys also had red hair, but not nearly this long.

"Esther?" Percival leaned down and brushed his lips across hers. "I would join my wife in our bed, if she'd allow it."

He was asking to bed her, to exercise his marital privileges, while his very clothing bore traces of congress with somebody else.

"Of course, Percival." Esther finished undressing her husband, wondering how it was that she could love a man whose casual behavior also had the power to devastate her.

When she was naked on her back, Percival braced above her and, joining their bodies with excruciating deliberateness, Esther tried to push the ugly, desolate thoughts aside:

Was it guilt—or something more arrogant and possessive—that drove him to make love to his wife while he was also keeping a mistress?

Should she wait out his renewed interest in the behaviors of an unmarried man, or accept that their marriage had served its purpose and separate lives awaited them?

Percival set up a languorous rhythm, tucking himself close and running his nose around her ear. "Where are you, Wife? Do you grow bored with your husband's attentions?"

He punctuated the question with a kiss, a hot joining of mouths that tormented as it aroused: *Did he kiss his mistress this way?*

As Esther's body undulated in counterpoint to her husband's, her imagination flashed on Cecily O'Donnell's bright red hair and full mouth. Even through the pain of that recollection, Esther felt her husband's passion shift from teasing to focused arousal. She responded—some part of her hated that she did; another part of her wept from the relief of it.

Percival levered up on his arms, regarding her by firelight as their bodies strained together. "I love you, Esther Windham. Only you, always you."

She traced her fingers over his jaw. He meant those words. Here, now, their bodies joined, he meant those words with his whole heart.

"Percival, I love you too."

This was a truth as well, one that might yield to what lay before them. As Esther gave herself over to her husband's pleasuring and felt the first quickening flutters deep in her body, she said a prayer that their love would somehow endure the coming storm.

❧

Lovemaking was different when a man was trying to get his wife pregnant, though Esther might kick him to Cumbria if she suspected that was his aim. Instead, she sighed and trembled and ran her hands over his backside and over his shoulders, in the light, warm caresses he'd learned to crave.

"Percival, I love you too."

The words were wrenched from her, as if against her will. As he plunged into Esther's body, Percival had the sense that her capitulation was also wrenched from her, a surrender she regretted even as the pleasure grew most fierce.

When he was sure her passion had been sated, Percival let himself fly free too.

A child, please, one more child so I might have reason to call on my wife when all other excuses have been exhausted.

The release was exquisitely intense, in part a function of long denial, but also, Percival suspected, a function of desperation. When he'd regained the ability to move, he pitched off his wife and drew her against his side.

"Percival?" Esther's fingers winnowed through his hair. "Did you intend that?"

That. Did he intend to risk conception, when for the past months they'd been avoiding it? The question was free of judgment on her part and reasonable, so he told a reasonable lie in response.

"I did not. My self-restraint grows weak from overuse, perhaps, or the pleasures we share overwhelm it." He kissed her cheek, drawing in the scent of roses and despair—he had sunk to lying to his wife in their very bed.

Something in Esther's silence told him his prevarications lacked conviction, so he troweled a layer of truth onto his falsehood. "You've seemed less tired lately, Esther, or am I mistaken?"

A few beats of quiet went by while Percival traced the curve of her jaw. The depths to which he would miss this woman were unfathomable. How did a man march off to war, leaving his wife and family behind?

How did a man *not* march off to war, when his wife and family were threatened?

"You are not mistaken. I am feeling somewhat better."

She sounded surprised, as if she were just realizing it. Percival sent up a prayer of thanks and reminded himself to renew his orders to the kitchen. Not a cow would be left standing in the realm if feeding his wife beef was restoring her health.

Except soon he would not be in a position to

dictate her menus. Percival closed his eyes and gathered his wife closer.

"Are you up to a trip back to Morelands, Esther?"

Another silence. She rolled out of his embrace to lie on her back. When she didn't reach for his hand, Percival reached for hers.

"You just sent Tony and Gladys to Morelands, and the children have only in the past few days settled in here, Percival."

She did not want to go. He took solace from that. Better she not want to go than that she leave him all too willingly.

"I'll follow soon, my love. The holidays will be upon us, Parliament will recess, and His Majesty will understand that my place is with my family." God willing, Cecily O'Donnell would understand too.

He waited, listening to the soft roar of the fire while Esther's fingers went lax in his. "Esther?"

She had either fallen asleep or was feigning sleep. In either case, she hadn't refused his request for a swift departure to the country—nor had she given her consent.

~⁊~

"How much do you want?" When he longed to wring Cecily O'Donnell's neck, Percival instead affected bored tones.

Cecily rested her fingers on the décolletage of a gown that barely contained her breasts, a gesture intended to call attention to the pink flesh peeking through pale lace just above her nipples.

"This isn't entirely about money, Percy. This is

about what's due the daughter of a man well placed in Society. I've heard you might stand for a seat in the Commons, and with your ambition and social stature, there's no telling how high you might rise in the government."

She threatened and flattered with equal guile, though as far as Percival was concerned, her words meant nothing compared to the documents she'd produced. Irrefutable evidence that the girl, Magdalene, could indeed be his daughter.

"Magdalene is a by-blow at best, madam. One you chose to keep from my notice until the moment suited you. Society will remark that and draw conclusions that will not devolve to the girl's benefit."

Cecily's rouged lips compressed, suggesting this line of reasoning had escaped her consideration. "Society will keep its opinions to itself if we're seen in company often enough."

"No."

The word slipped out with too much conviction, such that even Cecily couldn't hide her reaction.

"You are not in a position to dictate terms to me, Percival Windham. I spread my legs at your request, and you will honor the resulting obligations."

"I will never rise in government, will never even take a seat in the Commons if you're seen hanging on my arm. His Majesty takes a dim view of licentiousness, as does his queen."

Cecily rose from her sofa on a rustle of skirts and marched up to Percival, her heeled slippers making her almost of a height with him. "Then you won't take that seat. I've provided for this child every day of her life, seen her clothed, fed, educated, and disciplined. You will not turn you back on her without losing what reputation you have. I'll bruit about details of our liaison your own brother will blush to hear."

The scent of rice powder and bitterness wafted from her person. This close, Percival could see the fine lines radiating from her eyes, the grooves starting around her smile. He turned away and fixed his gaze on the clock that graced her mantel.

Esther was tired, her stamina and energy stolen by successive births. Cecily O'Donnell had given up her youth and her coin to nights at the theater, high fashion, and a succession of lucrative liaisons. Percival watched the hand of the clock move forward by a single minute and realized he could not leave the child in Cecily O'Donnell's keeping. If a woman was to end up exhausted, worn-out, and much in need of cosseting, then it should be because she'd sacrificed much to her children, and not to her own vanity.

And as for a seat in the Commons? Esther had not been enthusiastic about such a prospect. Percival tossed that ambition aside between one tick of the clock and the next.

He shifted his gaze to Cecily's face. "I shall visit with my daughter now."

Triumph flared in Cecily's calculating eyes. He'd admitted paternity, though it meant nothing without witnesses. On instinct, Percival whipped open the parlor door to find a footman crouched by the keyhole.

Bloody damn, he'd been stupid. "You, sir, will take me to the nursery, *now*."

Cecily sputtered several dire curses then fell into silence, though Percival knew she was merely planning her next series of broadsides.

Leaving the woman to sip her tea and plot his downfall, Percival went on reconnaissance through the upper reaches of the house. What he found disappointed more than it surprised. At the head of the stairs, Cecily's bedroom was still a temple to elegant indulgence. The bed hangings, curtains, and pillows were all done in matching shades of soft green brocade, and a single white rose graced the night table. Beyond the bedroom, the house grew increasingly chilly, and on the third floor, there was not a carpet to be found.

The footman knocked on the nursery door, which was opened by the child herself.

"Hullo."

Percival glowered at the footman. "Leave us."

The man withdrew, looking unabashedly relieved.

"May I come in?"

The child drew the door back, revealing a room made sunny—also downright cold—by the lack of curtains across the windows. In the middle of the bare floor sat a worn mess of fabric, yarn, and stuffing that might once have been a doll, along with five wooden soldiers, one of whom was missing part of a leg.

The grate held no fire.

"I was taking tea with the regimental officers. Would you like to join us?"

He'd freeze if he spent much time in this room. Maggie did not seem aware of the cold. Her braids were ratty, her short dress stained at the hem, and her pinafore fastened with a knot rather than a bow at the back.

"Tea would be lovely." He loathed the stuff.

Maggie took him by the hand—her little fingers were like ice—and drew him into the room. "I will make the introductions. You may sit there." She settled onto the floor with a fluffing of her pinafore and dress that bore a disquieting resemblance to her mother's pretentious manners. Percival lowered himself across from her, haunted by the memory of visits with his boys in their cozy, carpeted nursery—a room full of books, toys, and comforts.

While Percival felt despair clutching ever more tightly at his heart, little Maggie spun a fantasy of a polite tea with elegant service, crumpets, servants, and a cozy fire in the grate, which the imaginary footman tended about every two minutes.

When he could tolerate her play no more, Percival interrupted his daughter's diatribe on whose wig was the most ridiculous at last night's soiree.

"Maggie, where is your nurse?"

Her gaze narrowed on him, showing displeasure at having to give up her fictional tea party. "I haven't a nurse. Mrs. Anglethorpe is the housekeeper. Burton is our maid of all work, and if Mama wants me, Burton fetches me."

"Then who dresses you, child?"

Downy little brows twitched down. "I dress myself. I'm not a baby."

She was not. He knew exactly how old she was, and she was not an infant. She was a handful of months older than Bartholomew.

"Who cares for you, Maggie?"

She studied him with an expression of consternation. "Burton says Mama loves me, but I can take care of myself."

The despair weighting Percival's heart threatened to choke him. He could not abandon this child to the care of her mother. He simply could not—his honor would not allow it, and in some way, even his standing as Esther's husband would not allow it. For a moment, he considered confiding in his wife, but even if Esther were inclined to be understanding, there was nothing she could do to still Cecily O'Donnell's vile tongue.

Percival rose and shed his jacket. "I want you to have my coat." He draped it around Maggie's shoulders. It fell nearly to the floor on her, which was good.

She drew it closed at the lapels and gave it a sniff. "It smells like you, and it's warm."

"Exactly the point. When was the last time you ate?"

She glanced at the battered doll and the worn soldiers.

"I mean real food, for God's sake." At the exasperation in his tone, her expression shuttered, and that…went beyond causing him despair. No child of her years should have instincts like this, should have circumstances like this while her mother sat two floors below, swathed in lace and warmed by a blazing fire.

"Come with me, Miss Maggie. We're off to the kitchen."

When he'd seen the child seated before bread, butter, jam, and hot tea, Percival forced himself to rejoin Cecily in her lair. Her eyes went wide at the sight of him without his coat, but she said nothing until the door was firmly closed behind him.

"You've assured yourself the girl is well and hale, and you know she's yours. If I say you'll accompany me to the theater tomorrow night, Percival, then accompany me, you shall."

He hated this woman. Hated her with an intimate, burning passion that was not for himself but for the small child left shivering and alone hour after hour.

He was going to rescue this child, though he must wait until Esther had removed to Morelands to implement that plan. Hatred fueled the most ironically pleasant smile he'd ever manufactured. "I'll pick you up at eight. Try not to dress like the trollop you are."

Five

"SHE DIDN'T ASK HOW MUCH I WANTED, SHE ASKED how much I needed." Kathleen St. Just fell silent rather than try to explain to her son why desperate schemes were rioting through her brain.

Devlin glanced up from where he was laying out playing cards on his mother's bedspread, this room being the only one with even a meager fire. "The lady who gave me chocolate was nice. The horses were wonderful."

The deck he was playing with lacked several cards, and try as he might to pair each one with a match, his game was doomed. Being a child, he hadn't figured this out, and Kathleen wasn't about to tell him.

"That lady is your papa's wife. She's kind." And for that kindness, Kathleen wanted to hate her, which was of no moment whatsoever. "Also very rich."

They spoke Gaelic, which was a sign of how tired Kathleen was. Bad enough Devlin was illegitimate, worse yet if he sported a brogue as he got older. "I received another letter from Mr. O'Dea."

Devlin glanced at her when she switched to English. "Mr. O'Dea lives back home."

Back home was a place the boy would have little memory of, or so Kathleen hoped. She'd visited only once during Devlin's short lifetime. "He does. He asked after you."

Devlin made no reply, remaining focused on his cards. Billy O'Dea always asked after "the boy," but his sentiments regarding Devlin were one reason why Kathleen hadn't made any more trips back to Ireland. With the tolerant pragmatism of a man who knew exactly how Kathleen earned her livelihood, Billy— like Kathleen's own family—believed Devlin's best chance for a good start in life lay in throwing the boy on his father's charity, and Billy was not wrong.

He was also not going to offer marriage unless or until Kathleen heeded his advice. On that tired thought, wind rattled the glass and fluttered the curtains, bringing an icy draft into the room.

And winter was only getting started. Kathleen thought of the vile things Gregory Pelham had whispered in her ear as she earned her coin with him like a doxy in his mews, and wanted to retch.

"One day soon, we're going back to visit your papa's wife again."

Devlin turned up a pair of queens and smiled. "Will she give me more chocolate?"

"Yes. She'll give you more chocolate. As much chocolate as you can drink."

Without making a sound, Kathleen started to cry.

‿⟡

"Your papa has asked us to return to Morelands. You'll like that, won't you?" Esther adopted the cheery tones of a parent bent on deceiving small children, though from the look Bart and Gayle exchanged, she'd failed miserably.

Gayle kicked at the dead leaves on the frozen ground. Bart dropped Esther's hand and skipped ahead a few steps. "I like the park. If we go home, we can't play in the park. Papa visits with us more here too. I like when Papa visits."

Gayle echoed the complaint as they wandered along the Serpentine, cold winter sunlight bouncing off the water in the middle of the lake. Near the shore, ice had once again formed. Esther resisted the urge to find a rock and pitch it hard at the ice, lest the boys complain about missing the Serpentine too.

"Papa will be home at Christmas," Esther said, "and that's just a few weeks away." Though Percival hadn't *promised* to return to Morelands at Christmas.

Bart's face lit up with glee as he pointed at a rider coming down the path on a chestnut stallion. "There's Papa! Maybe he'll let me ride home with him!"

Predictably, Gayle planted his mittened fists on his little hips. "That's not fair! You got to ride with Papa last time, and it's my turn."

Percival Windham was so handsome, he nearly took Esther's breath away. Mounted, he had a sort of rugged elegance that the painted town dandies in their clocked stockings and high heels would never achieve. And yet that wasn't why she loved him. She loved him because when he spotted them, he swung off his horse and held out his hands to the boys.

"My first and second lieutenants, scouting the wilds of Hyde Park in search of the general's beautiful, lost daughter. I see you've found the poor, wandering damsel."

"That's not a damsel," Gayle said, grabbing his father's hand. "That's Mama."

"Why, so it is." Percival made her an elaborate bow, likely for the sake of his sons. Esther bobbed a curtsy for the same reason, when she wanted to tear a strip off her handsome, charming, randy husband for no reason in particular.

"Take me up, Papa!" Bart started. "I want to ride on Comet."

"It's my turn," Gayle bellowed over his brother's pleading.

Percival picked Gayle up and sat him on Comet's empty saddle, then swung Bart up behind his brother. "Hush, the both of you. If you spook my horse, you're likely to land in something objectionable, and your mama will not be pleased. Madam?" He winged his arm at her, and Esther felt a lump lodge in her throat.

"My thanks." She tucked her hand over his arm, while with his free hand, Percival led the horse—now sporting a pair of pirate princes intent on plundering London from the back of their equine ship.

"Are you prepared to leave for Morelands in the morning, Wife?"

No. "Almost. There are a few things that can't be packed up until shortly before we leave, and things the children will want in the coach."

"A storybook or two?"

"Several storybooks, their favorite blankets, their soldiers."

They strolled along, a young family to all appearances indulging the children's high spirits on a chipper day.

Esther spoke at the same time as her husband, their unison perfect.

"I'll miss you."

From Esther's perspective, they were both speaking the truth, but the missing would be very different for each of them. She would miss her husband with a bodily ache and a heavy heart, and more than a dollop of resentfulness. He would miss her with a passing wistfulness, particularly on the nights when his mistress could not accommodate him.

The thought sent a spike of nausea through Esther's belly.

"Madam, are you well?"

She'd put her hand over her middle. Behind them, Comet clip-clopped along, and the boys plotted terror on the high seas of Mayfair.

"I do not want to return to Morelands, Percival. There is no reason for it."

He remained silent until they approached the gate that would see them onto Park Lane. Percival paused, the horse coming to a halt behind them.

"Will you go because I ask it of you, Esther? I will join you at Christmas if I have to walk every step of the journey back to you in my bare feet."

Now was the time to tell him no, she would not go. She would not so easily let him drift into the liaisons and affairs that eventually attended every titled marriage, save the eccentric few. Now was when she should join battle, except Percival's eyes held such a grave request, she could not form the words.

She nodded, and they turned out of the park and onto the busy streets of Mayfair.

❧

"You're not off to the levee this morning, Husband?"

Esther looked tired to Percival, making him wonder if she'd waited up for him. When he'd dragged himself home after an execrable evening at the theater, Esther had been abed, and he hadn't been able to bring himself to wake her. His hesitance hadn't stemmed from consideration for a woman who'd be trapped in a freezing coach with her children all day but rather from guilt.

All evening long he'd fielded curious glances and raised eyebrows from men who would no doubt tell their wives that Lord Percy Windham had been in the company of a former mistress, and those wives would talk to each other, and eventually...

"I'm off to a meeting," Percival said. "His Majesty has some notion Wales ought to be kept informed of the committee's doings, though Wales is far more interested in chasing skirts than requisitioning uniforms."

"Then I'll bid you farewell. I've final packing to see to."

She did not. Percival knew his wife well enough to know that her own effects had likely been packed before she'd found her bed the previous night. Esther pushed her chair back, and Percival covered her hand with his own. "I've said my good-byes to the boys, but..."

She gazed at him, her expression so solemn

that guilt and frustration coalesced into shame. The damned beefsteak he'd been choking down threatened to rebel, and a life of such moments—ashamed, awkward, silent—rolled past in Percival's mind.

"Esther, I love you. I wouldn't be asking you to leave if I did not love you."

If she asked him why her departure was necessary, he would have no answer for her: Because a vicious woman was going to use a small child to wreak vengeance on an entire family; because a randy young officer had made foolish choices.

Because he could not bear to see Esther hurt.

He kissed her cheek. "Will you finish my steak for me? One doesn't want to be late, even if Wales will be more drunk than sober at such an early hour."

Something shifted in Esther's green-eyed gaze, something cooled and reassessed. "I don't care for beef at breakfast, Percival. Perhaps you'll serve yourself smaller portions in future rather than expect me to finish your meal."

Her tone was so perfectly bland, Percival had to wonder if she hadn't already heard with whom he'd been seen the previous evening. "I will try to recall your preferences when next we're dining at the same table."

He rose, held her chair for her, and hated what his life was about to become. Hated it so much, in fact, that when he'd managed to take his leave of his lady wife without shouting, breaking things, and rampaging through the house, he did not go to his meeting. Percival instead took himself to that address he most loathed in all of London.

"Good morning, your lordship." The same footman

who'd listened at Cecily's keyhole was now minding her front door. "Madam has not yet come down, though if you'll follow me to the parlor, the kitchen will send up a tray."

The words were right and the tone was deferential and brisk, but the fellow's gaze was nervous, more nervous than it had been even when he'd been eaves-dropping. Percival handed him his cloak, and noticed another gentleman's coat hanging from a hook in the foyer. The garment was well made, a soft, dark wool with crested buttons that suggested both wealth and good taste.

Also a complete lack of common sense on some poor fellow's part. Percival did not stare at the coat, lest the footman catch him at it, but the presence of that coat spoke volumes.

Percival took himself down the hallway toward the foyer, addressing the footman over his shoulder. "A tray would be appreciated, with chocolate and none of that damned tea."

Chocolate would take longer to prepare, and for what Percival intended, every moment counted.

"Very good, my lord."

The footman scampered toward the back stairs, while Percival kept right on going past the parlor. The plan he'd formed was daring and precipitous, but an eternity of nights toadying to Cecily O'Donnell was unthinkable. And as for Esther...

He pushed thoughts of his wife aside, knowing that dear lady was already on her way to the countryside. If the gods smiled upon a well-intended husband, then Esther need never know of what was about to transpire.

Cecily's bedroom door was closed, thank God, probably the better to hoard the heat from the only fire outside the kitchen. When he gained the nursery, Percival paused.

What he was about to do was in some way selfish, and in some way proper—it was also right.

"Maggie."

His daughter glanced up from the same pile of damaged toys he'd found her with previously.

"Papa." She scrambled to her feet but then checked herself, making a painful contrast to the way Percival's sons had greeted him in the park—to the way they always greeted him.

"Collect up your things, my dear. I'm taking you away from this house."

"We're going on an outing?"

"Something like that. Bring your doll and your soldiers and anything else that matters to you."

She disappeared into a cupboard and emerged with Percival's coat. "Burton said we could sell it for coal, but I didn't want to. I like how it smells, and the buttons have a unicorn on them."

Maggie held still while Percival fastened the frogs of a wool cloak under her chin, and she said nothing when he stuffed her doll and soldiers into his pockets. As they stole back down through the house—making only one brief stop in the parlor—Percival wondered if there was a greater comment on Maggie's situation than that all she really knew of her father was the scent of his cologne.

Six

ESTHER HAD WANTED TO LEAVE FOR MORELANDS AN hour ago, but the children were being recalcitrant, and the nursery maids—one of whom was enamored of the porter—were abetting them.

And while Esther waited for this favorite pair of boots to be found and an indispensable storybook to be tucked into the coach, she thought of her husband and of the solemn, dark-haired boy who bore her husband's eyebrows.

A man who was going to keep a mistress for all of London to see could afford to quietly support his son at some decent school in the Midlands. Winter was barely under way, and the boy's mother had already been reduced to begging. This was perhaps the inevitable fate of a woman plying the harlot's trade, except...

Except if Esther had been that boy's mother, she'd do much worse than beg if it would see him fed. Thinking not as a wife, but as a mother, Esther could not leave Town without making at least a short call on Kathleen St. Just, whose direction she'd obtained at their last encounter. Knowing that the traveling coach would still take at least an hour to pack, Esther called for the town coach and dressed in her plainest cloak and boots.

Kathleen St. Just opened the door to a perfectly nondescript little house on a perfectly nondescript street. "My lady, I am surprised to see you."

Surprised was a euphemism, likely covering shock and humiliation, as well as a quantity of resentment, though Esther did not quibble over it. The freezing house, the stink of tallow rather than beeswax in the foyer, and the fact that Mrs. St. Just had opened her own door announced the situation plainly enough.

Esther swept past her hostess rather than linger on the stoop. "I will not take up much of your time, Mrs. St. Just. Is your son on the premises?"

Fear, or something close to it, flitted through Mrs. St. Just's eyes. "He is."

"Shall we repair to a parlor, then? What I have to say affects the boy."

It would affect Esther's marriage too, though she brushed that thought aside and followed Mrs. St. Just to a parlor that surely had never been used for company. Had it been warmer, the room would have been cozy. An entire flower garden was embroidered and framed on one wall, species by species, in exquisite needle-work. A teacup and saucer sat on a low table near a workbasket, the saucer chipped but still serviceable.

"My lady, you will forgive the clutter, but this is the smallest parlor and the easiest to heat."

"You need not build up the fire for me," Esther said, and that was true, because she hadn't surrendered her cloak at the door, and Mrs. St. Just—who was wearing two shawls herself—hadn't offered to take it. "I will be blunt, Mrs. St. Just. My husband has banished me back to the countryside, the better to disport as a young man is wont to when in the capital. I have not informed him that you're raising his son, but I think some provision should be made for the boy sooner rather than later."

"You're leaving London?"

This did seem to occasion surprise. "My husband has asked it of me, so yes."

A shaft of anger accompanied those words, and yet Percival had *asked* it of her, he hadn't ordered her to go.

Mrs. St. Just squared her shoulders, which let Esther realize she and this woman were the same height—and what metaphor did that speak to? "Then you can take Devlin with you."

And this was cause for surprise all around, because Mrs. St. Just seemed as startled by her own pronouncement as Esther was.

"I beg your pardon?"

"You either take him with you, or I'll approach his lordship in public and make the same request. I'll demand money. I'll let all and sundry know Moreland's spare has a son on the wrong side of the blanket."

The woman was daring herself to do these things. Esther heard that in her tone and saw it in the wild uncertainty in her eyes.

"Sit down, Mrs. St. Just." Esther managed to settle onto a sofa with no little dignity, which was at complete variance with the wobbling of her knees. "What are you saying? That you'd expose your son to avoidable scandal? That you'd disgrace yourself and embarrass my husband over a bit of coin?"

The woman got herself to a chair, but half fell onto it, as if blind with drink or great emotion. "I'm saying that, yes. Devlin's father has obligations to him. Nobody would argue that."

No, they would not, though despite those obligations, despite the cold hearth and her obvious need, Mrs. St. Just had yet to inform Devlin's father he even had a son.

"When was the last time you ate, Mrs. St. Just?"

She shook her head.

"I gave you a bracelet, and that bracelet should have bought a load of coal and put food in your pantry." Esther let a bit of ire—ire for the boy—infuse her tone.

"That money is for Devlin. Where he sleeps, we keep a fire, and there's food enough for him. I bought him a coat too, because he's growing so quickly…"

She closed her eyes and stopped speaking. Esther watched in horror as a tear trickled down the woman's cheek.

"Here." Esther reached into her reticule and withdrew a shiny red apple, one of the many weapons a mother would arm herself with prior to a coach journey with children. "Eat this. Eat it right now, and we will talk about your son…about Devlin."

And they talked, mostly about the boy. Esther let Kathleen be the one to fetch him, the one to explain that he'd be staying "for a time" with the chocolate lady and that he was to be a good boy when he met his papa.

"Papa has the horses." To the little fellow, this was a point in Papa's favor.

"He does," Esther said, "and we've a cat too,

though I'm not supposed to know she sleeps in the nursery when she's done hunting in the mews."

From his perch on his mother's lap, young Devlin assayed a charming and all-too-familiar smile. "I like cats. Cats like to play."

"They do. Tomcats in particular are fond of their diversions." Esther rose, wanting abruptly to get on with her day and all the drama it was likely to hold. She did not doubt that she had made the right decision, though it would by no means be an easy decision to live with—for any of them. "Shall we be on our way?"

She did not reach for the child. Mrs. St. Just hugged him, whispered something in his ear, and let him scramble to his feet. He parted from his mother easily, secure the way every child should be secure in the idea that his mama would always be a part of his life.

Mrs. St. Just rose slowly. "Fetch your new coat, Devlin, and then come right back here."

He pelted off, his footsteps sounding to Esther exactly like Bart's and Gayle's... Like his brothers'.

"Your ladyship is wrong about something."

Esther regarded the other woman, seeing weariness and sadness but also peace in her gaze. "I think you are making the best decision for your son," Esther began. "And I will of course write to you, as promised, though I wish you'd agree to write back to him."

"A clean break is better. I don't want him to miss me. That's not what you're wrong about."

"You will enlighten me?" The defensive note was unbecoming, if understandable.

"Your husband, his lordship... He loves you. He is

not disporting with anybody, though I'll grant you the man is an accomplished flirt."

This, from Percival's former mistress?

Esther jerked her mittens out of her pockets. "Mrs. St. Just, a certain sympathy of feeling between us as mothers of small boys is not an invitation for you to presume in any manner—"

A thin, cold hand touched Esther's knuckles. "He loves you. He told me so in the King's English when he came here to ask me about your ailments. He was beside himself with worry, risking all manner of talk just to be seen stabling his horse in the mews. He said you were stubborn, but he said it like he admired you for it, and he did not want to be asking the physicians, because they spread gossip."

Esther abruptly sat back down. "Percival was *here*?"

"Just the once, and he went no farther than the parlor. He offered help before he left, and I did not… I did not want to take it, but then I realized my pride would not keep Devlin in boots, which was why you found me in your mews."

The child came banging back into the parlor. "I'm ready. We can pet the horses, right?"

"We can pet every one," Esther said, wondering where the ability to speak had come from. "Your papa can tell you their names."

A few beats of silence went by, while Mrs. St. Just hugged her son again. He wiggled free, clearly anxious to make the acquaintance of his papa's horses.

As they walked with him to the front hallway, Esther had to ask one more question. "What did you tell him—tell his lordship, I mean?"

The question apparently required no explanation. "I told him you were worn-out from childbed and pregnancy. You needed red meat and rest, also light activity and a time to repair your health before you carried again. I trust you're feeling somewhat better?"

"I am." All the breakfast steaks and misplaced menus made sense, though little else did. "I truly am."

She felt better still when she realized that presenting Percival with his son would likely generate a minor scandal. People would think they'd quarreled over the boy—which they well might—and pay less attention to the women Percival trifled with in Esther's absence.

❦

"You won't be staying at this house," Percival assured his daughter. "We will find you a nice accommodation and somebody to look after you who takes the job to heart. You'll like that."

Though Percival would not like it one bit.

"Why can't I stay with you?" Little Maggie rode before him through the park like she'd been around horses since birth, which had to be blood telling, because her mother would not have allowed it.

"I wish you could." He wished it with his whole heart, else how would he know she was safe from her infernal mother? And yet, if she dwelled under his roof, her mother—her legal custodian—would always know where to find her and be able to snatch her back. "This is a small house, and you would not have your own bedroom."

"I don't need my own bedroom. Burton used to sleep in my room, when I had a fire."

"Maggie, you will never want for a fire again, and your soldiers will all have two legs."

"I like Colonel George. He was very brave about losing his leg."

She chattered on about the colonel perhaps being considered for a knighthood, though he'd rather be a general. Percival turned Comet into the alley that led to the mews, glad in his bones that Esther had already departed for Morelands. With luck, he could have Maggie situated somewhere not too far away by sundown, and then he and Cecily O'Donnell would come to whatever understandings were necessary to keep the girl safe.

❧

"These are very big horses," Devlin remarked. His tone was casual, but Esther well understood the grip the child kept on her hand as they walked past the team hitched to the traveling coach.

"They are very *nice* horses," she said. "They particularly like little boys, because your brothers come visit them frequently."

Small fingers seized around Esther's hand painfully tight. "My brothers?"

"You have four, and they are capital fellows, just like you." Except those four had never known want, never known cold, never been expected to part with their mother's love with no possible explanation.

"That's a pretty horse." Devlin did not point—the boy had wonderful manners—but his gaze fixed on a chestnut stallion walking up the alley.

As the clip-clop of shod hooves grew closer, for an

instant, the picture before Esther's eyes did not make sense. She recognized Comet, she recognized Comet's handsome rider, but she did not... A small child, a red-haired girl, sat before Percival in the saddle. The child was vaguely familiar, and Esther had seen Percival wrap his forearm around his own sons with the very same vigilant protectiveness.

The horse shuffled to a halt. "Esther. You have not yet departed for Morelands."

His tone was so grave.

The hair on Esther's nape and arms prickled, and beside her, the boy was unmoving. "And you, my lord, have not been to any committee meetings."

A groom came out to take Comet, sparing them conversation while Percival swung down, handed off the reins, and hefted the child out of the saddle. She stood beside Percival, her hand in his, her gaze watchful in the way of children who grew up early.

"You're the Viking lady," she said to Esther.

"She's the chocolate lady," Devlin replied. "She's my papa's wife."

A thousand questions rose in Esther's mind while the chill breeze pushed dead leaves across the cobbles. One of the coach horses stomped its great hoof and tossed its head as if impatient with the two adults staring at each other in silence.

"Percival, who in the world...?"

"Madam, we will speak privately."

Of course they would, because if Percival thought to move his mistress and her offspring into Esther's house, Esther would need a great deal of privacy to disabuse her husband of such a notion.

"Devlin, ask the grooms to show you and this girl the stable cat. There's a kitty with only one eye, and she doesn't yet have a name."

A commotion by the back gate had all adult eyes slewing around as Bart and Gayle came barreling into the alley. "We're ready to board the ship!" Bart bellowed.

Gayle came to a halt beside his older brother. "Who are they?" His green eyes narrowed on the girl. "Who's *she*?"

Bart smacked his mittened hands together. "They can be the colonials! We can play Damned Upstart Colonials, and we'll have French and colonials both. We can slaughter them and take scalps and everything while Mama and Papa kiss each other good-bye!"

Gayle glanced at his parents as if he knew exactly how long two parents could kiss each other, and grinned. "Come on." He took Devlin by the hand. "There's a tiger in the stables, and we can hunt her down for our supper."

The red-haired girl fell in with the boys. "I want to be a lion who hunts down the hunters."

"You have to be the damned upstart colonial," Bart said. "I'm General Bart, and that's Colonel Gayle."

"Then I shall be a fierce, damned upstart colonial wolf named Maggie."

❧

What did a man say to the wife who'd come upon him riding along the alley with an unexplained by-blow up before him?

While Percival pondered that mystery, one of the children gave a shriek as a cat skittered around a corner of the stables, and small feet pelted off in a herd.

Percival stared at his wife, who stared back at him in visible consternation. He did not know what to say to her, did not know why she'd been in the company of that small dark-haired...

Images of the same child, warily clutching another woman's skirts, barreled into Percival's mind. He felt the impact physically, a spinning sensation that whirled through his body and changed everything in the blink of an eye.

Changed everything *again*.

There were two of them. Two small children who'd not known their father's love or protection. His knees threatened to buckle, and still he did not know what to say.

"Percival?"

Esther spoke his name in dread, which he could not abide. He held out a hand to her. "Esther, please listen. Please, please listen."

She aimed a puzzled frown at his outstretched hand, as if she did not comprehend what she beheld.

"Esther, you must listen to me." Or he'd shoot Cecily O'Donnell before witnesses, then shoot himself. "I did not want for you to be hurt. You must believe that."

Bart's voice pierced the cold around them. "We've got her! Blast, you let her go!" The coach horses shifted in their harnesses and still Esther merely regarded him.

"I think it possible I am not hurt after all. Who is the little red-haired girl, Percival?"

"My daughter and Cecily O'Donnell's—may God have mercy upon me. I became aware of the child—I met her—only a few days past. Her name is Maggie, and she's very bright."

Perhaps he shouldn't have added that last. Percival let his hand fall to his side, and yet still he held out hope that Esther might eventually forgive him. He knew from her expression that she was *thinking*, and that had to be encouraging.

She worried her lower lip while Percival uttered prayers more fervent than any he'd offered up in the Canadian wilderness.

"You know Devlin is your son?"

"I do now. His mother said nothing to me."

"She said a great deal to me, most of which I had to agree with."

From the barn, a girl's voice called out, "She's coming around the saddle room! Run, you lot!"

"Esther, may we continue this discussion where we have a measure of privacy?"

"Yes." She strode across the alley and took his arm. "We had best. Come sit with me in the garden."

His first thought was that a garden in winter was a depressing place, all dead flowers and bare trees. When Esther had him situated on a cold, hard bench, it occurred to Percival that here, while his marriage died a painful, civilized death, helpful servants would not intrude to ask if he wanted a bloody tray of perishing tea.

Esther took his hand. "Tell me about Mrs. O'Donnell, Percival, but be warned, I am not prepared to be reasonable where she is concerned."

Where to start? "First, you must know I loathe the woman. Second, you should also know I went to the theater with her last night."

Esther slipped her fingers free of his. Percival grabbed her hand right back and held it shamelessly tight.

"Husband, I do not understand you. You sport about before all of Polite Society with a woman you loathe, while the wife you profess to love is sent out into the countryside. You are generally very direct, Percival. You will have to explain this apparent contradiction to me."

In her exaggerated civility, Percival realized that Esther was nowhere near as composed as she wanted him to think—a fortifying thought.

"Mrs. O'Donnell threatened the girl," Percival began, "threatened to make a bad situation worse. If I lent the woman my escort, she would spare the child and allow matters to go forth as if we maintained a cordial liaison. If I refused her my attentions, she'd stir the scandal broth at every turn and ensure the child—my own daughter—had no chance at a decent life. I needed time to make provisions for Maggie and placated that woman accordingly."

Esther was silent for long moments, but she at least let Percival keep possession of her hand. "Vile woman. You must teach me some curses so I might better express my sentiments toward her when I am private with you."

His wife contemplated being private with him. The reprieve of that revelation was vast. Even so, Percival did not relax his grip on her hand. "I'll teach you every curse I know. Tell me about the boy."

This question seemed to relieve Percival's wife. She smoothed her skirts with her free hand, relaxing in a way that communicated itself mostly where they held hands. "He has your love of horses, very pretty manners, and he does not know he won't see his mother for some time. I thought you would be wroth with me for not consulting you, but I can see you had your hands full with other matters."

Percival brought her knuckles to his lips, and again did not know what to say. When he'd been busy skirmishing with the enemy and rescuing a princess, his staunchest guard had been protecting his flank.

Never had a man been so grateful to misperceive a situation.

The gate scraped open behind them, and the senior groom shuffled a few steps into the garden, hat in hand.

"Beggin' milord's pardon, but is we to unhitch the traveling coach?"

❧

Esther regarded her husband, waiting on his reply. Percival might well send her packing, might well sweep the children away from Society's notice until the gossip died down—which would happen only after several eternities.

"Unhitch the team," Percival said. "We won't be needing the traveling coach for some time. Is the cat still in one piece?"

The groom's lips twitched. "Grimalkin be in the straw mow, that racket be the children all burrowing after. The mice is laughing fit to kill." He left them alone, closing the gate behind him.

There were four children in that straw mow, and two more in the nursery, and they were *all* her husband's progeny. The notion was dizzying, so dizzying, Esther was grateful to hold her husband's hand.

"Esther, there is more we should discuss."

She peered over at him, because he'd spoken carefully, with a studied calm that presaged bad news. "Six children is rather a lot, Percival. Are there more?"

She hadn't been joking, but he smiled at her, a smile of such tenderness that Esther's insides stopped hopping about like a collection of March hares, for no man smiling like that could be hiding any further secrets.

"I have only six children that I know of, unless you're carrying. I was hoping to find decent quarters for Maggie before her mother comes, making a great drama on our doorstep, for I seized Maggie from her mother's house and didn't exactly ask permission first."

He sounded hesitant, not quite sure of his strategy, when it had been the only reasonable course. "You kidnapped her." Esther patted his knuckles with her free hand. "Of course you did, because the child was her mother's greatest source of leverage. I do not see that you had a prudent alternative, it being beyond bad form for a mother to use a child like that."

He studied their joined hands, his expression so serious as to emphasize a resemblance to his father. "I don't see what prudence has to do with our situation, my lady. Had I been prudent, none of this would have occurred."

He leaned back against the garden wall and stretched out his long legs before him. Though Percival didn't turn loose of her hand, in some way his posture suggested he was abandoning his wife so he could wallow in his guilt and misgivings.

They had no time for male histrionics if Mrs.

O'Donnell was maneuvering her cannon into place, and there was no point to Percival's dramatics, either. "Listen, Percival Windham, and tell me what you hear."

He closed his eyes. "I hear altogether too many small children making a lot of rumpus over one sorry feline."

"Those children are laughing. They are playing together without a single toy between them, and they are having great good fun. They met each other a few minutes ago, and already they know how to go on as a family. We must take our example from them and make a certain cat sorry she ever thought to go hunting on our turf."

❧

"Nobody prosecutes warrants for prostitution."

Cecily's attempt at disdain was undermined by the quaver in her voice as she stared at the document Percival had tossed onto the table before her. If the woman had any sense, she'd be more terrified than angry, but then, she'd *never* demonstrated appreciable common sense.

"Madam, I vow to you that I will see this warrant prosecuted, and have affidavits from a dozen witnesses of good birth to ensure the charges result in a conviction. I will also bring suit for slander if you suggest to a soul that a single, casual evening in a public theater box was indicative of any renewed association between us."

Cecily flicked the document aside. "You kidnapped my daughter. I am the child's legal custodian, and you've taken her unlawfully from my loving care. Perhaps you aren't even her father."

"In your loving care, she hasn't a single proper toy. She hasn't been inoculated for smallpox, her feet are covered with blisters because she outgrew her only boots ages ago. And I am very certain she is my daughter, thanks to the documents you so kindly provided me."

Something smug in his tone must have given him away, because Cecily rose from her artful pose on the green sofa and stalked over to her escritoire. She rifled the drawers and came up glowering.

Which purely delighted Percival. On his last raid into enemy territory, he'd made one stop before he and Maggie had left the premises, and that detail, that one small detail, justified years spent shivering on reconnaissance in the Canadian wilderness.

"You've stolen the documents, my lord. Shall I have you arrested for that?"

Percival settled his elbow a little more comfortably on her mantel and noted one of the green bows on Cecily's towering wig was coming undone. "By all means. You'll want your witnesses to lay information, provided you can find any who will malign a duke's son with their perjury. You procured the documents for me at my specific request, as the signatories on the documents would attest."

As they would attest *now*, now that Percival had met with each one and held pointed discussions with them.

Cecily slammed the last drawer closed hard enough to make the inkwell on the blotter jump. "You lying, conniving, sly—"

"Such flattery will surely turn my head, Mrs.

O'Donnell." He pushed away from the mantel, because if she came flying at him, he'd want to be able to step aside without letting her touch him. "You have an alternative, you know. My wife was insistent that you'd see reason eventually."

"Your *wife* isn't fit to—"

Before she could complete her insult, Percival harpooned her with a look that let her see every particle of savagery in him. To protect his wife and children, to protect even his lady's good name, he would cheerfully murder this woman on the spot. Esther had been very clear he was not to indulge in such an impulse, though Esther was also demonstrating a marvelous ability to deal with the occasional marital disappointment.

Cecily took a seat at her escritoire. "What is this alternative?"

Percival tossed documents before her, like he'd throw slops before a hog. "Sign those papers giving me authority over the child, and that bank draft is yours to do with whatever you please."

No sow had ever regarded her dinner with such a gleam of avarice in her eye. Cecily traced her fingers over the figures on the draft. "All I have to do is sign the papers?"

"Immediately."

She didn't like that. From the scowl on her face, Percival surmised she'd planned on absconding with the money, and at some future date, perhaps absconding with the child.

"Fine, then. Take the brat, and I wish you the joy of her." She reached for the inkwell, and Percival went to the door. "What are you—?"

"Witnesses, Mrs. O'Donnell. A proper legal document, to be binding, requires proper witnesses, doesn't it?"

She made no effort to hide her rage as John, Duke of Quimbey, strode into the room, very much on his dignity. Anthony came after that, followed by a marquess and an earl whom Percival had known since his years at Eton.

Quimbey took the time to make sure Cecily was signing freely and voluntarily and that she understood what she was signing—a nice touch, that, but then Quimbey had acquired his title before he'd gone to university, and was a genuinely good friend.

The deed was quickly a fait accompli, and with thanks all around in the mews, Percival mounted his charger and prepared to report to his commanding officer that the enemy had been thoroughly, absolutely, and permanently routed.

❧

"Maggie will help me civilize them," Esther said as they closed the nursery door. "She's had to think for herself from a young age, and a lot of cosseted boys will not slow her down one bit."

Beside her, Percival studied the closed door. "You consider Devlin to have been cosseted?" He hoped it was so. Distracted by his siblings, Devlin seemed to be fitting in easily, but Percival saw worry in the boy's eyes.

Time to go shopping for some ponies.

Esther slipped her arm through his and walked with

him toward the stairs, probably to prevent him from suggesting they read the children just one more story.

"You must not fret, Husband. In some ways, Devlin has been cosseted the most. His mother could not provide lavishly for him, but he had her love all to himself, no siblings to compete with, no father to distract Mama from her darling son. He'll be fine, Percival. We'll all be fine."

Because Esther believed that, Percival could believe it too. Kathleen St. Just had taken ship for Ireland, where a second cousin was willing to marry her. Cecily O'Donnell was reported to be taking a repairing lease at Bath. In some ways, the Yule season that approached would be the happiest of their marriage so far.

Esther leaned a little closer. "What did Tony have to say?"

Tony had said surprisingly little, and all of it encouraging. "Anthony could barely spare me the time of day, so anxious was he to return to his bride." Percival opened the door of their private sitting room. "He did say Peter seems to be doing much better for trying the foxglove tincture."

"Arabella writes to the same effect. Are we returning to Morelands for the holidays?"

For all the upheaval in the past few days, and for all the honesty and closeness it had brought between Percival and his lady, he still could not tell if she was asking to go home or asking not to.

He closed the door behind them and drew his wife into his arms the better to communicate with her. "His Grace's spirits are also reported to be much improved."

They were all in better spirits, and who would have thought such a contretemps might yield that result? Against his shoulder, Esther yawned.

"Surely, that your father's situation might admit of any improvement qualifies as a miracle."

"Peter conceived the notion to provide Papa with a young, buxom nurse. Arabella found some village girl with a kindly disposition toward 'the old dear,' and His Grace is reported to be pinching the maids and threatening to appoint himself Lord of Misrule." Percival rested his chin against Esther's temple. "Will you do the same for me, Esther, when I'm old and crotchety?"

The idea that they'd grow old and crotchety together loomed like the greatest gift a man might aspire to—though Esther hadn't a crotchety bone in her lovely body.

"Of course, Percival. You shall have all the buxom nurses and giggling maids you desire, because I know you'll not begrudge me my handsome footmen and flirting porters, hmm? And my doctors will be the most attentive and doting too."

She patted his chest, while love for her expanded to every corner of his heart. A month ago, she would not have teased him thus. A month ago, she would have given him a look he could not read, and gone about taking her hair down as they exchanged careful small talk.

"I love you, Esther Windham. I will always love you."

"I love you too, Husband." She yawned again but made no move to leave his embrace; nor was he about to let her go.

A thought popped into Percival's tired, happy

mind. A thought that might have terrified him only a few short weeks ago. "You took a nap yesterday, Esther, and again today."

"All by myself, which was a sorry waste of a large bed."

"We shall put that bed to mutual use presently, but tell me: Are you carrying?" She sighed softly, and that was not a no. "Esther?"

"You adore your daughter, Percival. You study her as if she were some treasure unearthed from exotic antiquity, and you delight in the way she manages the boys."

Percival inhaled through his nose, the better to catch Esther's rosy scent, and it hit him: an undernote of nutmeg graced her fragrance. "I love all my children, and I love my wife, and if my wife is carrying yet another child, I will love that child too. And you're right, I am fascinated by little Maggie and her way with her brothers. I am fascinated with all of them, but mostly, I am in love with my wife."

He waited for her to tell him she was carrying. Instead, she kissed him, and because he was her husband and he did love her to distraction, that was answer enough.

Epilogue

THE DOOR TO ESTHER'S BEDROOM CRACKED OPEN AS the baby stirred in her arms.

"Quiet now, you lot," came a whispered admonition. "If the baby's sleeping, we mustn't disturb her, or your mama will be wroth with us."

Percival Windham, His Grace the Duke of Moreland, had rounded up his lieutenants to make a raid on Esther's peace.

"Mama's always wroth with us," Gayle observed.

"She's not wroth with *me*," Bart countered.

Percival pushed the door open another few inches and peeked around it. "Hush. The next man who speaks will be court-martialed for conduct unbecoming."

"No pudding," little Victor piped. "No pudding."

Victor was very particular about his pudding, much like his father and his late grandfather.

"Come in," Esther said, pushing up against her pillows and cuddling her newest daughter close. "I've been telling Louisa to expect some callers."

Percival held Louisa's older sister Sophie in his arms, and Devlin walked at his side, while Bart charged ahead, Victor clutched a fold of his father's coat, and Gayle kept Valentine by the hand. Maggie, as always, hung back, though she was smiling, as was her father.

Another healthy girl child safely delivered was an excellent reason to smile.

"Can I see the baby?" Victor asked.

As small as he was, he could not see his mother in her great bed, much less the new baby. Percival tucked Sophie in against Esther's side and hoisted the children onto the bed one by one. They arranged themselves across the foot of the bed, never quite holding still, but demonstrating as much decorum as they were capable of.

"There, you shall all have a look," Percival said when he'd positioned his troops. "But no shouting or bouncing around lest you rouse your baby sister Louisa."

"She'll mess her nappies," Gayle observed. "You named her for Uncle Peter, because his real name was Peter Louis Hannibal Windham."

"We did," Esther said, though she shared a smile with Percival over the scatological preoccupations of the young male mind.

Not to be outdone, Bart gave his next-youngest brother a push. "You named Sophie for Grandpapa, and that's why she's Sophie George Windham."

"Sophie Georgina," Gayle said, shoving back.

Percival scooped up wee Sophie and settled with her, his back to the bedpost. "The next fellow who shoves, pushes, or interrupts his brother will be sent back to the nursery."

"No pudding," Victor said again, grinning at his older brothers.

Percival tousled Victor's dark hair. "Heed the young philosopher, boys, and follow Maggie's example of juvenile dignity." He winked at Maggie, which always made the girl turn up bashful. "Esther, how do you fare?"

This had become a family ritual, this bringing the older siblings to see the new arrival, and what a darling new arrival she was. Louisa had Victor's swooping brows, which on a newborn made for a startlingly dramatic little countenance.

"I am well, Percival. Childbearing is not easy, but it does improve with practice. Would you like to hold your daughter?"

They exchanged babies with the ease and precision of a parental drill team, and Esther beheld the Duke of Moreland give his heart, yet again, to a lady too small to understand the magnitude of such a gift.

Gayle also watched his father gently cradle the newborn in his arms. "If you have another baby, Mama, will you name her Cyclops?"

"Cyclops is a stupid name," Bart started in. Percival silenced his firstborn son and heir—Bart was arguably Pembroke now, though no parent in their right mind would tell the boy such a thing yet—with a glower, while Esther waited for Victor to pronounce sentence on the pudding again.

"Cyclops is not a stupid name," Gayle replied with the gravity peculiar to him. "Sophie was named for Grandpa, and he died. Louisa is named for Uncle Peter, and he died right after Grandpa. Nobody has seen Cyclops for days, so she must be dead too, and that means we can name a baby after her."

Percival left off nuzzling the baby long enough to smile at Gayle's reasoning. "I think if you climbed up to the straw mow on a sunny morning and were quiet and still long enough, you'd find that Cyclops has finished her own lying-in and has better things to do than let little boys chase after her and threaten to take her prisoner."

"Girls don't like to be taken prisoner," Maggie said. "May I hold the baby?"

The idea made Esther nervous, though Maggie would never intentionally harm her siblings.

"Come here," Percival said, patting the bed. Maggie crawled across the mattress to sit beside her father. He placed the baby in Maggie's lap and kept an arm around his oldest daughter. "I think she looks a little like you, Maggie, around the mouth. She's very pretty."

Characteristically, Maggie blushed but did not acknowledge the compliment. "Sophie was bald. Louisa has hair."

Little Valentine squirmed closer and traced small fingers over the baby's cheek. "She's soft."

"She'll mess her nappies," Gayle warned.

Bart apparently knew not to argue with that eternal verity. "Can we go now?" He looked conflicted, as if he might want to hold his baby sister and didn't know how to ask without losing face before his brothers.

In Esther's arms, little Sophie squirmed but did not make a sound. "Take Thomas with you if you're going to the mews, and mind you big boys look after Victor."

Four boys who'd needed help to get up onto the bed went sliding off it, thundering toward the door, while Valentine remained fascinated with the infant.

He stroked his sister's dark mop of hair. "Soft baby."

"She is soft," Percival said. "And you, my lad, are smarter than your brothers for choosing the company of the genteel ladies over some nasty, old, shiftless cat."

"She's heavy," Maggie said, passing the baby back to Percival. "I'm going to watch the boys."

"Take Valentine." Percival used one hand to balance the baby and the other to help Maggie and Valentine off the bed. "He'll make enough noise that Madam Cyclops will be able to hide before her peace is utterly destroyed."

"Come along, Valentine. We've a kitty to rescue." Maggie left at a pace that accommodated Valentine churning along beside her, leaving Esther with her husband and her two baby daughters.

❧

Percival shifted to recline against the pillows with his wife, one arm around Esther and Sophie, the other around Louisa. He leaned near enough to catch a whiff of roses, and to whisper, "Do you hear that, Your Grace?"

"I hear silence, Your Grace."

They addressed each other by their titles as a sort of marital joke, one that helped take the newness and loss off a station they'd gained only months before.

"That is the sound of children growing up enough to leave us in privacy from time to time. Good thing we've more babies to fill our nursery."

He kissed Esther's temple, and Sophie sighed mightily, as if her father's proximity addressed all that might ail her—would that it might always be so.

"I wish Peter and His Grace had lived to see this baby, Percival. They doted so on Sophie."

Percival went quiet for a moment, mesmerized by the sight of yet another healthy, beautiful child to bless their marriage. A man might love his wife to distraction—and Percival did—but love was too paltry a word for what he felt for the mother of his children.

"In some ways, their last year was their best, Esther. That tincture gave Peter quite a reprieve, and His Grace perked up considerably when you presented him with a granddaughter."

His nursemaid had perked him up, though the young lady had been Esther's companion in the late duke's mind, and nobody had disabused him of this idea.

"Percival, it's Thursday."

"It's Louisa Windham's birthday," he replied, kissing Esther's cheek. "Two months from now, if I'm a good boy, I may have some pudding."

Esther turned to kiss his cheek. She was wearing one of his dressing gowns—the daft woman claimed the scent of him comforted her through her travail, and because she came through each lying-in with fine style, Percival didn't argue with her wisdom.

"Today is Thursday, Percival, and your committees meet on Thursday. You never miss those meetings. The government will fall if you neglect your politics. George himself has said nobody else has your talent for brokering compromises."

That the King admired such talent mattered little compared to Esther's regard for it. Percival traded babies with his wife, then gently rubbed noses with

Sophie, which made the infant giggle. "Am I or am I not the Duke of Moreland, madam?"

Esther loved it when he used those imperious tones on her, and he loved it equally when she turned up duchess on him.

"You are Moreland, and it shall ever be my privilege to be your duchess." His duchess had labored from two hours past midnight until dawn, and could not hide the yawn that stole up on her. Even a duchess was entitled to yawn occasionally.

"And my blessing to call you so. But, Esther, as that fellow standing approximately sixty-seventh in line for the throne, I'd like somebody to explain to me why it is, when all I need are three more votes to carry the bill on children in the foundries, I am incapable of seeing such a thing done."

He should not be bringing his frustrations up to her now, but in the past few years, Esther had become his greatest confidante, and for the first time in months, he did not want to attend his meetings.

"When do you expect the vote to come up?"

Right to the heart of the matter, that was his duchess. "Too soon. I'm sure if I could turn Anselm to my way of thinking, then Dodd would come along, and then several others would see the light, but they won't break ranks."

Esther stroked her fingers over Louisa's dark mop of hair. "Lady Dodd was recently delivered of a son."

Percival had learned by now that Esther did not speak in non sequiturs, not even when tired. She was the soul of logic; it remained only for Percival to divine her reasoning.

"I know. Dodd was drunk for most of a week, boasting of having secured the succession within a year of marriage. The man hasn't a spare, outside of a third cousin, and he thinks his succession ensured."

Children died in foundries, died and were burned horribly. How could Dodd not know his own offspring were just as fragile?

"How old is Anselm's heir?" Esther asked.

Percival raised and lowered his tiny daughter and cradled her against his chest, because Esther's question was pertinent. He wasn't sure how, but it was very pertinent.

"He has a boy in leading strings. His lady believes in spacing her confinements, which imposition he reports to all and sundry before his third bottle of a night."

"Not every couple is as blessed as we are, Your Grace. Who else would you consider to be susceptible to a change in vote?"

The Duke of Moreland left off flirting with his infant daughter and offered his duchess a slow, wicked smile. "My love, you are scheming. I adore it when you scheme."

He suspected Esther rather enjoyed it too, though she no doubt fretted that somewhere there was a silly rule about duchesses eschewing scheming. What duchess could fail to aid her duke, though, when it made him so happy to have her assistance—and was such fun?

"A lying-in party, I think," Esther said, smoothing a hand over Louisa's hair. "I will have their ladies to tea, ask after the children, and mention your little bill."

"You won't mention it. You'll gently bludgeon

them with it. They'll leave here weeping into their handkerchiefs." And God help their husbands when the ladies arrived home.

"We'll follow up with dinner," Esther said, her tone suggesting she was already at work on the seating arrangements. "We'll invite Anselm one night, and Dodd the next, and you can drag them up to the nursery to admire the children before we sit down."

"We have very handsome children." Percival ran a finger down Louisa's tiny nose. "And I have a brilliant wife. It could work, Esther."

"Divide and conquer. Pull Dodd aside one night, tell him your wife is haranguing you about this bill, and she's recently delivered of another child. He'll sympathize with you as a husband and papa like he'd never bow down to you as a duke."

When a man should not be capable of holding any more happiness, Percival felt yet another increment of delight in his duchess. "Because Dodd's naught but a viscount, and they are a troublesome lot. I'll do the same thing with Anselm the next night and imply Dodd would capitulate, except he feared losing face with his fellows. My love, you are a marvel." He turned to kiss her then drew back. "A tired marvel. I see a flaw in your plan, though."

She cradled his cheek against her palm, looking tired—also pleased with her husband. "One anticipates most plans will benefit from your thoughts, Your Grace."

He kissed her—a businesslike kiss that nonetheless nurtured his soul. "You will be lying-in. No political dinners for you for at least a month."

She'd eschewed the old tradition of a forty-day lying-in several babies ago. Inactivity was not in the Duchess of Moreland's nature.

"Two weeks ought to be sufficient, Percival. This was not a difficult birthing, and as that lady married to the fellow approximately sixty-seventh in line for the throne, I've decided I need practice at making royal decrees."

What she needed was a nap. Percival didn't dare suggest that.

"Planning is one of your strengths, Esther. Though I do worry about your health. With each child, the worry does not abate, it grows worse. What proclamation are you contemplating?"

She kissed his wrist. "You need not fret, Husband. Every duchess has a carnivorous streak if she knows what's good for her. I'll soon be on the mend, or you'll be slaying hapless bovines to make it so. Now attend me."

"I am helpless to do otherwise, as well you should know."

"The government will topple without you, I know that, your king knows it, and I suspect all of Parliament—when sober—understands your value, but I saw you first."

She was tired, she was pleased with the night's work—very pleased, and well she should be—but Percival also saw that his wife was working up to something, something important to her that must therefore also be important to him, even on Thursdays.

"Esther, I love you, and I will always love you. You need not issue a proclamation. You need only ask."

"Then I am asking for my Thursdays back."

"I wasn't aware Thursdays had been taken from you, Your Grace." And yet they had—they'd been taken from him, too, and given to the ungrateful wretches in the Lords.

"Percival, I recall that trip we took up to Town only a few years ago, when Devlin and Maggie came to join our household. I was so worried then, for us and for our children, and one of the ways I knew my worry was not silly was that you'd forgotten our Thursdays. I'm not worried now, but I think we need our Thursdays back."

Something warm turned over in Percival's heart. He loved his wife, but it was wonderful to know he was still *in love* with her too—more than ever.

"Parliament can go hang," Percival said, stroking a hand over his duchess's golden hair. "We shall have our Thursdays back, and no one and nothing shall take them from us, or from our children."

The duchess's proclamation stood throughout shifts in government, the arrival of more babies, the maturation of those babies into ladies and gentlemen, and even through the arrival of grandbabies and great-grandbabies—though given the nature of large, busy, families, Thursday occasionally fell on Tuesday or sometimes came twice a week.

Whether Thursday fell on some other day or in its traditional position, Esther knew she would always have her husband's Thursdays, and his heart—and he would forever have hers.

**Introducing True Gentleman,
Grace Burrowes's gorgeous new
Regency romance series featuring the
Haddonfield ladies and their loves.**

An Excerpt from

Tremaine's True Love

"THE GREATEST PLAGUE EVER TO BEDEVIL MORTAL MAN, the greatest threat to his peace, the most fiendish source of undeserved humility is *his sister*, and spinster sisters are the worst of a bad lot." In the corridor outside the formal parlor, Nicholas, Earl of Bellefonte, sounded very certain of his point.

"Of course, my lord," somebody replied softly, "but, my lord—"

"I tell you, Hanford," the earl went on, "if it wouldn't imperil certain personal masculine attributes which my countess holds dear, I'd turn Lady Nita right over my—"

"*My lord, you have a visitor.*"

Hanford's pronouncement came off a little desperately but had the effect of silencing his lordship's lament. Quiet words were exchanged beyond the door, giving Tremaine St. Michael time to step away from the parlor's cozy fireplace, where he'd been shamelessly warming a personal attribute of his own formerly frozen to the saddle.

Bellefonte's greeting as he strode into the parlor

a moment later was as enthusiastic as his ranting had been.

"Our very own Mr. St. Michael! You are early. This is not fashionable. In fact, were I not the soul of congeniality, I'd call it unsporting in the extreme."

"Bellefonte." Tremaine St. Michael bowed, for Bellefonte was his social superior, also one of few men whose height and brawn exceeded Tremaine's.

"Don't suppose you have any sisters?" Bellefonte asked with a rueful smile. "I have four. They're what my grandmother calls *lively*."

So lively, Bellefonte had apparently bellowed at one of these sisters for the entire ten minutes Tremaine had been left to admire the spotless Turkey carpets in Belle Maison's formal parlor. The sister's responses had been inaudible until an upstairs door had slammed.

"Liveliness is a fine quality in a young lady," Tremaine said, because he was a guest in this house, and sociability was called for if he was to relieve Bellefonte of substantial assets.

His lordship was welcome to keep all four sisters, thank you very much.

"Fat lot you know," Bellefonte retorted, taking a position with his back to the fire. "If every man in the House of Lords had rounded up his *lively* sisters and sent them to France, the Corsican would have been on bended knee, seeking asylum of old George in a week flat. How was your journey?"

Bellefonte had the blond hair and blue eyes of many an English aristocrat. The corners of those eyes crinkled agreeably, and he'd followed up Tremaine's bow with a hearty handshake.

Bellefonte would never be a friend, but he was friendly.

"My journey was uneventful, if cold," Tremaine said. "I apologize for making good time down from Town."

"I apologize for complaining. I am blessed in my family, truly, but Lady Nita, my oldest sister, is particularly strong willed."

Bellefonte's hearty bonhomie faded to a soft smile as feminine laughter rang out in the corridor.

"You were saying?" Tremaine prompted. When would his lordship offer a guest a damned drink?

"Nothing of any moment, St. Michael. My sister Kirsten and my sister Della have taken note of your arrival. Shall we to the library, where the best libation and coziest hearth await? Beckman gave me to understand you're not the tea-and-crumpets sort."

When and why had his lordship's brother conveyed that sentiment? Another thought intruded on Tremaine's irritation: Bellefonte knew his womenfolk by their laughter. How odd was that?

"I'm the whiskey sort," Tremaine said. "Winter ale wouldn't go amiss either." Not brandy though. Not if Tremaine could avoid it.

His lordship was too well-bred to raise an eyebrow at tastes refined in drovers' inns the length of the realm.

"Whiskey, then. Hanford!"

A little old fellow in formal livery stepped into the parlor. "My lord?"

Bellefonte directed the butler to send some decent sandwiches 'round to the library, to fetch the countess to her husband's side when the fiend in the nursery had turned loose of her, and to inform the housekeeper that Mr. St. Michael was on the premises earlier than planned.

His lordship set a smart pace down carpeted hallways, past bouquets of white hothouse roses and across gleaming parquet floors, to a high-ceilinged, oak-paneled treasury of books. Belle Maison was a well-maintained example of the last century's enthusiasm for the spacious countryseat, and whoever had designed the house had had an eye for light.

The library was blessed with tall windows at regular intervals, and the red velvet draperies were caught back, despite the cold. Winter sunshine bounced cheerily off mirrors, brass, and silver, and here, too, the hearth was blazing extravagantly.

The entire impression—genial Lord Bellefonte; his dear, plaguey sisters; roaring fires even in empty rooms; the casual wealth lined up on the library's endless, sunny shelves—left Tremaine feeling out of place.

Tremaine had been in countless aristocratic family seats and more than a few castles and palaces. The out-of-place feeling he experienced at Belle Maison was the fault of the sisters, whom Bellefonte clearly loved and worried over.

Commerce Tremaine comprehended, and even gloried in.

Sisters had no part in commerce, but the lively variety could apparently transform an imposing family seat into a home. Bellefonte's sisters inspired slammed doors, fraternal grumbling, and even laughter, and in this, Belle Maison was a departure from Tremaine's usual experience with titled English families.

"I know you only intended to stay for a few days,"

Bellefonte said, gesturing to a pair of chairs beneath
a tall window, "but my countess declares that will
not do. You are to visit for at least two weeks, so
the neighbors may come by and inspect you. Don't
worry. I'll warn you which ones have marriageable
daughters—which is most of them."

"A few days might be all the time I can spare, my
lord," Tremaine said, seating himself in cushioned
luxury. "The press of business waits for no man, and
wasted time is often wasted money."

"Protest is futile, no matter how sensible your argu-
ments," Bellefonte countered, folding his length into
the second chair. "My countess has spoken, and my
sisters will abet her. You are an eligible bachelor and,
therefore, a doomed man."

The earl crossed long legs at the ankle, the picture
of a fellow to whom *doom* was a merry concept.

"Her ladyship will ply you with delicacies at
every meal," he went on. "Kirsten will interrogate
you about your business ventures, Susannah will
discuss that Scottish poet fellow with you, and Della
will catch you up on all the Town gossip. The
Haddonfield womenfolk are like faeries. A man falls
into their clutches and time ceases to have meaning."

Avoid faeries as if your life depends on it. Tremaine's
Scottish grandfather had smacked that lesson into his
hard little head before Tremaine had been breeched.

"What about your sister Lady Bernita?" Tremaine
asked. The sister putting the worry and exasperation
in her brother's eyes, and inspiring the earl to raise
his voice.

"Oh, her." Bellefonte's gaze went to the window,

which looked out over terraced gardens in all their winter solemnity.

A tall, blond woman marched off toward the stables along a walk of crushed white shells. She wore a riding habit of dark blue—no clever hat or pheasant feather cocked over her ear—and her briskly swishing hems were muddy.

Bellefonte's gaze followed the woman, his expression forlorn. "Lady Nita is very dear to me. She will be the death of us all."

~

The baby was small and vigorously alive, two points in her favor—possibly the only two.

"Your mother is resting," Nita said to the infant's oldest sibling, "and this is your new sister. Does she have a name?"

Eleven-year-old Mary took the bundle from Nita's arms. "Ma said a girl would be Annie Elizabeth. Ma wanted a boy though. Boys can do more work."

"Boys also eat more, make more noise, and run off to become soldiers or worse," Nita said. Boys became young wastrels who disported with the local soiled dove, heedless of the innocent life resulting from their pleasures, heedless that the soiled dove was a baronet's granddaughter and a squire's daughter. "Have you had anything to eat today, Mary?"

"Bread."

Thin, freckled, and wearing a dress that likely hadn't been washed in weeks, Mary looked younger than her eleven years—also much, much older.

"Your mother will need more than bread to

recover from this birth," Nita said. "I've brought butter, sausage, jam, sugar, boiled eggs, and tea, in the sack on the table."

Nita would have milk sent over too. She'd been distracted by her altercation with Nicholas, and in her haste to reach Addy Chalmers's side, she'd neglected the most obvious need.

Mary pressed a kiss to Annie's brow. "She's ever so dear."

Would that the child's mother viewed the baby similarly. Nita went down to her haunches, the better to impress on young Mary what must be said.

"When Annie fusses, you bring her to your mother to nurse. When Annie's had her fill, you burp her and take her back to her blankets. She'll sleep a lot at first, but she needs to sleep where it's quiet, warm, and safe." Though the little cottage wouldn't be warm again until summer.

Mary cradled the newborn closer. "I'll watch out for her, Lady Nita. Ma won't have any custom for weeks, and that means no gin. Wee Annie will grow up strong."

Nita rose, feeling the cold and the lateness of the hour in every joint and muscle.

"I'll send the vicar's wife by next week, and she'll have more food for you and your brothers, and maybe even some coal." The vicar's maid of all work would, in any case. "You store the food where nobody can steal it, and here…" Nita withdrew five shillings from a pocket. "Don't tell anybody you have this. Not your mother, not your brothers, not even wee Annie. This is for bread and butter, not for gin."

"Thank you, Lady Nita."

"I'll come back next week to check on your mother," Nita said. "If she runs a fever or if the baby is doing poorly, come for me or send one of your brothers."

Mary bobbed an awkward curtsy, the baby in her arms. "Yes, Lady Nita."

Then Nita had nothing more to do except climb onto Atlas's broad back and let the horse find his way home through the frigid darkness.

≈∞≈

"They are charming, the lot of them," Tremaine said. "I'd forgotten what a big, happy family can do to a man's composure." Particularly a big, happy, healthy family with Saxon good looks and a thriving appreciation for life's finer comforts.

"Bellefonte is besotted," Tremaine went on, scratching William's hairy withers. "As is his countess."

"I'm told it works better that way."

William hadn't spoken—William was a gelding and the voice was decidedly feminine.

A tall, blond female, rosy cheeked from the cold, led a saddled specimen of plow stock down the barn aisle. The flame of the stable's single lantern gilded red-and-gold highlights in her hair, and the hem of her dark blue riding habit was damp.

She brought the beast to a halt outside William's stall. "I don't recognize you, sir."

Tremaine recognized her though. The sculpted cheekbones, defined chin, height, and bearing—and the muddy hem—proclaimed the late-night arrival to be Lady Nita Haddonfield, oldest of the late earl's daughters, and the selfsame woman who'd marched across the barren gardens hours ago.

"Tremaine St. Michael, at your service, my lady. I am visiting your brother to discuss common business interests."

Something about his recitation bothered her. She was too tired to hide it, or perhaps she didn't care if she offended him.

"May I take your horse, my lady?" Though why the grooms weren't thundering down from their quarters above the carriage house, Tremaine could not guess.

"Why would you do that?" she asked, stuffing her gloves into a pocket.

The great beast at her side let out a gusty sigh, as if to say debate and discussion could wait until he'd been unsaddled.

"I'd see to your horse because you are a lady and I am a gentleman," Tremaine said, which was half-true, "and you should not have to manage your own mount at this late hour." She should not be *allowed* to do a groom's work at any hour.

Her ladyship patted the horse's shaggy neck. "Atlas and I have kept much later hours than this. I'll unsaddle him, but if you'd make sure he has hay and water, I'd appreciate it."

What manner of lady went about unescorted after dark with what looked like bloodstains on the cuff of her sleeve?

Tremaine made short work of the hay and water, and Lady Nita was equally efficient removing the horse's saddle and bridle. Atlas ambled into his stall without being haltered or led, and commenced a friendly sniffing through the slats with William.

"Your gelding is very handsome," Lady Nita said, closing the stall door. "Atlas's charms are more subtle."

Nothing about Atlas was subtle. He had feet the size of tea trays and quarters suitable for displaying an entire service.

"Charms such as?" Tremaine asked.

"Atlas has never been known to buck or spook. Steadiness in a fellow is a fine quality."

Very likely the horse was too lazy to buck or spook, though he applied himself to his fodder with singular diligence.

While Lady Nita's eyes were shadowed with fatigue.

"Your absence was remarked at dinner, my lady."

"You know who I am, then. Nobody warned me you were coming, Mr. St. Michael, or I might have sent my regrets to dinner."

Suggesting her ladyship would not have attended, even if she'd known the family was entertaining.

"May I escort you back to the house?" Tremaine asked. "I've assured myself William's not kicking down a wall or dying of thirst, and the day has been wearying." Dinner with the Haddonfields had been every bit as wearying as the trip down from London, though significantly warmer.

"My thanks for your courtesy."

Her ladyship's thanks were tired though sincere. Why had no one come out from the house to see to her well-being?

Tremaine took the lantern down from its peg, causing shadows to grow and dance. He did not offer his arm. A woman who could ride the countryside by moonlight was well equipped to negotiate the paths of her own garden.

"Is my presence at Belle Maison an unpleasant surprise, my lady?" he asked.

Her sisters would have turned Tremaine's question into a joke or a flirtation.

"Please do not be offended if I say your presence is a matter of indifference to me now," her ladyship informed him as they left the stable for the chilly air of a winter night. "Not so very long ago, I was the one who would have made sure your room was prepared, a bath waiting for you, refreshment and cut flowers in the chamber I'd selected for you."

Tremaine appreciated honesty more than he did the laughter and banter of the Haddonfield dinner table.

"I do not presume to know you, my lady, but arranging flowers and ordering a tea tray could not be much of a challenge for you."

His observation pleased her ladyship enough that a hint of a smile flitted across her features, while somewhere in the distance, a dog commenced barking. In the manner of winter nights, the sound carried, lonely and annoying.

Lady Nita moved along the garden path far more slowly than she had hours earlier. Either she was exhausted, or she wasn't looking forward to returning to her home.

"I'd like to sit for a moment," she said as they approached a gazebo. "Seek your bed, if you wish. I'll be fine alone."

Tremaine took a seat beside her, ignoring the siren

call of his quilts and pillows because, in another sense, she was not fine.

"The child lived," Lady Nita said. "I want to wake up each and every member of my family and inform them of that. The mother was also resting comfortably when I took my leave of her."

"You attended a birth." The only acceptable reason for bloodstains on a lady's attire.

"The midwife can only attend one birth at a time," Lady Nita said. "The babies are rude though. They do not appear one at a time. I have explained this to my brother repeatedly. In fact, when the weather changes, the babies conspire to arrive all at once, and the midwife, understandably, will go where her services are remunerated. The women with the least consequence deliver with the least support, and yet they need the most help."

Despite Lady Nita's calm and euphemistic summary, she was all in a lather. Her emotional fists were raised, and she would make her blows count.

Though she wouldn't rain them down on Tremaine.

"You are a reproach to your family, then," Tremaine concluded.

The lantern sat on the bench opposite them, casting little light because the wick was low. Even so, Tremaine had the sense his words earned him the first smidgen of genuine regard from the lady beside him.

"I am a reproach, Mr. St. Michael? They've certainly become free with chides and scolds aimed in my direction."

Now they were. Now that she'd been deposed as lady of the manor. Bellefonte probably had not the first inkling of the hurt he'd done Lady Nita when he'd acquired a countess.

Tremaine's backside ached from hours in a cold saddle, and yet he remained on the equally cold bench a moment longer. He withdrew the lady's gloves from the oversized pocket in which she'd jammed them and passed them to her.

"A great debate ensued after the fish course, my lady, as to whether country assemblies should permit the waltz when so few know how to dance it properly. While this inanity held the company's entire attention, you helped a new life get a start in the world. Yes, you are a reproach to your family, and to all who think Christian charity is a matter of Sunday finery and Boxing Day benevolence."

A great sigh went out of her ladyship, interrupted by a sneeze. She leaned her head back against a support and closed her eyes. She hadn't put on her gloves.

"You're Scottish," she observed.

What Tremaine was, was cold. He put his handkerchief on the bench between them, in case the sneezing, tired, honest lady had need of it.

Despite Lady Nita's willingness to wrestle demons on behalf of the newborn parish poor, she was attractive. The local beauties would refer to her as "handsome" in an effort to denigrate her features politely, but she was lovely nonetheless. Her brows were the perfect graceful complement to wide, intelligent eyes; her eyes, nose, and mouth were assembled into a face that deserved excellent portraiture and needed no cosmetics.

The beauty of her features was such that even weariness was becoming on her.

"I can sound Scottish," Tremaine said, "particularly when in the grip of strong sentiment. My mother was born in Aberdeenshire." He could hold a grudge like a Scot too, and endure cold and handle strong drink.

"And your father?" She had a good ear, did Lady Nita. Also pretty ears.

"French." Tremaine waited for her to put more questions to him, but she instead turned the lamp wick down until the light extinguished.

"We were wasting oil," she said.

"The hour is late and the night cold. We should go in. If you'd like to linger here in solitude, I'll bid you good evening," Tremaine said, rising.

To be found alone with him in the dark would cause greater problems for the lady than to be found alone with her discontents.

He bowed over her bare, cold, elegant hand. "A pleasure to have made your acquaintance, my lady."

Tremaine left Lady Nita the unlit lamp and his handkerchief and made his way to the house. Nita Haddonfield was an earl's daughter who understood the practicalities, and she didn't dress her sentiments up in tedious dinner conversation. She was easily Tremaine's favorite Haddonfield of the lot.

What a pity he'd have no time to get to know her.

Daniel's True Desire

"WHY MUST ALL AND SUNDRY ENTERTAIN THEMSELVES by telling me falsehoods?"

Daniel Banks's teeth chattered as he put that conundrum to his horse, who had come to a halt, head down, sides heaving, before the only building in sight.

"'Ye can't miss it,'" Daniel quoted to himself. "The only lane that turns off to the left half a mile west of the village."

This lowly dwelling was not Belle Maison, the family seat of the Earl of Bellefonte. Daniel had listened carefully to the directions given to him by the good folk at the Queen's Harebell. They'd sent him, in the middle of a roaring snowstorm, to a mean, weathered cottage, albeit one with a light in its single window.

"I'll be but a moment," Daniel promised his gelding.

Daniel's boots hit the snowy ground and agony shot up limbs too long exposed to the cold. He stood for a moment, waiting for the pain to fade, concocting silent epithets when he ought to have been murmuring the Twenty-Third Psalm.

"Halloo, the house!" he called, thumping up three

snowy steps. The porch sheltered a small hoard of split oak firewood. Somebody within burned that oak, for the frigid air held a comforting tang of wood smoke.

The wind abated once Daniel ducked under the porch's overhang, while the cold was unrelenting. He longed for a fire, some victuals, and proper directions, though only the directions mattered.

A man of God was supposed to welcome hardships, and Daniel did, mostly because his store of silent, colorful language was becoming impressive.

He raised a gloved fist to knock on the door. "Halloo, the—!"

The door opened, Daniel's sleeve was snatched into a tight grasp, and he was yanked into the warmth of the cottage so quickly he nearly bumped his head on the lintel.

"I said I'd be home by dark," his captor muttered, "and full dark is yet another hour away. I was hoping this infernal snow would slow down." The woman fell silent, for Daniel's sleeve was in a young lady's grip. "You're not George."

Alas for me. "The Reverend Daniel Banks, at your service, madam. I lost my way and need directions to Belle Maison, the Bellefonte estate. Apologies for intruding upon your afternoon."

Though, might Daniel please intrude at least until his feet and ears thawed? Beelzebub was a substantial horse who grew a prodigious winter coat. He'd tolerate the elements well enough for a short time.

While Daniel was cold, tired, famished, and viewing his upcoming visit to the earl's grand house as a penance at best.

"Your gloves are frozen," the lady noted, tugging one of those gloves from Daniel's hand. "What could you be thinking, sir?" She went after his scarf next, unwinding it from his head, though she had to go up on her toes. She appropriated his second glove and shook the lot, sending pellets of ice in all directions.

What had he been thinking? Lately, Daniel avoided the near occasion of thinking. Better that way all around.

"You needn't go to any trouble," Daniel said, though the warmth of the cottage was heavenly. A kettle steamed on the pot swing, and the scent of cinnamon—a luxury—filled the otherwise humble space. Somebody had made the dwelling comfy, with a rocking chair by the fire, fragrant beeswax candles in the sconces, and braided rugs covering a plank floor.

"I can offer you tea, and bread and butter, but then surely we'll be on our way. I'm Kirsten Haddonfield, Mr. Banks, and we can ride to Belle Maison together."

Haddonfield was the family name that went with the Bellefonte title.

"You're a relative to the earl, then?"

She wore a plain, dark blue wool dress, high necked, such as a farmer's wife would wear this time of year. Not even a cousin to an earl would attire herself thus unless she suffered excesses of pragmatism.

"I am one of the earl's younger sisters, and you're half-frozen. I hope those aren't your good boots, for you've ruined them."

"They're my only boots."

Swooping blond brows drew together over a nose no one would call dainty, and yet Lady Kirsten Haddonfield was a pretty woman. She had good facial bones, a definite chin, a clean jaw, and blue eyes that assured Daniel she did not suffer fools—lest her tone leave any doubt on that score.

Daniel was a fool. Witness the ease with which the yeoman at the inn had bamboozled him. Witness the ease with which his own wife had bamboozled him.

"At least sit for a moment before the fire," the lady said, arranging his scarf and gloves on pegs above the hearth. "Did you lose your way because of the weather?"

Daniel had lost his way months ago. "The weather played a role. Are you here alone, my lady?"

She folded her arms across a bosom even a man of the cloth acknowledged as a fine bit of work on the Creator's part.

"I am on my family's property, Mr. Banks, and they well know where I am. The weather is not only foul, it's dangerous. If you must prance out the door to die for the sake of manners, I'll not stop you. The groom or one of my brothers should be here any minute to fetch me home. We'll note into which ditch your remains have fallen as we pass you by."

The fire was lovely. Her ferocity, though arguably unchristian, warmed Daniel in an entirely different way. Nowhere did the Bible say a Good Samaritan must be excessively burdened with charm.

"You aren't much given to polite dissembling, are you, my lady?" For an earl's daughter was a lady from the moment of her birth.

She marched over to the sideboard and commenced sawing at a loaf of bread. "I'm not given to any kind of dissembling. You should sit."

"If I sit, I might never rise. I've journeyed from

Oxfordshire, and the storm seems to have followed me every mile."

"Why not tarry in London and wait out the weather?"

Because, had Daniel spent another night in London, he'd have been forced to call on a bishop or two and explain why his very own helpmeet hadn't accompanied him to his new post.

"I am here to assume responsibility for the Haddondale pulpit," Daniel said, moving closer to the fire. A copy of *A Vindication of the Rights of Woman* lay open facedown on the mantel. "I was given to understand filling the position was a matter of some urgency."

Her ladyship swiped a silver knife through a pat of butter and paused before applying the butter to the bread.

"*You're* the new vicar?"

Amusement made this brusque, pretty woman an altogether different creature. She had mischief in her, and humor and secrets, also—where on earth did such thoughts come from?—kisses. Fun, generous kisses.

When she smiled, Lady Kirsten looked like the sort of female who'd pat a fellow's bum—in public.

The cold had made Daniel daft. "Do I have horns or cloven feet to disqualify me from a religious calling, my lady?"

She slapped the butter onto the bread, her movements confident.

"You have gorgeous brown eyes, a lovely nose—though it's a bit red at the moment—and a smile that suggests you might get up to tricks, Mr. Banks. You could also use a trim of that brown hair. Ministers aren't supposed to look dashing. I have two younger sisters who will suffer paroxysms of religious conviction if you're to lead the flock."

Olivia had found Daniel's nose "unfortunate." Daniel found his entire marriage worthy of the same appellation.

Feeling was returning to his feet, and hunger writhed to life along with it. Lady Kirsten passed him the bread without benefit of a plate.

"It's not quite fresh, the bread, that is. The butter was made this morning. I'll fix you some tea."

Daniel took a small bite, then realized he'd forgotten to send grateful sentiments heavenward before he'd done so. *I'm grateful for this bread—also for the company.*

"Your tea, Mr. Banks. Drink up, for I hear sleigh bells."

Daniel downed the hot tea in one glorious go, the sweetness and substance of it fortifying him, much as Lady Kirsten's forthright manner had. She swirled her cloak around her shoulders, then draped his scarf, warm from the fire and redolent of cinnamon, around his neck.

"Let me do the explaining," she said, passing him warmed gloves when he'd bolted his bread and butter. "The sleigh will afford us hot bricks and lap robes, but once we get to Belle Maison, we'll hear nothing but questions. Nicholas is protective, and my sisters are infernally curious."

She crossed the room to bank the fire, then blew out the candles one by one.

Lady Kirsten had been gracious to him, and Daniel wanted to give her something in return for her hospitality. Something real, not mere manners.

An impoverished vicar had little to give besides truth.

"I'm not lost," he said. "I was misdirected by some fellows at the inn. I asked for the way to Belle Maison, and they sent me here. I did not confuse their directions, either, because I made them repeat their words twice."

He'd been taken for a fool, in other words. Again.

"The joke is on them, isn't it?" Lady Kirsten said, blowing out the last candle and enshrouding the cottage in deep gloom. "They might have entertained an angel unaware, and instead they'll have a very uncomfortable moment when it's their turn to shake the new vicar's hand. I will enjoy watching that. My sisters will too."

She wrapped up the bread and butter and stuffed it in a brown brocade bag, then set the teakettle on the mantel.

The sleigh bells went silent, and Daniel sent up a few more words of gratitude. Hot bricks and lap robes were paradise itself compared to Beelzebub's cold saddle. After he'd tied his horse behind the sleigh, Daniel climbed in beside Lady Kirsten, who wasn't at all shy about sharing the lap robe with him.

And that was a bit of paradise too.

❧

You're not George.

Had a woman ever uttered a stupider observation? Kirsten put aside her self-disgust long enough to arrange the lap robe over her knees. Mr. Banks was on her right, Alfrydd, the head lad, on her left, at the reins.

A great deal more warmth was to be had on her right.

They reached Belle Maison in what felt like moments, before Kirsten could mentally rehearse the version of events she'd offer to her siblings. Not lies.

She never bothered lying to them, though they doubtless often wished she would.

"Come along, Mr. Banks. Alfrydd will spoil your horse rotten, and very likely the countess will do the same with you."

"I'll be but a moment," Mr. Banks said, untying his shaggy black beast from behind the sleigh. Ice beaded the horse's mane and tail, and balls of snow clung to its fetlocks. "Beelzebub has seen me through much this day. I can at least unsaddle him."

A parson who named his horse Beelzebub?

Kirsten's brothers typically handed their horses off with a pat and a treat, then went striding away to the house, there to track mud, make noise, call for their brandies, and otherwise comport themselves like brothers.

Mr. Banks wasn't George, wasn't a brother to Kirsten of any variety but perhaps the theological.

"I'll help," she said, "but you need not fear your reception with the earl. Unless you hurl thunderbolts from the pulpit and insult women in the street, you'll be an improvement over your predecessor."

Mr. Banks led his mount into the dim, relatively cozy stable, the scents of hay and horse bringing their familiar comfort. Kirsten didn't share her sisters' love of all things fine and pretty, though Mr. Banks had an air of careworn male elegance.

"If you'll take the reins, I'll tend to his saddle," Mr. Banks suggested.

Kirsten obliged, stroking her glove over a big, horsey Roman nose. "Why did you name him after an imp?" An imp of Satan.

"He's blessed with high spirits and a fine sense of humor, though little stops him when he settles to a job."

"Your owner treasures you," Kirsten told the horse. The gelding had dark, soft eyes, much like his owner's, and equally fringed in thick lashes. On both man and horse, those eyes had a knowing quality, nothing effeminate or delicate about them.

"I treasure my horse, while Zubbie treasures his fodder," Mr. Banks said, unfastening the girth and removing the saddle but not the pad beneath it.

Mr. Banks's words held such affection, Kirsten envied the horse.

"Have you had him long?" she asked, for there was a bond here, such as Nicholas enjoyed with his mare and George with his gelding. Kirsten's brothers confided in their horses, were comforted by them, and fretted over their horsey ailments as if a child had fallen ill.

Men were sentimental about the oddest things.

"Beelzebub was a gift," Mr. Banks said, taking the reins from Kirsten and looping them over the horse's neck. "A parishioner getting on in years foaled him out and saw that Beelzebub would be too big and too energetic for an older couple. He was given to me when he was a yearling, and we've been famous friends ever since."

Mr. Banks produced a disintegrating lump of sugar from a pocket, and held his hand out to his horse until every evidence of the sugar had been delicately licked away.

He patted the gelding, slid the saddle pad from its back, and led the animal into a loose box boasting a veritable featherbed of straw. The bridle came off, and some sentiments were imparted to the horse as Mr. Banks stroked its muscular neck.

"Alfrydd will see that he's properly groomed," Kirsten said, because under no circumstances would she allow Mr. Banks to announce himself. She and the vicar would storm the sibling citadel together.

Susannah would be especially vulnerable to the kindness in Mr. Banks's eyes, a patient compassion that spoke of woe, sin, and the magnanimity of spirit to accept them both. Della would like the friendliness of those eyes, and Leah, though besotted with Nicholas, was ever one for intelligent conversation.

"He likes the chill taken off his water," Mr. Banks said, giving the horse another pat, "and he's a shy lad around the other fellows."

"Nicholas prides himself on a well-run stable, Mr. Banks. Beelzebub will be fine. He's nigh three-quarter ton of handsome, equine good health, not a sickly boy on his first night at public school."

A shadow crossed Mr. Banks's features, bringing out the weariness a day of winter travel inevitably engendered.

"You heard the lady," he said, tweaking one big, equine ear. "Be a good lad, or I'll deal with you severely." He turned to go, and the horse made a halfhearted attempt to nip at his sleeve, which Mr. Banks ignored.

"Biting is dangerous behavior," Kirsten said as Mr. Banks left the stall and closed the door. "Why didn't you reprimand him?"

She'd wanted to smack the horse. How dare Beelzebub mistreat an owner who plainly loved him?

Mr. Banks pulled his gloves out of his pocket and tugged them on. "He wants me to tarry in his stall, and if I turn 'round and spend another minute shaking my finger in his face, he'll have succeeded, won't he? You must be cold, my lady. May I escort you to the house?"

He winged an arm. Bits of hay and straw stuck to his sleeve, as well as a quantity of dark horse hairs. Kirsten longed to tarry with him in the barn, to put off the moment when she had to share him with her family.

She was not a mischievous horse, however, intent on pursuing selfish schemes that had no hope of bearing fruit. She took Mr. Banks's arm and walked with him out into the gathering darkness.

About the Author

New York Times and USA Today bestselling author Grace Burrowes's bestsellers include *The Heir*, *The Soldier*, *Lady Maggie's Secret Scandal*, *Lady Sophie's Christmas Wish*, and *Lady Eve's Indiscretion*. Her Regency romances and Scotland-set Victorian romances have received extensive praise, including starred reviews from *Publishers Weekly* and *Booklist*. *The Heir* was a *Publishers Weekly* Best Book of 2010, *The Soldier* was a *Publishers Weekly* Best Spring Romance of 2011, *Lady Sophie's Christmas Wish* and *Once Upon a Tartan* have both won RT Reviewers' Choice Awards, *Lady Louisa's Christmas Knight* was a *Library Journal* Best Book of 2012, and *The Bridegroom Wore Plaid* was a *Publishers Weekly* Best Book of 2012. Two of her MacGregor heroes have won KISS awards. Grace is a practicing family law attorney and lives in rural Maryland.

She loves to hear from her readers, and can be contacted through her website at graceburrowes.com.